Campaign Heat

Governor Bryce owed so many things to so many women that he'd lost count how much to whom. At least here, on this one occasion, he could give a little payback.

Lindsay writhed beneath him, holding his head tight just where she wanted it. Then she exploded, covering him with a sweet emission. Damn, she'd been a squirter to boot.

'Oh, Governor,' she cooed, kissing him afterward. 'Are you sure you don't want to marry me?'

'Can't.' He smiled rakishly. 'We both have spouses already.'

Five minutes later, they were back in the main room, back to their separate friends, their separate lives. Such was politics. Such was life.

'Sir?' It was Cray, looking for a status report.

Bryce gave him an affirmative nod. 'Mission accomplished,' he assured the man.

Cray pursed his lips. 'She looks like she'd be quite a pistol,' he observed.

'You don't know the half of it,' he said smiling.

Cray knew enough not to pursue the matter. If there was one thing you could say about Governor Bryce Clarkson, for all his carryings on, he didn't ever kiss and tell.

Other books by Gabrielle Marcola:

Bedding the Burglar

Campaign Heat
Gabrielle Marcola

BLACK LACE

Black Lace books contain sexual fantasies.
In real life, always practise safe sex.

First published in 2005 by
Black Lace
Thames Wharf Studios
Rainville Road
London W6 9HA

Copyright © Gabrielle Marcola, 2005

The right of Gabrielle Marcola to be identified as the Author of
the Work has been asserted by her in accordance with the Copyright,
Designs and Patents Act 1988.

Design by Smith & Gilmour, London
Printed and bound by Mackays of Chatham PLC

ISBN 0 352 339411

1

Governor Bryce Clarkson turned into the dimly lit parking lot of the Thunderbird Motel and immediately doused his headlights. Double-checking for any potential witnesses or pesky paparazzi, he pulled the nondescript sedan in front of room seven, where Queenie was waiting for him. He knew his behaviour was incredibly self-destructive. If there were a list of things not to do to be re-elected Governor, sneaking away from your own security men and going off to meet with a known madam had to be the worst. OK, he could come out against the flag or apple pie, but this was still pretty damned close to the top on anybody's list.

Making one more visual inspection, he turned up the collar of his trench coat and put on his sunglasses. It was now or never. He could only hope the coast was clear. These days there could be cameras anywhere, not to mention spies working for his elitist, unscrupulous opponent, Lamar Jankinson.

He opened the car door as quietly as possible and stuck out a foot, pressing the sole of his imported Italian loafer (earned honestly through income fully declared on his taxes, thank you very much) onto the cracked asphalt. It was unlikely that the surface of this parking lot had ever been treated to such expensive shoe leather but, then again, you never knew what sorts of men found themselves after midnight at places like this, nestled off lonely exits of the interstate.

Stuffing his hands in his pockets, trying to look as unlike his normally statuesque self as possible, the square-jawed, blue-eyed forty-one-year-old Governor skulked to the door. So far, so good. Only two other cars parked nearby and no lights on in the adjoining rooms. He was nearly home free. His heart pounding like a gavel during budget season at the state house, he put his hand to the cold, damp knob of door number seven.

Excitement poured through him as the knob turned. It was unlocked. That meant she was inside. Already waiting. In a moment he would be in her presence again, after eighteen long, dry months.

It was impossible to explain why he was doing this, throwing caution to the wind – not to mention a potential bid for the White House in two years – for what appeared to be little more than another in an endless series of cheap and easy screws, but the fact was that this former model and stripper had the one quality in the world none of the other women he'd bedded had ever possessed.

Queenie Amazon could make him beg.

This wasn't a small thing for a man whose combined good looks, charm and up-and-coming political power had ranked him in the top ten sexiest men in America for the last two years. It was a classification he took full advantage of, too, with the full, albeit grudging, awareness of his wife Lydia. Bryce couldn't help that he liked pretty women. Some called it an addiction, but that was foolishness. Every woman who swapped bodily fluids with him got something deeper from him and he from them. It was a sharing of souls – of energy, and spirit, and drive. It was what made this country great. Men and women coming together, free of bounds, full of hope. His own dreams being passed on, in a way, and theirs being fulfilled.

Of course, more than one woman had attempted to charge him with creating some new little constituents as a result of their activities. Naturally these were spurious claims as the Governor always practised exceedingly safe sex. Still, he made sure to have a viable legal staff as well as a battery of state-of-the-art spin-doctors to keep publicity favourable.

Over and over they'd told him it would be a whole different league when he ran for president. Cowell Owens, his crotchety septuagenarian Secretary of State, had been particularly blunt.

'If that pecker of yours so much as peeks out of your boxers except for a piss during the national campaign,' he drawled, 'I'll whack it off myself.'

The man would probably have to stand in line behind a number of others, his own dear wife included.

It was dark inside the motel room. Bryce licked his lips in anticipation. Queenie was the most fabulous, gorgeous and physically fit forty-year-old woman in the world, with the possible exception of his own Lydia. Her long legs, bare, with a pair of stiletto heels, could still stop a tank. As for making any man her willing slave, all it took was a little flash from her eyes, a tiny smile or a whiff of her perfume.

Bryce would never forget the first night he met Queenie as long as he lived. He was a mere state senator then, attending a party at the home of a wealthy financier. On the way in he was getting the usual briefing – who to shmooze, who to pass over after a quick handshake and so on – when he spied a gorgeous redhead with upswept hair and a magenta gown baring most of a fabulous bosom. His eyes ran up and down the hourglass figure, noting in particular the group of drooling men around her.

'Who's that?' he'd asked his press secretary, ever-faithful and long-suffering Ron Wyman.

A frown had come over Ron's pudgy face instantly. 'That's nobody. She's a friend of the host. Ignore her. Avoid her like the frigging plague.'

Naturally the mysterious, elegant woman was his first stop. 'I couldn't help noticing,' he told her. 'You're not like anyone else here.'

'No,' she agreed. 'I'm not. Which is why I'm going to cut through the bullshit. You're going to make some clever small talk, try and get me to have a drink or two, then invite me back to your suite or some apartment somewhere and screw my brains out. Is that about right?'

He flashed a sly smile. 'I was raised never to contradict a lady,' he said, inclining his head.

'In that case,' she continued, 'you should know that I would say yes to you, though I don't think it would be quite your cup of tea.'

'Really?' He attempted coyness. 'And what makes you so sure of that?'

She took a sip of her martini. 'I like to take charge, Senator Clarkson. And I expect to be worshipped, as well. A man must earn his way into my bed.'

Bryce was hooked from that moment on. Queenie became his obsession, a thirst he could not quench. Five times he saw her in the next month alone, each time playing the woman's sexual games. Mostly this involved teasing, and his pleasuring her at great length. They would talk, too, sometimes for hours. The best part, though, was the wicked torture she put him under. The last time he had seen her was over a year and a half ago, just before she'd left for Europe, supposedly for good. Apparently she'd opened a brothel in Paris with a French woman, who'd since been arrested.

Then, a week ago, she'd announced she was back in the US and that she needed to see Bryce at once. The Thunderbird was her choice of meeting place and he had felt powerless to refuse. Queenie was like a drug. An itch that you'd happily drive yourself half mad trying to scratch.

Softly, in the pitch black, he called her name.

'Slide the chain on the door,' came her sultry reply.

Bryce's cock was throbbing in his pants. There never had been any moderation with this woman. He was, as always, a horny, dumb goat in her presence, a total slave awaiting his orders. Obeying, he engaged the mechanism, the clinking of the metal links reminding him of the chains she used on him sometimes when she wanted him confined for teasing.

'Good boy, Bryce. Now face me.'

He heard the striking of the match. By the time he'd turned there was a soft glow in the air from the candle she'd lit. He could see her sleek silhouette, her thick fiery hair, her shapely body, deliciously coated in some kind of black Lycra, like liquid, poured on. It left the crotch bare and her breasts, too. Gold rings gleamed in her nipples.

In her hand was the riding crop, that thin, stinging thing he both loved and feared for what it could make him do and how it made him feel. It was raw energy, raw power.

'Take off your coat,' said Queenie. 'Crawl to me.'

He shed the trench coat. Underneath he wore a dress shirt and slacks, no tie. The remains of his business day. With startling ease, his knees plunged to the carpet. He thought of her beautiful sexy feet, wondering if he would be allowed access to them tonight, to lick and suck at her toes.

For now, though, he must concentrate on his given task. Lowering himself to all fours, he moved forward, one palm in front of the other. The only sound was his own heart beating. He yearned to tear off his clothes, to pull out his cock. God, he was so desperate.

'Were you followed?' she wanted to know, as he reached her red toenails.

'No, I don't think so,' he said to her beautiful foot, encased in the wispy thin leather straps of her black shoe. 'I passed the exit the first time going north and doubled back just to be sure. Don't worry. It's covered.'

'I hope not,' said Queenie. 'You're in for enough of an ass-whipping as it is.'

His cock was ready to explode in his pants. Without waiting to be told, he pressed his lips to the surface of her polished nails. Delicately, fervently, he kissed them.

'Were you given permission?' she snapped as she pulled back her foot.

The Governor put his head to the floor, reprimanded. 'No, ma'am.'

'Stand up,' she said, her tone brooking no nonsense.

Bryce obeyed, restoring his six-foot frame to upright position. The five-foot-three-inch woman went immediately for his belt. Hands at his sides, he made no move to resist as she worked the buckle.

'Don't expect a medal just for showing up tonight, Bryce.' She opened his belt, then undid his pants and pulled down the zipper. In seconds she had his naked shaft in her hot little fingers. 'That is minimal obedience. It gets you in the front door, nothing more.'

'I understand,' he rasped, the blood surging up and down his turgid rod.

Queenie whipped his thigh, a tingling, erotic sting.

'You understand nothing, slave, except what I tell you to understand.'

Bryce felt the familiar rush of sexual surrender. Just being called a slave was enough to trip it off. This was by no means the only turn-on for the sexually adventurous politician, but it was certainly one of the strongest and most intriguing.

'Yes, mistress.' He gave Queenie her due title in return.

'Unbutton your shirt,' she ordered.

His fingers moved quickly down the front of the dress shirt, craving to expose his bare skin to her deliciously wicked touch.

'Still wearing undershirts,' she complained, noting the layer of white cotton beneath. 'Rip it open.'

Bryce knew better than to hesitate to obey an order from his mistress. Grabbing at the collar, he sheared the fabric down the middle.

'Off.' She tapped his belly with the whip.

He shed both of the shirts to the floor, baring his lean, muscular chest and tight abdomen. Bryce had been on the rowing team at college and he'd made a point of keeping physically fit ever since. Three miles a day of jogging, and fifty laps in the swimming pool of the Governor's mansion. Not to mention the exercise he got from his extracurricular activities between the sheets.

'Nice and hard,' she said, noting his nipples. 'What a slut you are.'

'Thank you, mistress.' He winced as she nibbled them. Ever the cruel-to-be-kind bitch, she stroked his cock at the same time, making him take his pleasure with a nice dose of pain. Employing her tongue and nails over the rest of his chest, she was able to reduce him to a whimpering wreck in seconds.

'Get a hold of yourself,' she chided. 'You call yourself a chief executive? What are your constituents supposed to think if you can't even hold back your ejaculation for five minutes?'

'Need to . . . come,' he groaned.

'Well, we don't always get what we want in life, do we?' She pushed him back, her palms firmly on his chest. 'Go lie on the bed on your back. I'm going to tie you down. Any trouble from you and I will leave you right now and never see you again. Is that clear?'

'Yes, mistress.'

Bryce walked immediately across the room and crawled onto the king-sized bed. If this were anyone but Queenie, he'd have her underneath him on this very mattress by now, moaning and begging for release. But there was something about this woman that brought out his submissive, masochistic side. Maybe it was her red hair, like his mother's. Or her moxie. Who knew where her power over him came from? But it was undeniably real.

Lying down on his back, he waited, helpless.

'Close your eyes,' she snapped, whipping his stomach. The riding crop made him squirm. He'd have a pink mark there for another hour. Maybe it would even last till he got back home, having snuck through the theoretically impregnable security of the Governor's mansion. Fortunately (or unfortunately) he had a chief of security who turned a blind eye whenever his employer wanted to sneak off and play.

Bryce's dimly lit world grew even dimmer as he obeyed Queenie. His other senses sought quickly to fill the vacuum left by his closed eyes. Queenie was near him; he could smell her soft, sweet scent. Lace mixed with jasmine in his nostrils while his skin tingled with the wild feel of the Lycra. He groaned as her lips grazed his. A second later her long, silky hair swished across his face.

'Would you like to be fucked?' she asked, as if there were any possible doubt as to how he would answer.

'Oh, God,' he moaned, his cock begging attention. 'Yes, please, mistress.'

This was the good part, the prolonged teasing.

'No.' She denied them both. 'Not till I've made you suffer some more.'

'Yes, mistress.' His toes were curling. He could think of nothing but her sweet, sweet sex. He would do anything, say anything for her favours. A dangerous position, he thought, for a politician.

'Lift your ass.' Queenie wanted his pants and under-wear and shoes and socks off. To put it simply, she wanted him naked.

The Governor complied, surrendering the remainder of his clothing.

This accomplished, she lashed his thigh hard with the whip. 'Legs apart, slave.'

He opened himself, exposing his precious hard-on and tight, fully loaded balls.

'Such a good boy,' she teased, putting her finger to his lips. 'I think that deserves a special treat.'

The finger was wet and fragrant. Greedily, he slurped at the fluid, fresh from her sex.

'Save your energy,' she said, popping it back out of his mouth. 'You'll need it.'

She put a leather cuff around his wrist. He extended his fingers as she pulled it semi-tight and sealed the Velcro. A moment later, after climbing across his over-sensitised body, she was doing the same to the other wrist. Her next step was to draw the cuffs tight above his head. Presumably she was attaching him to the headboard.

She had cuffs for his ankles, too, heavier, sturdier ones. She pulled them wider apart, fixing something – probably a wooden dowel or spreader bar – between them. This would make it virtually impossible for him to lift his legs, while leaving them helplessly open. The sensation made his whole body tingle. One touch to his cock and he would shoot off.

'Lift your head,' she whispered.

She slipped the silk around his head, knotting it tight. It was a blindfold, snug and sweet-smelling, like Queenie herself.

Bryce released small moans as she smoothed the silk with a feather-light touch, then moved to tickle his ear with the tip of her tongue. 'Are you ready?' she asked.

He lifted his ass from the bed, bucking his manly hips to show just how ready he was. 'Mistress, yes, God, yes.'

'Lie still.' Queenie flicked the whip against his cock, inducing a high-pitched yelp. Sensations surged up and down his spinal column, a dozen emotions raging at once. He feared her, he hated her, hell, he damned near loved her. But above all he wanted to be slamming his cock home into her. Silencing her, reducing her gloating to groans, her cat-like hisses to soft, sweet purrs. But that was the charm and the magic, wasn't it? The fact that she dangled before him just enough of that other side of herself, pliant and weak in the classically female way, to keep him enticed, and ultimately to make him come crawling back.

Back into her web.

She always had been the one woman he couldn't get enough of. There was one other woman he might put in that class, and that was Cassie. But Cassie would forever be her own chapter, her own category. He'd

felt things for her he'd never admitted, not to the woman herself, not even to his own consciousness. In the end there'd been decisions to make. She deserved better than the kind of hit-and-miss affection he was able to offer as a potential boyfriend or husband.

Marrying Lydia was the best thing he could have done. For both their sakes. Cassie had pretended to understand, though in his heart he knew she wondered if she would ever forgive him.

It was a pain, and a lust he preferred to bury as deep as it would go in his consciousness.

'That's better,' she whispered, running the tip of her finger up his side, sending a tiny, sweet tug of electric charge down his body. 'Now, how about you lie nice and still and let Mistress Queenie bring you a special surprise?'

'Yes, I'll do what you say, mistress . . . just hurry.'

Her question was obviously rhetorical, though he gave his affirmation anyway. She rewarded him with an open-mouthed kiss that nearly melted his lips. Queenie was an aggressive kisser, passionate but decisive, placing her tongue where she wanted and directing his head back just as she wished. He met her with full force, holding nothing back. He could feel the throbbing in his cock, his every muscle tensing. He wanted her to need this as badly as he did, to be overcome with lust for his body, to be unable to keep from throwing herself on top of him, linking their sexes, pelvis to pelvis, a frantic pounding leading to mutual satisfaction.

But Queenie Amazon, unlike him, had willpower. She had class, too. Few knew she was the daughter of a French diplomat and an English actress, raised in the States by a distant cousin in Boston. Her real name was Abigail Auvignon, though she'd been using this

stage name of Queenie Amazon for over two decades. Many considered her a frivolous tart, but Bryce knew better. She was a woman of incredible intelligence and humour, too sensitive for a world as bleak and sexless as this one. She played her little games, made her living in the most passionate and interesting ways she could think of, to keep boredom at bay.

'Such a good, good boy,' she crooned, running her fingers through his rich dark hair, perfect hair, black with sprinklings of silver. Bryce was the kind of man who'd only get better looking as he got older. Smarter, too, wiser and more mature. More presidential. The majority of the pundits thought he would secure the party's nomination next time out, as long as he didn't screw it up. The presidency was his to lose. Sooner or later, in other words, it would come down to Bryce vs. Bryce. His own worst enemy.

'Be right back, darling.'

Just like that she was gone. The highly compromised Governor clenched and unclenched his fists. He was trapped. Tied down for real. He really hadn't thought this through, had he? His libido had run him straight him into a damned messy spot. Again.

'Mistress?' he called out into the empty space.

Every second seemed like a lifetime.

'Queenie? ... Abigail, are you there?'

The motel room door opened and closed.

This was not good. Not at all. You really didn't expect or appreciate people coming or going when you were tied down naked and blindfolded in the company of a woman very much not your wife. And in a thirty-dollar-a-night motel room, no less.

'Abby, is that you? Is someone else here?'

He pulled at the bonds, testing their strength. Bryce Clarkson was not a weak man by any means, but these

straps weren't exactly lightweight either. Grunting, he strained his wrists as hard as he could. If he could just get one free.

Damn it, someone was turning the lights on. He could hear Abby talking. Who was it in the room with her?

'Smile,' chortled a sickeningly jovial voice. 'You're on video.'

Thick, puffy fingers pulled away the blindfold. A fat man in black turtleneck and jeans was leaning over him with a video camera, sweeping up and down, alternating quite pointedly between the Governor's face and his swollen member.

Bryce looked desperately at the woman lying beside him on the bed, now brightly illuminated. 'Abigail, what's going on?'

'I'm sorry,' she said softly. 'I had no choice.'

'That's enough,' snapped the cameraman. 'Time for you to finish your end of the bargain.'

'You mean you are doing this for money? As long as we've known each other?' he exclaimed. It wasn't possible. Not Queenie, anyone but her.

'Stop sounding so idealistic,' snorted the increasingly annoying fat man. 'You're as sleazy they come.'

'Just finish your disgusting sex film,' said the Governor flatly, 'and get the hell out of here.'

'You think I'm some cheap director? *Au contraire.*' He pronounced the French badly in his New Jersey accent. 'My work has been viewed by some of the most powerful people in the nation – though they don't often enjoy it too much. OK, Queenie, let's see if we can get him a little more worked up, shall we?'

'Abigail,' he said, tensing. 'Don't do it.'

'I'm sorry,' she repeated, her eyes showing genuine sadness. 'I haven't any choice.'

Bryce sucked in a ragged breath as Queenie kissed her way down his stomach to his genitals. Dear God, she was going to suck his cock. He'd never be able to hold his tongue under that kind of pressure. They could make him confess to anything.

'All right, Mr Governor, to start with, how about you state your full name and title for the camera.'

'I am Bryce William Clarkson.' He gasped as she kissed the head of his uncircumcised manhood. So much for maintaining his dignity. Pushing up his buttocks, he sought and was denied deeper penetration. 'Governor of the great state of –'

Queenie bit down, just hard enough to turn his words into a mild howl.

'Never mind, we all know who you are. How about telling us how many women you slept with, say in the last year?'

'I'm a happily married man,' he protested, writhing, trying to push away the sensation of her teeth nibbling at the protruding veins. 'And an upstanding … Christian … churchgoer.'

Queenie pulled her mouth away, leaving a trail of saliva.

'No, don't stop,' he wailed, knowing what a bad case he was making for himself as a moral paragon. 'Suck my cock, please.'

The whip cracked down on his belly. 'Don't piss me off,' said Queenie, returning to dominatrix mode. 'Answer the question.'

She played with his cock, using one hand while striking with the other. They were sharp, stinging blows, enough to bring his every nerve fibre to life.

Bryce moaned, hot shivers passing up and down his spine. Suddenly the very flushing of his own career down the toilet became part of the dark excitement of surrender. There was simply no limit to this woman's ability to manipulate him sexually, even after revealing a level of treachery that ought to leave him cold as the grave.

'I – I don't have an exact count,' he fudged.

Queenie climbed across his thighs, moving her limber body within striking position of his cock. 'Bullshit,' she retorted, teasing the length of his cock with her glistening wet pussy lips. 'You're way too proud of your indiscretions not to keep tabs. You're like a big game hunter.'

A little higher up, he thought, then you can slip me right inside yourself and ride me like a fucking maniac.

'I'm waiting.' She leaned forward to pinch both nipples with her long nails.

'One hundred,' he groaned. 'And fifty-three.'

'Does that include tonight with me?'

'No,' he grimaced. 'We didn't ... finish. Plus, you're a repeat.'

Queenie released his nipples. 'How about your wife?' She swathed some juice from her pussy on his cock. 'Did you fuck her this year?'

He shook his head to and fro, his eyes rolling somewhere up in his head. 'Not ... this year,' he managed to stammer.

'How do you get your women, Governor?'

Bryce swallowed. This particular part was not going to make him look good. Not by a long shot. 'Is there any way ... we can work ... something out ... and stop your taping?' He managed to keep his presence of mind.

'Don't even insult me,' said the blackmailing cameraman. 'I'm an artist.'

Queenie immediately took possession of him with her cunt, sheathing his cock inside her. At first he felt only relief from his long plaguing itch. She was hitting the sweet spot. Like an old dog getting scratched behind the ear, he was feeling a warm animal satisfaction. Except this was building, rising at the speed of light to what was going to be one of his best orgasms of all time – right up there with his mile-high meeting with Miss January and the time he had those twins from the Dallas Steers football cheerleading squad.

'Oh, Jeezus,' he cried, taking in vain the name of the Lord he was supposed to be so adamantly following. 'Oh, my fucking Jeezus ... fuck me, Abby.'

Queenie was good, getting him fully worked up. When he was close to coming, however, she broke contact, leaving him in suspense, his glistening cock thrusting up into the air.

'Abby,' he cried piteously, 'please don't stop.'

'Tell us what we want to know, Governor, and you'll get your precious pussy back,' the cameraman bargained.

He watched her, sultry as hell, leaning back, still astride his thighs, both hands on her full globes, massaging. The tummy undulating, the red-hot cunt dripping, inviting him back inside. His own mother's secrets wouldn't be safe with him now, not with a chance to come inside that heavenly box at stake.

'I use interns,' said Bryce. 'And my security men, they get me women, too. Call girls.'

'Your security men?' asked the cameraman innocently. 'But aren't they state police? Paid for with taxpayers' money?'

Queenie had her eyes closed. She was running her fingers through her hair, long red flames. Was she thinking about her dancing days? Or how she was going to spend whatever money she was getting for betraying him?'

'You know they are, you bastard,' the Governor blurted.

'Temper, temper,' the fat man lectured. 'Any more outbursts and I won't let you have your sleazy little orgasm with your sleazy little whore.'

'She's not a whore,' Bryce heard himself defending her.

Queenie's eyes melted in a rare show of emotion. 'Oh, Bryce, that's so sweet. I can't believe you'd defend me. Here and now after all this.'

He wasn't sure whether to laugh or cry. In a flash, Queenie was moving back on top, her eyes ablaze, locking on Bryce's, letting him know she wanted him and wanted this.

'What the fuck are you doing?' demanded the cameraman. 'No sex till he talks. That was the deal.'

'I'm sorry, Ian.' She resheathed his cock in one smooth motion. 'I have to do this now.' Bryce couldn't believe the heat. Her vaginal canal was red hot and tight as any eighteen-year-old's. He only hoped she'd move fast enough to achieve her own orgasm, because he wasn't going to last more than a few strokes himself.

Funny that he should care about her pleasure after all she'd put him through. If anything, he should want her rather seriously deprived of pleasure for a good long time, and yet, at this moment, he wanted nothing more than for them to come together, blocking out the rest of the world with all its troubles and miseries. Yes, he'd give himself fully to her, to them, allow himself to surrender everything to their mutuality.

She'd make it all right, Queenie would. She had him pinned down, she'd secured his body, and that meant at some level he must have trusted her in an unshakable way. It was irrational, but it was all he had to hold on to, especially with a spasming cock getting ready to shoot itself deep into the woman's sex, and a hostile camera two feet away catching every last bit of the action.

'Queenie.' He bucked up to meet her. 'Tell me ... you didn't ... do it just for money.'

She squeezed her strong pussy muscles, pushing herself forward and back. 'Mmmm,' she moaned through gritted teeth. 'Just shut up and ... fuck.'

Bryce didn't need to be told twice. He pushed his cock up to meet her, bending his body to fit her passion. Just in time, he found the rhythm as she rode him with wild abandon, screaming out her final explosion. What a vision she was, her hair wild, her amber eyes flashing like alien moons. She was so damned perfect, so damned chiselled. It just wasn't right that so much beauty could be so deadly. Then again, look at the diamondback rattler.

'Queenie ...' He filled her with his hot semen, their pelvises locked and sealed in a primal quake. It was beyond language, beyond all social niceties. No friends or enemies now, there were only the sheer animal requirements for orgasm, the mindless, passionate blending, yin and yang.

They moved together for several minutes afterward, postponing the inevitable collapse, sweat coating their skin, exhaustion dogging their limbs. It was as if neither wanted to admit the inevitable reality, the falling back down into individual consciousness and individual responsibility.

There was sin here, enough to go around. A seamy underside to the politics of the time. Treason to meet the naked eye, along with a bevy of other crimes that ought never to see the light of day.

'Get off him,' demanded Ian, the fat man. 'You've

had your fun. It's time to call it a wrap. That is, unless you want to have some fun with me, too?'

'Touch her and I'll kill you,' said Bryce, speaking with a vehemence he'd not known himself capable of.

'Listen to him,' chortled Ian. 'I think the old boy's in love. Maybe after he resigns as Governor in disgrace you two can go out on the road, do an act in a sex club somewhere.'

'Leave him alone, Ian. Just get the fuck out. You got what you wanted.'

Ian was still laughing as he walked out of the room. Abigail undid the bonds on Bryce, tears streaming from her eyes the whole time. When the job was done, she left, too, without another word.

For the longest time he simply lay there, staring at one of the tears, which he had captured on his fingertip. He hoped she would be all right, tonight, no matter what she had done.

Bryce sat up and soon he was crying, too. How long exactly had it been, he wondered, since he'd thought like this – cogitating on another's needs ahead of his own?

Too long. And therein, he thought, lies my true sin.

2

Cassie Dane absorbed the last few seconds of the music video, the titillating images of half-naked, cavorting men and women flickering at last off the monitor screen that had been wheeled into her plush, liberally air-conditioned office. She took a moment to gather herself, not wanting to deal yet with the four sexy young guests who'd been watching with her. Despite the cool temperature, it had gotten decidedly hot in here, red hot, and Cassie was finding it a little difficult to concentrate on the business at hand.

She attempted an appeal to reason. These gorgeous bodies represented clients, not bed partners, she told herself, and she was trying to guide them, not seduce them.

'Well, what do you think?' inquired the lean, muscular young artist responsible for the video – a dark-skinned man with the charming name of G Killer Vice. 'Will it fly?'

The owner and founder of Dane Imaging & Consulting took a deep cleansing breath and leaned back in her Corinthian leather chair, a beautiful match to her mahogany desk. The handsome furniture was one of the perks of being her own boss. So was the right to take an extra moment to park her libido and then speak her own mind as freely as she liked.

'Will it fly?' She regarded the sweat-suit-wearing Vice, who looked barely old enough to have tied his two-hundred-dollar sneakers. 'Sure. Just long enough to be shot down by every morals group within a thousand miles. Have you not been watching the news? Half-a-million-dollar fines for every blue word so much as muttered under your breath? Warning labels that make your music sound more dangerous than smoking cigarettes with chasers full of acid? Any of this ring a bell? The Gilded Age is over, ladies and gents. It's back to Puritans in long stockings and public floggings.'

G Killer Vice, who was wearing enough gold necklaces to re-sink the Titanic, turned to his sneaker-wearing advisor. The move was a little difficult, what with the two young women hanging all over him on the couch. They were delectable, slinky young things, with short skirts and tight half-shirts revealing cute little belly-button rings. They had lots of make-up on, too, and long, elaborately painted nails. The motions of their well decorated fingertips over Vice's sculpted, muscular body left little doubt about their purpose in the musician's entourage.

'What's she saying, C Money?' Vice wanted to know, sounding genuinely perplexed by Cassie's words.

C Money, who was sitting next to them, all on his own in a wing-back, tried to translate her remarks using the kind of street lingo popular among musicians of his generation. Vice shook his head, looking every bit the suffering artist as he swallowed the cold, hard truth.

'Man, all I want to do is make my art,' he lamented as the two young women vied for the right to caress his bulging crotch, the contents ill-disguised by his tight leather pants.

Cassie found herself wondering just how big that package might be when unwrapped. There was no way these two little tarts deserved that kind of meat.

They were barely legal. Though, admittedly, Cassie wouldn't mind going down on one of them for good measure when she was done with the rap star. She paused and mentally chastised her unhelpful genitals, then plodded on, attempting to eliminate this temptation as quickly as possible.

'Be that as it may,' she said, biting her tongue at the man's attempt to equate his songs with art, 'lyrics such as ...', and she paused to refer to the sheet of paper on her desk, '... "Bitch don't fight no more, spread it now, get down, take it hard" are really not going to win the hearts and minds of an increasingly morals-conscious society.'

'I sing what I live,' he said proudly. 'And I ride till I die.'

Cassie watched his hand creep under the hem of one girl's skirt. A black-skinned beauty with huge breasts, she proved her obedience to the man's lyrics by spreading for him instantly, revealing her naked pussy. Cassie squeezed her own thighs together. She had a funny feeling she was going to end up cleaning that leather couch before the morning was over.

'That's right. Vice don't trip on nobody,' C Money confirmed, pointing his finger animatedly.

The black starlet was leaning back now, openly moaning as the rapper's finger moved easily between her puffy sex lips. She was wet and ready. The very fact that she was a little slut ready to spread at the musician's command was making Cassie as horny as hell. It was all she could do to keep from digging her fingers under her own skirt – which was of a more dignified business length – to find her needy clit.

'You like this,' observed Vice, noting Cassie's hard nipples under her white blouse. 'You want it, too, don't you? You want to be G Killer Vice's woman.'

The thirty-year-old Cassie rocked her pelvis as subtly as possible. 'My fantasies ran more in the direction of Stephen Tyler and Aerosmith, I'm sorry to say. I'm afraid you'll have to take your little ride till you die without me.'

'Don't be so sure, Image Lady.' Vice snapped his fingers, ordering the other girl to her knees on the floor. She was pale-skinned, with long brown hair and long legs. Her lips were wide and ruby red and Cassie had a pretty good idea what she'd be using them for.

'It takes two bitches to swallow my meat,' bragged Vice as he continued to make the black girl buck and writhe like a possessed doll.

'At least two,' said the increasingly annoying and toadying Mr Money, holding up his fingers. 'Sometimes three.'

'I'll keep that in mind, thank you,' Cassie said drily. Her eyes were fixed on Vice's zipper. It was like watching the snake exhibit at the zoo. As much as she might want to turn away, she couldn't. She was fascinated, in a dread, totally helpless kind of way.

'No bitch can resist this,' Vice was telling her. 'You'll be begging for your chance to service me, too.'

It was a ridiculous, megalomaniacal approach to seduction. Cheesy. Amateurish. But, damn it, oh, so fucking kinky. You could hear a pin drop as the little brown-haired girl tugged down the zipper, one catch at a time. Vice wore no underwear. Like a jack in the box, the compressed organ sprung out, fully awake.

Cassie swallowed hard. He was big all right. No wonder he had so many women. No wonder they were practically worshipping him in that video.

'You ever seen a dick like that?' C Money wanted to know.

Cassie was really wishing there was something that

big to put in Money's mouth right now. 'It's really not your concern, with all due respect, what my experience is with genitalia. I really think you should go, actually, all of you.'

No one believed Cassie really wanted them to go, least of all herself. As a matter of fact, a moment later she was telling the obsequious C Money to make himself useful and lock the door. This was another perk of being your own boss: the right to sequester yourself for some very improper contact with a client.

'But what about my image?' Vice reminded her. 'Not to mention the cash I need to keep flowing.'

The brown-haired girl licked the head of his big, bad cock, making it glisten. The dark hue against her white skin made for a most sexy contrast. That could so easily be me down there, thought the blonde, blue-eyed public relations consultant, lapping it up, like a kitten after a saucer of milk.

'Vice, how about throwing me a little action?' C Money had his eye on the black girl and his hand on his cock through the velour sweatpants. 'You can see I got a little situation.'

'Deal with it yourself,' said his boss.

Cassie secretly smiled at how easily Mr Money had been put in his place. Finally, she thought, something to really appreciate about G Killer Vice.

The dark-skinned girl was close to orgasm. Vice ordered her to pull up her shirt and bare her bouncing tits. She closed her fingers around them greedily, squeezing. At the same time she was moving on his knuckles, taking what she needed from him to get herself off.

It was scandalous, really, the way the girl was letting herself be used, allowing herself to be displayed and paraded in front of a stranger, in a totally inappropriate setting. It was more than acquiescence, though, because unless she was a very remarkable actress, she was doing more than putting up with this treatment; she was loving every minute of it. Vice was so cool about it, too, manipulating her, even as he received his slobbering kisses from the other girl, equally beautiful, equally subjugated.

This kind of submissive imagery went against everything Cassie believed about the equality of the sexes. This man's whole career, in fact, with his talk of gangsters, guns and macho men, was anathema to her. And yet there was another part of her, deep and secret, that longed to be dirty like this, to be treated as little more than a sex animal, good for pleasure, good for getting off on. A pure female creature, meant to serve a pure male one. No complications, no relationship bullshit.

Now there was a refreshing thought. No more dates and innuendoes. No more mama's boys and married men. No more hypocrites and egotists. No more conniving, using backstabbers and pretty boys. Just simple down-and-dirty exploitation.

At least with Vice you knew up front how you were being fucked, she thought sardonically. Compare that to the men whose circles she moved in, where it took weeks, months to figure out their games. And often then it was too late. You'd already given your heart away.

Then, too, maybe it was just the teenager in her again, coming to life. The late-night sighing dreams of being with one or another rock star. Rubbing against his tight pants, running fingers through his big, larger than life hair. They didn't have such big hair now as they did in the 8os. In fact, G Killer Vice had no hair at all. Also, the rockers from her day weren't so developed physically. They weren't like statues with bodies that moved on stage, covered in glistening sweat you wanted to lick off.

'That's it, Lateesha,' said Vice. 'Give it up, just like the little whore you are.'

His lewd command seemed to be just what the girl needed to push her over the top. This was how they talked in the rap star's circles. This was how they got each other off. Who was Cassie to argue with the results? Lateesha's head was thrust all the way back and her body ramrod-straight, her teeth gritted, her fingers pinching her nipples, hard as sin, as the orgasm overtook her.

It was a spectacle to behold. Vice had barely had to wag his finger over her clit and she was transported into some electrified world beyond the visible horizon. Cassie was jealous. She wanted that hand on her. She wanted her clothes off, too, in a big way.

'Oh, baby,' moaned Lateesha when she could talk again. The girl nibbled at his neck, wanting to thank him in as physical a way as possible. Not one to waste the attentions of a willing female admirer, Vice pulled up his tight T-shirt and attached her head to his nipple.

Lateesha sucked greedily, putting an instant smile on the rapper's dark face. Meanwhile Vice pushed the white girl onto his cock, winding his fingers in her brown hair. Cassie bit her lip as she noted Lateesha's juices still on the star's hand as he pumped the white girl's head. He was marking her hair with it, deliberately, it seemed, and she didn't even seem to mind. Part of the game, Cassie supposed.

'This is Jenny,' said Vice, introducing the white girl. 'She ran away from home, ended up turning tricks. I took her off the street. Made her my bitch when she turned eighteen.'

'Attitudes like this,' said Cassie, feeling rather as she did every time she touched down breathless in mile-high Denver, 'don't help your image any. People say you take advantage of helpless women.'

As if she didn't want the charismatic singer to do a little exploiting of her right now.

'I make people happy,' he said with a grin. 'I tell it like it is. I give them what they want. Lateesha, go and give Miss Dane what she wants.'

And how exactly was Lateesha supposed to know what Cassie needed at that moment?

Mesmerised, Cassie watched the girl lower herself to the floor and begin to crawl on all fours. The bypassed C Money made a protest, the complaints inducing Vice to tell him to take out his dick and start stroking it. The manager muttered something under his breath but did as he was told, pulling his sweat-pants down to release his cock. The shaft was thinner than Vice's and maybe an inch shorter. Still, it was a tempting treat in itself.

'Let's get you relaxed, Image Lady,' Vice advised.

Vice probably thought she was uptight. Actually, Cassie was trying to hold herself back. These kids really didn't want to see her at full throttle. It would not be a pretty sight.

Lateesha got up on her knees and pulled back Cassie's rolling chair. Next thing she knew she was facing the girl, leaning straight back as if she was at the gynaecologist's office.

'Her panties are sopping wet,' Lateesha reported to her boss.

What did she expect – the Sahara Desert? A moan escaped Cassie's throat as Lateesha's finger wormed between her thighs. Her legs were up on the girl's shoulders. Her calves were flexed.

'Squirm, little girl,' said Lateesha encouragingly to the woman who was her senior by a decade. 'Show us what you got.'

Lateesha knew how to play with a pussy. That was for sure. Even working around the edge of Cassie's panties, she was rapidly driving her to the edge of desperate sexual need.

'You already know what I got,' she replied, challenging the girl and her boss. 'The question is, can you handle it?'

She was all about the weird and wonderful. Exotic encounters with movers and shakers. Anything goes in the sheets or on the backseat. But as her assistant Stephanie was so fond of telling her, casual sex wasn't cool anymore, and anyhow, she wasn't getting any younger. A woman her age needed to look at settling down. No more married men, no more heartbreakers and bad boys. From now on, it was supposed to be standard, behind-closed-door missionary sex, with politely timed and exquisitely faked orgasms. She would leave her real adventuring for the alone times she spent with her vibrator.

What would the pert, bobtailed young Stephanie make of this? Cassie could just picture the look on her face when Vice and his crew eventually tramped out of the office later and past her reception desk. Assuming she ever got them out of here today at all.

'Oh, fuck,' Cassie moaned. She was squirming all right, trying to push herself down on the girl's hand to impale herself.

'Take off her panties,' said Vice.

Good idea, thought Cassie. Lifting her well-toned buttocks off the chair, she allowed Lateesha to yank down her silk underwear. They were indeed more than a little fragrant with her liquid essence.

'She needs it bad,' grinned Lateesha, putting them to her nose. 'Don't you, little girl?'

Cassie gushed, this time directly onto the seat. 'You're too young to know what I need,' she quipped, though there wasn't much left to the imagination at this point, as her hands raced to undo the zipper of her skirt. Cassie needed to be nude. Cassie needed to be fucked.

'Strip her.' Vice read her mind. 'And lay her on the floor.'

Lateesha pulled down Cassie's skirt and went to work on her blouse. Cassie blushed as the wispy pink demi-bra was exposed beneath the blue silk. The bra had 'fuck me' written all over it, as did the tiny, provocative panties.

'Whooee,' Lateesha whistled. 'She sure is planning on giving it to somebody today.'

'Is that for your boyfriend?' asked Vice. 'Did you do that on your own or did he tell you to wear it for him?'

Cassie said nothing. They'd never believe her if she told the truth. The sexy little underwear was for no one but herself. All part of Cassie's new one-woman campaign to prove she could feel sexy and desirable without having to actually have sex with everyone she came in contact with. So far, things had gone well. Though it was only the first day.

The bra was front-clasping. Lateesha flicked it open, baring Cassie's C-cup breasts. They were firm and resilient, the pink nipples tight, swollen buds, more than ready for sexual attention. Holding her breath, she watched as Lateesha began to play with them.

'She's not bad,' the lovely black girl reported. 'For an old woman.'

Cassie arched her back. All of a sudden Lateesha didn't think she was a little girl any more. The Irish in her wanted to fight back, showing this pretty young thing just how an old woman like her could really handle herself.

'I think we need less mouth from you,' Cassie declared, 'and more action.' She pulled the girl's head back by her hair and landed a kiss on the brightly painted lips.

Lateesha's eyes went wide, the kiss catching her off-guard. Cassie had had some lesbian experiences before, dating back to college. She wasn't afraid to take on a woman and show her who was boss.

Lateesha tried to resist as Cassie reached for her exposed breasts, but a quick pinch to her thick dark-pink nipple rendered her quickly docile. Rising from her chair, withdrawing her tongue from Lateesha's plundered mouth, Cassie pushed her down to her knees. 'Lick,' she commanded, indicating where the girl's tongue was to insert itself.

Lateesha's insolent mouth disappeared between the older woman's legs. Cassie sighed in satisfaction, having put the youngster in her place.

'That is off the hook,' laughed Vice, using a phrase that Cassie knew meant she had done well in his estimation. 'Tell it, C Money. Tell her it's off the hook what she's doing to Lateesha.'

C Money, eyes bulging, hands on his swollen cock, proceeded to tell her just how off the hook this really was. 'Vice, I'm with you, my homey.'

'Image Lady, how about if I let C Money fuck that pretty mouth of yours?' Vice inquired mischievously, still enjoying his deep-throat servicing from Jenn.

'How about if I bite C Money's cock off instead and we rename him Plug Nickel?' she countered.

Vice slapped his thigh, loving her spunk. 'Plug

Nickel. That's off the *chain*. You hear that, C? I may just rename your punk ass that one of these days.'

C Money grimaced, trying to deal with the insults at the same time as he was working on his hard cock. 'G, I can't take this no more,' he complained. 'I gotta blow my load.'

Vice shook his head. 'No discipline, C. None at all.' He snapped his fingers. 'Lateesha, go take care of Plug over there.'

'Plug?' C Money whined vehemently at the newly applied moniker, clearly terrified it might stick. 'Vice, why you playing me like this? I been down with you since the start. I'm your dog, man.'

Lateesha popped her head out from Cassie's crotch. Cassie knew better than to try and stop her leaving. She answered to Vice and nothing Cassie did would change that. Still, she intended to teach the nineteen-year-old rap star a little lesson about the sexual powers of the older generation.

'You took my toy away,' she rasped. 'Any idea how we can replace it?'

Vice licked his lips, the look in his eyes indicating that C Money and his name problems had just been totally blocked out. Who could blame him, what with Cassandra holding her pussy lips open for him, her lean, well-toned legs spaced wide apart, her shapely body clad in nothing but a pair of high heels. 'I don't go south,' he said, shaking his head all macho-like, though Cassie was pretty sure he'd crumble like the Berlin Wall with just a little more effort on her part.

'Too bad,' she said teasingly. ''Cause you'll never get it this good again.'

'I can get any box I want, Image Lady.'

Cassie ran her finger over her clit, inducing a fresh

trickle. 'So go,' she crooned, and put the finger to her mouth. 'Who's stopping you?'

It had been a long time since she'd tasted a pussy, let alone her own. It brought back memories – of kinky games in the dormitories late at night, after way too many beers, under the influence of hunky boys, cheering the girls on as they flopped their huge cocks in the breeze.

'You go flashing that thing,' Vice warned, 'and I'm liable to come at you armed and ready.'

She spasmed just thinking of the man's cock filling her thirsty hole. That was as good as his tongue. Better, in many ways. 'You talk the talk,' she said, reminding him of his lyrics, 'but do you walk the walk? Gonna make me spread, huh, big boy? Gonna lay it on me, make me moan, gonna give me inches all night long?'

Vice tapped Jenn on the shoulder. 'Go help Lateesha. I got business to take care of.'

Cassie smiled, cat-like. Son of a gun. She still had it. She was actually seducing the rap star.

'But I wanna suck you,' Jenny whined, sounding like she needed a firm spanking and a nap. 'Not C Money.'

'I ain't asking you to suck him. Just hold the tweezers while Lateesha sucks him.'

C Money started in with the abandoned homey/dog/brother business again, despite the fact that he was getting what looked like a very nice blowjob from the kneeling Lateesha. There really was no pleasing some people, Cassie decided.

Vice spread his legs on the couch. 'I hope you know what you just did,' he said, 'cos this cock is all yours to deal with now.'

'And this is yours,' she said, displaying her pussy in return, 'if you can fill it.'

Truth be told, she'd never had a man that big inside

her. She'd slept with an ex-baseball player once, who was running for Congress. He was almost this big, though unfortunately for both of them he'd spilled himself on her belly before ever reaching home base. He felt terrible about the whole thing. She wasn't really surprised when he lost the election, by a landslide.

'Oh, I can fill it,' he assured her. 'The question is, can you take it?'

'Only one way to find out.' Cassie's blood was pounding. She was walking toward him. She was on her way, naked, to her own office couch to fuck one of the biggest rap stars on the planet.

Big in more ways than one.

Cassie didn't stop till she was standing directly against the edge of the couch, her thighs between his knees.

'You got a tight little body,' said Vice admiringly, running his hands up her hips and around to her ass. 'Do you work out?'

Cassandra shivered at his touch. The man was good at what he did. Damned good. 'I do aerobics,' she told him. 'And kick boxing.'

He clamped her ass, hard. 'I'm gonna work your body today, Image Lady. And I'm gonna work it hard.'

She felt her knees go weak. 'I want to suck you,' she said. 'Please?'

Vice pushed her willing head down onto his shaft, still wet from the mouth of young Jenny. Cassandra popped the head of him into her mouth, tasting his sheer masculinity. He was so much bigger up close. She sure as hell was going to get a workout. But it would be a labour of love. Or rather one of lust.

There was no way she could take all of him. Even pulling him to the back of her throat, two thirds was left exposed. Wrapping both hands around the base, she gave him oral pleasure, foreshadowing as best she could what it would be like inside her pussy.

Cassie did not see herself as submissive, though she was most apt to enjoy sex with a man of superior strength or power who could make her feel a bit overwhelmed. Ordinary dating had never seemed to interest her. As a pretty, petite blonde, she had plenty of opportunities, but she preferred to keep things superficial. When she got to college and discovered sleeping around, she was in heaven. The sorority was perfect for her in that regard. So was her choice of political science as a major. The two internships she landed, one at the state legislature and the other at a local campaign office, kept her more than busy between the sheets.

She'd had her share of politicos, most notably the state's current Governor. He was without a doubt the most dangerous and the hardest to walk away from. She still had her dreams where Bryce Clarkson was concerned – or nightmares, as the case might be. He'd branded her, quite simply, touching her in a way no other man ever had. The bastard had gotten deep all right, just because he could. And then, having opened her to the depths of her heart, he'd left it empty, expecting it to stay that way.

Empty, broken promises with the expectation of your continued support in the next election. Wasn't that what politicians were best at? She only regretted not having had the gumption to tell him to go fuck himself long before he came to her with his happy little scheme to marry Lydia Davenport, the conveniently available heiress to a huge hotel chain. Lydia was just his cup of tea. A pretty face with a bottomless purse and a non-existent personality.

Cassie had gotten wise in a hurry to the ways of the world. She'd become hard-nosed and had used the next eight years to look out for number one, parlaying her consulting work into an independent business. Yes, Bryce Clarkson had made her what she was today in many ways. For that she should probably thank him.

'You're good with a cock, Image Lady. You must have done this a lot back in the day.'

Back in the day, indeed. Cassie bit down, just hard enough to immobilise the smart-talking thug. She'd show him that dinosaurs still had teeth.

'Ow,' he cried. 'What are you doing, you crazy bitch?'

See, there was this other side of Cassie, too, and it was the very opposite of submissive. She let him wriggle a moment or two more and then released him. 'Keep it spread,' she advised. 'And don't get in my way.'

Cassandra Dane climbed up onto the rap star's lap. Parting her pussy lips, she placed his impressive specimen of manhood below her opening. This was it, the moment of truth.

'Oh, yeah, now you're gonna get it,' said Vice, wild-eyed. 'Now you're gonna get your little mind blown.'

She was determined to keep control of the situation. Sucking in her breath, she lowered her pelvis, impaling her pussy. Oh, God, the man was gigantic. A fucking log.

'Take it,' said G Killer Vice, grabbing her hips. 'Take my big black cock, Image Lady.'

Cassie moaned, completely and thoroughly fucked. 'Omigod,' she moaned. 'Oh my fucking God.'

'All the way,' he insisted. 'Every last inch.'

Cassandra swallowed him whole, crying out as her pelvis crashed down on his. She was filled with cock – her womb, her belly, up to her eyeballs in man-meat. 'Soooo ... big,' she gasped.

Vice grabbed her tits, massaging them. 'Told you I was gonna give you a workout. You ain't felt nothing yet, though.'

Cassie whimpered, running her hands through her hair. She wanted to beg for something more, but what?

'I got staying power,' he warned. 'You're not going anywhere in a hurry.'

She didn't want to. She wanted to stay like this for ever. She wanted to die here. To come on this mammoth penis and then to die, fulfilled. 'Use me,' said Cassandra Dane, acknowledging the man's power over her. 'Fucking use me.'

G Killer Vice lifted her up a bit, easy as a rag doll. So slow and so sweet. She whimpered as he nearly emptied her pussy. 'Need . . . need it back,' she said.

'Beg for it,' said the rap star.

Cassie flooded in response. He intended to make her act like a slut, with her full and absolute consent. 'Please,' she said. 'May I have your cock back?'

'What are you?' Vice asked.

She moaned, knowing the admission she was required to make. 'I'm your . . . bitch,' she confessed. 'Your little bitch.'

The word just seemed appropriate at the moment.

'That's right. Now you're talking.' Vice put her back in place, privileging her with his erection.

'Thank you,' she breathed, leaning forward to smother him with kisses. 'Thank you.'

'Sit up straight,' he said harshly. 'Hands behind your neck.'

Cassie complied, putting herself into a position of exquisite vulnerability.

'See? I can tame any woman just like that,' bragged Vice to C Money. 'She's my little pet now, aren't you, Image Lady?'

'Yes,' purred Cassie, the little show of domination being fully consensual and pleasurable. 'I'm your pet.'

'Fuck me, pet. Bounce that pussy up and down.'

She lifted herself, moving her body as ordered. In seconds, she was panting with need.

'You ready to fuck C Money?' he asked. 'And Jenny and Lateesha, too? Cause I'm gonna give you to all of them, pet.'

'Meow, meow,' she creamed in reply, playing the perfect pet pussy. 'Sir.'

'You'll do a good job on them too, pet, or I'll spank that tight little ass till it's nice and red.'

'Yes, Vice,' she gasped, rocking her body, pressing her clit against his cock. 'You know I will.'

'I want her ass,' said C Money. 'I want to take her in the ass.'

'Shut the fuck up,' said Vice, not interested in a discussion with his underling.

Cassie ground her teeth as Vice reached back to pinch her butt. 'Faster,' he ordered.

She obeyed, her body rocking and hair flying. Sweat was collecting on her skin. She was indeed a naked pet, fucking in her high heels, a total slut in her own office. Not marriage material, not dating material, just a hot body like in Vice's music video. And, damn, did it feel good, despite the lectures from Stephanie.

'The question,' said G Killer Vice, glorying in his position, 'is where I want to come. Should I do it right now in your little pussy or maybe in your ass? Or should I come on your breasts and on your face? Would you like that, pet?'

'Anywhere,' she said, as if in a trance. 'I'll take it anywhere.'

'That's because you're a little pet,' he confirmed. 'You come when I call. You crawl for me. You spread for me. You swallow for me. Dance for me. Just like in my fucking songs, right?'

'Yes, Vice, just like the songs.' Cassie would never be agreeing to this if she weren't so aroused. It was like a drunkenness, a haze of permissiveness allowing her to be this other person, wanton, totally wicked and sluttish.

'Maybe I'll put you in my next video. This could be your audition.'

She thought of herself in a micro miniskirt, displaying her wares for an audience of millions of pimply boys, hanging all over the rap star, pushing her barely covered body against him for his callous attentions. Fuck, she needed to come. She needed to feel his sperm deep inside her. She needed them both shooting off together.

'Please, Vice, come inside me. Come inside me fast and hard.'

'Why should I?'

'Because . . . I'm a good pet.' She rubbed herself. The friction was flesh on flesh, nerve on nerve, bone on bone. 'I'm a good lay. I'm a hot fucking little cunt.'

What were his trigger words, anyway? Surely there was something she could do to push him over the edge.

'I'll be in your next video, Vice. I'll bump and grind. I'll crawl. I'll be the best little pet. You know you want me. You know you want to own my ass, spank it red and keep me in line. Yours, yours forever.'

Vice was groaning, the sound deep and guttural. He was over, all right, and there was no bringing him back. He wasn't talking or singing exactly, he was rapping, spitting out rhymed words to a down-and-dirty staccato beat. Was this going to be his next hit?

She couldn't follow the words he was saying, but

there was no mistaking the explosion of come deep inside her. She was right there with him, yielding herself up to a ragged sawtooth ride of ecstasy as he pumped her full of his power, his juice. She took it all, revelling in the big man's beautiful orgasm. So good. So overpoweringly, deliciously good.

'Fuck,' said Vice as she fell against his chest, expended. 'You sure know how to get busy.'

She savoured the feel of his muscles as he wrapped his arms around her. 'I'd say I got you a little busy, too, on your next number one song.'

He moved underneath her, indicating he fully intended to be hard again and soon. 'Damn straight. You're a true inspiration, Image Lady. And you're gonna keep on inspiring me, starting by showing me how well you can suck C Money's little dick.'

She grinned wickedly. 'Yes, sir.'

C Money had yet to come. The girls, it seemed, had gotten more interested in each other than they were in the hapless manager. He was just sitting there playing with himself, as he watched the two girls in a standing embrace, kissing and fondling each other's luscious young bodies.

Cassie, too, would have preferred the girl-on-girl action, but she had her orders. Besides, she was starting to feel sorry for old Plug Nickel.

'I'll handle that,' Cassie murmured, kneeling sweetly between his legs.

'I ain't fixing to get played no more,' he proceeded to tell her, as if she were Vice. 'And that's straight up.'

She suppressed a giggle as she gobbled him down. A few good sucks and he'd be singing a different tune.

Cassie was just getting into things when Steph buzzed over the intercom. She knew at once it was important, because Stephanie never disturbed her, no matter what. There could be a full-fledged terrorist attack in the building, and the young woman would try and handle it with a broom and dustpan before she would interrupt a meeting with a client.

Cassie sprang to her feet, clearing her throat on her way to the intercom. True to form, Stephanie fell all over herself with apologies the moment her boss pressed down on the speaker button. 'This just won't wait, though,' she said. 'It's someone pretty high up wanting to see you.'

Cassandra could have made a hundred guesses – hell, maybe a thousand – as to who might need to talk to her this urgently. Still, she would have been entirely unprepared for what her young assistant was about to say.

'It's the governor's office, Cassie. You're wanted there. Immediately.'

She leaned heavily on her desk, images of Bryce Clarkson floating through her mind. Some clothed, some not. 'Tell them ... tell them I'll be there as soon as I can,' she replied, more than a little shell-shocked.

'Um, actually, that won't be necessary,' said Steph, the sheepish tone indicating she had a pretty good idea what had been going on in Cassie's office. 'They've sent a car for you. There's a pair of state troopers out here waiting for you right now.'

Cassie tried to keep her pulse under control. Great, she thought. Just fucking great. Eight years I've been trying to get this man out of my mind and now he wants me in his office right now, with me smelling and looking like something that just crawled out of a Mexican brothel. Talk about Murphy's Law. She'd have to add a whole new one. Any fuck that can go wrong will go wrong, being interrupted by the most difficult, mind-blowingly sexy ex-lover you've ever had. 'Tell them I'll be right out, Steph.'

G Killer Vice and his crew didn't wait for an invitation to sneak out the back door. Having pressed a quick kiss on Cassie's lips, the rap star hauled ass with his entire crew. 'Nothing personal,' he said with a wink, 'but cops make me nervous.'

'Thanks,' smiled Cassie. 'For an excellent ... if incomplete meeting. Shall we try again next week? Same time?'

He shook his head, like she was crazy. 'Whatever you say, Image Lady. But I ain't paying for this by the hour.'

'Don't worry,' she quipped. 'If it's anything like today, I'll be paying you.'

Cassie slipped immediately into her private bathroom for a quick shower. This wasn't the first time she'd had to hide the evidence of an office tryst. It was, however, the first time she'd had to do so for a meeting with the chief executive of the state.

She ran over in her mind all the things the man could want from her. Anything was possible, of course, but when it came right down to it, Cassie's money was on just one.

Bryce Clarkson's libido had gotten him in trouble again. With his re-election for Governor coming up in November and the presidential primaries just two years away, the man couldn't afford any more slip-ups.

Which is where she came in. Cassie Dane was an expert in cleaning up messes. Everybody's, that is, except her own.

3

The troopers were young but cute as hell. Mere babes in the woods, all 'ma'am' this and 'ma'am' that. They apologised a million times for the cramped quarters in the back of the patrol car.

'It's no problem,' she assured them, delicately adjusting the hem of her skirt as they closed her in. 'I imagine you don't want your usual riders to be all that comfortable.'

'No, ma'am,' blushed the taller of the two, a strapping blond, as he tried to keep his eyes off her legs.

She smiled inwardly, not minding at all that these twentysomething hunks were going ga-ga over her thirtysomething chassis. Cassie was never so superficial as to care only about her looks, but she was a woman, a blonde woman at that, and that meant she was entitled to a certain amount of vanity.

To that end she was a fanatic for exercise, desperately staving off the inevitable ravages of time. Her greatest enemies in the world were doughnuts and French fries, and, after that, each and every man who'd ever lied to her, stood her up or broken her heart.

'Hold on tight,' advised the other trooper as he got behind the wheel. This one was a shorter, barrel-chested man, about five ten, with stubbly dark hair. They were both quite scrumptious in their uniforms, their khaki pants crisply creased, their leather gun belts and boots shiny and black.

'To what?' she couldn't help asking as the car eased out into traffic. 'All the good stuff is up front.'

The driver missed his opportunity to hit her up with a sexual innuendo. 'There's a seat belt, ma'am,' he said, as he flipped on the bar lights and sirens to allow them smooth passage through the traffic.

It was an exhilarating feeling, watching the cars dive left and right to avoid the oncoming police car. These boys were too young to know the effect this kind of horsepower and badge power could have on a female her age. Or were they?

'So tell me at least one of you doesn't have a girlfriend,' she quipped. 'Or a happy little fiancée waiting at the altar.'

She would have asked if they were married, but being the good little Girl Scout she was, she'd already noted the lack of a wedding ring on either left hand.

The dark-haired trooper looked at the blond and chuckled. 'Mike here's the one with the sentence hanging over his head. How many days you got left as a free man, buddy?'

'Fifty-three,' said Mike. 'I get married in fifty-three days. And I can't wait either. No matter what Jones here says.'

'Keep telling yourself that,' Jones said. 'Maybe you'll believe it.'

'You must be very much in love,' said Cassie.

Mike passed back a picture of a pretty auburn-haired girl with ribbons in her locks. 'Her name is Marissa. We've been together since high school.'

'She looks lovely,' Cassie acknowledged, fighting little jabs of jealousy. Sure, Trooper Mike liked Cassie's legs, and he'd probably fuck her if she tried hard enough, but she'd never be loved by the man that way.

Never cared for and treasured like Marissa. In sickness and in health. Till death do them part.

She handed back the photo, snapping herself out of her sudden dip into self-pity. You can't have everything in life, she told herself. And what she had was plenty already, more than most women could ever dream of.

Trooper Jones eased the cruiser onto the onramp of the expressway, heading for the Governor's mansion to the north of downtown. 'Marissa's really a great gal,' confirmed the teasing Jones. 'Loyal, beautiful. Too bad she has to settle for this loser.'

'Don't worry, Jones, somewhere out there is a woman for you, too,' Mike assured him. 'Of course, she's got to be legally blind.'

'Screw you,' said Jones, good-naturedly barrelling past an eighteen-wheeled tractor-trailer.

'What about you?' Cassie asked the brown-haired, muscular Jones impulsively. 'Haven't you ever been in love?'

Jones looked in the rear-view mirror. 'Who, me? You gotta be kidding. My old man was in the Marines. We moved every freaking year till I was eighteen. Then I joined up myself. Came out with a hell of a lot of bruises, but no harps and violins.'

She noted the dropping of the 'yes, ma'am' decorum. This Trooper Jones was letting it all hang out. He was her kind of man, she could tell. 'So I gather you don't believe in love?'

His deep brown eyes glared intensely. 'You want that on the record, or off?'

'Off.' Cassie's heart thumped in her chest. Things were going to get inappropriate, she could tell.

'No offence to Mike here, because I believe he's a

sincere man,' replied Trooper Jones. 'But in my humble opinion love is a crock of shit.'

'Interesting,' said Cassie, her finger trailing down her neck to remove a drop of sweat that had settled between her breasts. 'So do you believe in lust, then?'

The square-jawed trooper gave her another look in the mirror, his smile venturing in the distinct direction of a leer. 'At first sight.'

Cassie beamed, totally in her element. 'Would you say you feel lust for me . . . hypothetically speaking?'

'You want that on the record, miss, or off?'

'Oh, off, Trooper Jones, definitely off.'

'In that case, Miss Jones, off the record I would say, given half a chance, I would take you somewhere nice and remote, put you over the hood of this cruiser, bare that little skirt-wearing ass of yours and fuck your brains out.'

'Jonesy, are you insane?' Mike protested. 'This is a VIP. She's on her way to see the Governor himself.'

'It's all right, Mike, I don't mind. In fact,' she said, as she began unbuttoning her blouse, 'I was rather hoping to turn the both of you on. After all, you gentlemen risk your lives protecting me every day . . . me and my little skirt-wearing ass.'

'Ma'am, I have to ask you to stop this at once,' said Mike. 'This is public indecency.'

Cassie kept on unbuttoning. 'What's the matter?' she asked. 'Afraid you'll see something you won't like . . . or something you will?'

Jones laughed low and deep. 'She's got you there, Mikey boy.'

'Ma'am, this is your last warning.'

'I'm a bad girl,' observed Cassie, parting the halves of the silky material. 'A total slut, don't you think?'

Jones had slowed the vehicle down and cut off the lights and siren, apparently deciding to make the trip last a little bit longer. 'If it makes you feel any better, Mikey, we can use these on her.'

Cassie bit her lip as Jones held up the pair of silver handcuffs he'd pulled from his utility belt.

'Yes,' she said huskily. 'I need to be restrained.'

Jones chuckled, tossing them back. 'I'll just bet you do.'

She caught the manacles in mid-air, and clicked them shut on her wrists.

'You're both crazy,' groused Mike. 'And you're gonna get us in a shit storm of trouble.'

'We'll be fine as long as the little lady here keeps her mouth shut.' Jones looked at her pointedly.

'You have my word, officers. Cross my heart and hope to ... die.' Cassie lifted her tits to the troopers. It wasn't death she was hoping for, except maybe the little death, the *petit mort*, that was the French term for orgasm.

'It's not her I'm worried about,' declared Mike nervously. 'It's all these fucking civilians out here. You got any idea how many eyes are on us right now?'

'Maybe we ought to go somewhere nice and remote,' suggested Cassie. 'Just like Trooper Jones said.'

'Screw that,' said Jones. 'I want some action right here and now. Take down the bra, Miss VIP, let's see those nice tits of yours.'

'Jonesy, fer crissakes!'

'Chill out, Mikey. We got nothing to worry about. As far as anyone's concerned she's just some whore or a nutcase we picked up.'

Cassie's heart thundered in her chest. There was no reason for her to do this, and no possible way they could make her do it, either. She had everything to risk and nothing to gain. Someone could see her out here, someone she knew. Her business could be ruined overnight.

Then again, this was America. Land of second chances. One career down the tubes, if flushed spectacularly enough, could give rise to another, ten times more lucrative. Like the phoenix from the ashes. Played right, a scandal could be your best friend.

Anyway, she was horny, exhilarated from the sheer danger and ethical shakiness of the whole thing. She suspected Jones was in the same boat. Mike would be, too, any moment now.

Shivering from the heat up and down her body, Cassie pushed herself beyond the point of no return. Shrugging the blouse over one shoulder and then the other, she pinned her own arms with the material, just below her barely covered breasts.

'Holy shit,' whistled Jones, getting a load of the lace demi-bra. 'She's a VIP all right. No wonder the guv wants to see her. I'll give you three guesses what about, too.'

Cassie's nipples were hard as rocks. She was itching to show them, burning to make these cops blow their corks. Raising her cuffed hands, in an attitude of prayer, she pulled each mound from its fragile pink covering. 'Do you like what you see?' she asked, needing their affirmation, their dirty praise.

'Like it? Honey, I'm like a frigging steel rod up here,' Jones volunteered first.

Mike was trying to keep his eyes on the road, hiding behind a typical cop expression and a pair of mirrored cop shades. He was the one she really wanted to win over because he was trying to fight her so hard.

'Touch me,' she begged, leaning forward. 'Touch my breasts. Please, officer?'

With her hands shackled, she made an inviting package, her arms framing her bosom and displaying her cleavage to maximum effect. Still, he was unmoved. Again, she made her plea, doing her best Scarlett O'Hara-meets-Mae-West-meets-*Casablanca*.

'Just a little touch, Mike. Marissa won't mind. She'll have you her whole life. I'll have ... only this.'

'Touch yourself,' said Officer Jones, unwilling, it seemed, to have her paying so much attention to his partner. 'Put your hand in that sweet cunt of yours.'

'Mmm.' She smiled. 'Yes, sir, Mr Officer.'

Interesting, she thought. Was Jonesy a little jealous?

Thanks to her antics with G Killer Vice and his crew, Cassie was sans panties now, which made it a thing of ease to part her legs for penetration. It was the metal chain of the cuffs she felt first, cold and smooth against her hot pussy lips. 'Oh my frigging God,' she moaned, collapsing forward against the front seat at the sensation.

Mike frowned. He'd had all he could stand. Without actually looking over his shoulder, he felt for and found Cassie's left tit behind him. She whimpered as he massaged it, handling it with firm, manly fingers. It was sort of comical, the way he was trying to act as if he wasn't doing anything, his eyes still focused on the road.

'Yes,' she sighed, trying to get more of his attention. 'Oh, yes, Mike ... that's it ... please don't stop.'

'Careful,' Jones said, again sounding a trifle irritated. 'Don't want to go giving yourself a heart attack just before the wedding.'

Mike told his partner where to get off, and kept right on caressing Cassie's tit.

'Do you do this to her?' Cassie had to know. 'Do you play with Marissa like this?'

'She's saving herself,' the groping cop said grimly. 'For our wedding night.'

Cassie pushed her fingers into her slick sex, desperate to come. 'I'm not saving anything,' she said. 'It's all here for you. Right now.'

'I'm not going to cheat on her,' said Mike, even as his fingers continued to play with another woman's breast.

'This isn't cheating.' Cassie bucked against her own penetrating fingers. 'This doesn't mean anything. It's just . . . watching, mostly.'

'Look at the bitch go,' Jones said to his partner. 'Man, you're not even watching this.'

'Look at me,' Cassie hissed, grabbing his uniformed sleeve with her shackled hands. 'Watch me . . . fuck myself.'

She was writhing like a wild thing, panting like some female beast. They had her caged, these officers, and shackled. She couldn't leave this car against their will, nor could she cover herself up again. It was a perfect, wicked surrender, the kind of thing she dreamed of in the dark recesses of the night under her covers, the vibrator turned up to full, an extra set of batteries held in reserve as she rocked herself to a sweat-coated ecstasy, a sheer, savage passion that no man could ever hope to keep up with.

'Holy Christ,' guffawed the wide-eyed Jones. 'She's going apeshit.'

Cassie was dimly aware of herself screaming, and of Trooper Mike leaning over the seat trying to quiet her. They pulled off two exits early into a restricted truck-weighing area. It was Jones who got in the back with her and brought her back down, gripping her upper arms and looking her in the eye, sternly but with compassion.

What the hell had happened? he wanted to know. Did she always get this wild? The answer was no. It was as if something inside her had come unglued. A carefully suppressed sex-fiend gene, maybe. There was no mistaking it: it was an orgasm like none she'd ever had in her life. She'd squirted all over the patrol car, for heaven's sake. And all without a cock. Just her own fingers. In front of uniformed strangers. No bed. No wine, no candles. No sweet talk.

They had cloths in the trunk and water with which to clean up. The car had borne the brunt of the damage, though it came off fairly easily. Her own clothes, thankfully, had been spared. All in all, it was not too much of a disaster.

Jones, proving more of a gentleman than she could have hoped, forestalled her apology. 'Not a word,' he said, kissing her hand. 'You're a lady in our book. Now and always. Isn't that right, Mikey?'

Trooper Mike hesitated for only a second. 'Yeah,' he sighed, meaning it. 'You're a lady.'

She gave the man a hug. 'Marissa is a lucky lady,' she said. 'I'm jealous as hell.'

To Jones, whom she was a little afraid to embrace, she said, 'I know you're thinking of proposing to me, but I have to tell you, I snore.'

'Thanks for the warning.' He grabbed her for a hug himself, a little more lingering, the way a man holds a woman he's thinking of going to bed with, while knowing it will never happen in real life.

'You better get me to the mansion,' she said, breaking away, 'before we all get our asses kicked.'

Jones grinned, giving her a salute off the brim of his stetson. 'Yes, ma'am. Your wish is our command.'

If only, she thought, lamenting their lack of a little

more time and a nice motel room for the afternoon. If only.

The troopers brought Cassie to the front gate of the mansion. A uniformed guard waved them through a post at the large wrought-iron gates. Security was heavier these days, as it was everywhere at government offices and residences. The stately white Georgian-style structure at the end of the long driveway, with its columns and sweeping, majestic roof and porches, made Cassie think of simpler times, bygone days before terrorist alerts and pre-emptive military strikes.

Smelling the fresh blossoms on the trees and looking at the clear blue sky, you could almost put yourself back a century or two. A different breed of man had occupied the mansion then: stronger, nobler, simpler men. Men who knew how to harness ploughs and hew cabins using their bare hands – and then compose long, heartfelt letters with nothing but quill and ink. Letters to wives and sweethearts far away, as they went off to do their duty, over mountains and across high seas, with nothing but sails and horses to move them, nothing but musket ball and bowie knife to defend their lives.

Cassie smiled at her own reverie. The reality was, of course, quite different. Rustic those men might have been, but they were filled with the same sins as the men of today. Political scandals, corruption in high places and endless calls for reform – throw the rascals out!

Bryce William Clarkson was no worse than the rest. In many ways, he was typical, the epitome of the everyman, always managing to sidestep the critics and the scandalmongers. Oh, but he'd seemed different to

Cassie, once upon a time. She was just twenty-one then, a mere babe in the woods. Clarkson was thirty-one, a state senator, on the fast track to higher office. She was manning the phones one day in his office when he paid the staff a visit. He shook every hand, making everyone there feel like the most important person on the face of the earth.

But it was her he really took notice of. One feel of his enveloping hand and she was lost to him. 'I'd like to discuss some of my ideas with you,' he said, blurring the line between campaign work and a date. 'If you could find the time.'

Find the time? She'd sell her blood or her body in the street for a chance to answer the call of the charismatic young leader with the gorgeous blue eyes and cleft chin.

'Would tonight be too soon?' she blithered, trying not to sound like a total moron.

He laughed lightly, covering her over-eagerness. 'That would be great. Thanks for being so accommodating.'

She accommodated him, all right, in a hotel room across the street from the four-star restaurant he took her to. Till four in the morning she accommodated, giving the man full access to her lithe body. He was as passionate in bed as he was in politicking. It was like being fucked by an ideal. Each orgasm was a platform point, leading to a rising crescendo, a mind-blowing *über*-climax that left her whimpering, on the verge of tears and shaking almost uncontrollably.

True to form, the man told her how to feel about this, too, talking her down to a place of soft, lazy twilight, halfway between dreams and wakefulness.

'I love you,' said the very pathetic, hopelessly naïve intern Cassandra Dane.

The handsome politician dipped immediately between her legs, tickling her to yet another kind of orgasm. At the time she thought it was his way of telling her how he loved her back. It was only later she saw it for the trick it was. A classic diversion. Razzle dazzle at its finest.

Though she'd wanted to be fooled, hadn't she? That was the magic of youth. A steadfast refusal to allow reality to cheat you of your fantasies.

'The Governor is expecting you,' said a businlesslike man as he opened the rear door of the police cruiser the moment they arrived in front of the mansion. Cassie recognised him as the sort of conservative, right-wing-looking man she'd never had any use for. Yet – call it karma, or the result of the mixed-up day she'd had – for some reason, she was finding herself really turned on by the guy. She identified him immediately as security from the earpiece in his ear and his skull-hugging brush cut. The moustache was tightly clipped, too, a perfect match for his bleak expression. With the dark-blue suit, white shirt and red tie, the whole look screamed ex-military. Probably Marines, if she had to guess. Like Trooper Jones' dad.

And Cassie's dad, too, though she hadn't mentioned the point. Truth be told, there were similarities between the cocky lawman and her old man. Spooky ones at that.

'I was hoping to freshen up a bit,' she said, though she didn't really expect a favourable response.

The man with the moustache frowned, as if she was a raw recruit threatening to go AWOL. 'The Governor is on a tight schedule, Miss Dane. You will have to come with me directly.'

Cassie followed him and two similarly attired men fell in behind. She pegged the senior man as being in his late forties. Military men his age tended to have chips on their shoulders, having missed out on what they considered the real wars. Too young for Vietnam, they'd hung on for something else big, only to find themselves too old for the new anti-terrorist wars when they finally came.

Cassie's father had been there for the bulk of the East Asian campaign, right up to the fall of Saigon. As an intelligence officer, he wasn't allowed to talk about it much, but sometimes she and her little brother would hear him at night, sobbing and even screaming as their mother tried to comfort him.

Mostly their mother tried to keep things nice. Cassie was to be the pretty daughter, Andy the strong, capable son. Together they made a model military family, as good as any on the bases they traipsed through. Never mind Daddy's drinking and Andy's drug problems. And her own little problem with saying no to boys.

It was all about appearances. Making the Corps proud. Representing the age-old traditions. Cassie didn't presume to understand such things when she was growing up, and she still didn't. Mostly she kept her mouth shut and tried to be as productive as possible. Other than that, she just fucked around a lot. Dad felt too much guilt, so he either avoided her or spoiled her. Mom was in over her head, too submissive herself to take on the vacant role of acting, functioning head of household.

The Governor's mansion was like a museum. She could scarcely imagine living inside such a place. The entrance alone, with its gold dome and circular staircase, was enough to take away the breath of even the most seasoned Marine brat. Sure, she'd seen a few bigger, more splendid places in other parts of the world, but nothing to match the combined power and history of this place.

The portraits on the wall were of the fathers of the state and of the colony from which it was formed. Together they represented nearly three centuries of wisdom – and more than a dash of human folly, too. What did Bryce make of it, she wondered? What did he think about every time he came down the polished cedar steps, grasping the thick banister, on his way to the dining room with its hundred-foot table, so he could drink his famous morning cocktail of raw egg, milk and nutmeg? Did he feel like an ant in the home of giants? Did he cower beneath all these sombre, staring eyes? Or did he know himself to be up to the challenge?

Cassie suspected the latter. In fact, as the security men led her down the rich red-carpeted hallway with its finely crafted arch, she became more and more convinced of the matter. Bryce wasn't one to back down or be intimidated. Her gut told her he was that kind of man. Her belly, too.

Not to mention her memories. Being made love to by a man of ambition was like nothing else on the planet, and now she was feeling it all over again. She wasn't sure if all of this nakedly displayed power, from the arrogant portraits to the security men with pistols in shoulder holsters, was designed to make women feel horny, but it was certainly having that effect on her.

If she'd had panties left, to put it bluntly, they'd be wet.

The whole way Clarkson had arranged things, from start to finish, was sexy as hell in her mind. He'd sent armed, uniformed men to pick her up, compelling her presence, bringing her here to what was in essence his palace. And now she would go before him, attending to whatever need he'd deemed to be so crucial.

On the other hand, a woman would have good reason to be pissed off, too. Bryce was using his authority to bully her, was he not? And, lest she forget, she had a good reason for never wanting to be in this man's presence again. Eight years was a long time not to have seen him but, in many ways, a lifetime would not be long enough. You didn't put a time limit on that kind of betrayal. You didn't put a statute of limitations on that kind of intimate violation of trust. No matter how handsome and charming the man might be, or how many incredible excuses he might come up with.

All in all, it was an older, wiser Cassie Dane who allowed herself to be ushered through the double doors into the Governor's personal study. Since seeing the man last, she'd had nearly a decade of life experience. Emotionally, it had felt like a century. Just riding here in the police car, walking into this house, had made her aware of how far she'd come.

I'm ready, she thought. Ready to stare down this demon. Ready to move on to a bright shining future, completely free of the past. No more secret dreams in the dead of night, starring Bryce. No more flashes of desire, seeing him on the TV screen. No more running from her own long-dead feelings.

They were bold, well-meaning words, ready to be crafted into a fine speech. Unfortunately, one look at the Governor in the flesh was all it took to send them collapsing to the ground like a house of cards.

What did the eight years or all the insight matter in the end, when Bryce Clarkson was still the sexiest man she'd ever laid eyes on? If anything he was more gorgeous, more chiselled, more distinguished, with a dash of silver-grey in his hair and tiny laugh-lines bespeaking wisdom and the ability to love a woman's flesh even more. Even his eyes were deeper and fuller. All that and a body that had not lost an ounce of its lean strength.

The miserable bastard.

He rose from behind the desk of state and moved to greet her, a study of grace in motion in his grey silk suit. 'Thanks for coming on such short notice,' he said, pressing her hand.

Cassie flushed as she thought of her experience in the police car. She'd certainly come for the officers, hadn't she? 'Just doing my duty as a citizen,' she said, thinking of the two gorgeous troopers. 'I'd expect the same of anyone.'

His smile was complicated, a mix of emotions some of which she recognised and some of which, surprisingly, appeared to be new – acquired responses, she gathered, from the strain of holding public office in the wake of their tumultuous, doomed-from-the-beginning affair. 'You have a high estimate of the average citizen's sense of duty,' he observed. 'Then again, you always were an optimist.'

Until you came along and smashed my hopes, she was tempted to say. 'Just trying to see the glass half-full and not half-empty,' she replied with a careless shrug. 'You know the drill.'

'Indeed.' He raised a perfect brow. 'So I do. You know Ron and Cowell, I believe?'

She followed the sweep of his arm to the two men who had risen from their seats, along with their boss, when she entered the luxurious, book-lined room. She wasn't exactly on a first-name basis with the pair, since she worked largely with members of the opposing political party these days, but she certainly knew them by reputation. The older one, with distinguished, hard-earned wrinkles, a crop of white hair and a sort of permanent, thick-browed half frown, was Cowell Owens, Bryce's Secretary of State and one of the truly venerable institutions in state government. It was said that Cowell was the only man who could tell Bryce to his face that he was full of shit and get away with it. Not that a man of his breeding would ever stoop to such language.

'It's about time such beauty graced this office.' He kissed her hand with surprisingly vibrant lips. 'Bryce, you've been holding out on us,' he chided.

Cassie grinned, liking the man at once.

'He was only trying to protect her,' chimed in Ron, the Governor's long-time Press Secretary. 'From your notorious predations.'

Cowell winked at Cassie. 'They're just jealous because all the young ones still chase after me instead of them.'

'Who could blame them?' she riposted. 'You are obviously a man of both charm and good looks.'

Cowell nodded with great satisfaction. 'I can see why you wanted her for the job, Bryce. She's a genius all right.'

Bryce forced a smile. Again Cassie saw the strain on his face. Damn it, how was she supposed to not feel anything for a man who was looking this pathetic?

'Won't you sit down?' asked Ron, offering her a wingback, a far more upscale, antique version of the ones in her office, complete with genuine Victorian red velvet upholstery.

'Thank you.' She took her place gingerly, aware of all the things that had been happening of late between her legs. Seeing the gorgeous Governor in the flesh certainly wasn't helping matters any in that regard.

She watched him resume his place behind the desk. How heavy his brow looked as he steepled his fingers below his chin. Whatever was going on, it didn't appear that he was going to be able to talk about it himself.

'Miss Dane, all kidding aside, I am going to lay this out for you as plain as I can,' said the pudgy and balding Ron. 'As you know, we are in a sensitive time here. With the re-election and all. The Governor has certain enemies, as you can imagine. I think it's safe to say, really, that anyone of his stature would be a target for, shall we say, certain extortionary practices.'

'Confound it, boy, stop beating about the bush,' Cowell chastised. 'It's high time somebody stopped dressing up the sows and passing them off as blue-ribbon hogs. What we've got, my dear lady, is a case of *in flagrante delicto*, to wit a video-recorded liaison between the Governor and a certain party which stands to ruin the man's career if we don't deal with it.'

A videotape ... of Bryce screwing someone? Now that was news. Bad news, if you were the man himself or anyone in his organisation. 'You've seen it, I gather?' Cassie asked.

'Yes, and we've a copy for you.' Ron inclined his head to the edge of the desk where Bryce was continuing to brood. 'You may view it at your leisure.'

Cassie considered the black cassette then returned her gaze to the Governor and his aides. 'That's an interesting offer,' she said drily. 'Though I suspect you had a little more in mind when you brought me here than renting me a stag film?'

Ron cast a look at Cowell, indicating he was uncertain how much to tell her. 'We're talking blackmail, Miss Dane. We've been made to understand there are a hundred more copies of this, ready to be released to every media outlet in the state – unless the Governor tenders his resignation.'

'Why wait on him to do that?' Cassie wondered aloud. 'Why not use the tape and ruin him now?'

Ron flashed Cowell a slightly guilty expression, one that gave Cassie the distinct feeling this was going to come down to some jealous woman having had a tiff with the married Governor, which they now wanted her to smooth over.

'Well,' Ron said, screwing up his face as if he was getting ready to launch into one of his notoriously long press statements, 'as you know, Miss Dane, politics often operates on a number of levels, and –'

'Confound it, Ronald,' said Cowell. 'We need to call a spade a spade. The woman is too smart to listen to any gobbledygook. Look, Miss Dane, we all know that Bryce has messed up here, bigger than ever. But we also know the man has managed to do a few decent things while in office and we'd like him to do a few more. If there is any way to save him, damn it, we'd like to do it, in spite of himself.'

'We know the woman,' said Ron. 'She's the one we want you to contact. We will provide you with whatever you need, and through you the Governor will convey his deepest –'

'Blast it, Ron, I can't go through with it.' The Governor had suddenly come to life. 'I can't ask Cassie to do this. Hell, maybe I should resign.'

'Sir, really, we have this under control,' Ron insisted.

'It's not about control,' said the Governor, shaking

his head. 'It's about doing what's right for the people of this state.'

Cassie gripped the armrests of the chair. Oh, God, those eyes of his were lifting up and pointing right at her, in all their splendid sapphire brilliance.

'Cassie, you have my deepest apologies for allowing you to be dragged into this. I will have security take you home.'

'Not so fast,' said Cowell, talking to him the way only he could. 'Before you go trying to mount any high horses here, let me remind you that you're a bit rusty in that department. Frankly, you don't have the luxury of bowing out gracefully any more. You're in a fight and you'll stick it out. Win or lose. As for what the people need, that's up to them to decide – in the election. Don't you dare take that right away from them.'

Bryce looked about five years older as the tension drained from his face. 'All right, I will withdraw my objections, so long as Cassie agrees.'

Oh, great, now it was all up to her.

'Let me just get this straight.' She opted to buy a little time as all three pairs of eyes settled expectantly upon her. 'I am being asked to put my reputation on the line in order to help Bryce make nicey-nice with some woman he's been having adultery with so she won't ruin his career?'

Ron sighed heavily. 'That's a bit less diplomatic than the way I would put it, but, essentially, yes, that is the case.'

'Thank you for your honesty. I'm curious, though. Why me?'

'That was Bryce's doing,' said Ron. 'He insisted it be you.'

'How kind of you, Bryce,' she said sarcastically. 'To what do I owe the honour?'

What's the matter, she thought, didn't you kick me around enough the first time?

It was Ron who answered. 'Bryce knows you're the best. He also feels, for reasons he will not divulge, that you will be the most honest and the least likely to defend him if he doesn't deserve it.'

She felt a little lump in her throat. The last thing she needed was for the man to be showing signs of nobility right now. 'In that case,' she replied, 'I accept . . . also for reasons I will not divulge.' She looked at Bryce pointedly. If he was feeling the guilt she wanted him to feel, he betrayed no signs of it.

'The people are in your debt,' said Cowell.

Cassie was in a daze when they all rose to their feet a few moments later. She dimly remembered Ron passing her a large manila envelope with the tape in it, along with information as to how to contact the woman on the tape.

'You can call us any time,' Ron told her as he shook her hand. 'Day or night.'

'It's been a genuine pleasure.' Cowell gave her another kiss on the knuckles.

Bryce came out from behind his desk and kissed her hand as well. His flesh was warm, every bit as alive and vibrant as she remembered. Her knees went weak as she tried to say something clever by way of good-bye. All she could think of was melting into his arms, drawing upon his strength and, at the same time, comforting him too.

The next thing she knew, the sexy head security man was leading her out of the room and back down the hallway. Cassie was disappointed to find it wasn't the trooper car waiting for her but a taxicab. The security man slipped the driver fare money and opened Cassie's door.

'Are they always that uptight in there?' she asked him, craving conversation with someone less high and mighty.

The man managed a wry smile. 'Actually you caught them on a good day. Usually they're worse.'

'Thanks for the tip. I'm Cassie, by the way, in case you didn't know.'

'Cray Wilder,' he replied, in what was no doubt a show of extraordinary warmth and reciprocity for a man like him.

'Pleased to meet you,' she said. She caught herself wondering what he'd look like with his shirt off. Not to mention his pants. A man like that would be all muscle. He might even have a tattoo, two or three of them, tasteful and discreet, and probably some kind of scar as well.

Would her troopers have tattoos? They'd have fine bodies. Especially Jones. Making a mental note to try and find all this out for herself, she waved goodbye, watching Wilder's stark figure disappear from sight as the cab took off down the drive towards the front gate. All in all, it had been quite a day – from brand-new lusts to a rekindled flame from long ago. And from here on in, it would only get more interesting.

So many men, decided the 'Image Lady' with a sigh, and so few angles to spin.

4

Bryce had thought he could handle seeing Cassie again, but he'd been wrong. In reality, she'd nearly devastated him, blowing him wide open with desire. You would think, after nearly a decade, the woman would lose her appeal. Hell, it hadn't been a very long relationship at that. She was beautiful and all, but so were a lot of the women since. Time and distance should have been on his side, but instead it had only made her more alluring in his eyes. What was it about her now, with her air of maturity and wisdom? Damn, it was as if she wore her political savvy like a fragrance.

And talk about sexy. She moved like a cat. Who said a woman looked best at twenty? That was like drinking a two-year-old brandy instead of giving it time to age to perfection. He could only imagine her in ten more years, or even twenty.

It was not a good idea to be working with her and he knew it. She was a temptation *par excellence*. Cowell had already warned him in unusually blunt terms behind closed doors that when he was around her he must keep his pecker zipped at all costs. They simply could not afford another slip at this point, no matter how many horses had already escaped the proverbial barn.

Cowell didn't have his libido, though. He didn't have to deal with the hard-on after she'd left. God, one touch of her hand and he'd been ready to sweep her off her feet and make love to her right there in the office, with the other two watching.

That image stuck in his mind for the rest of the day as he went through the motions of meeting with various advisors and community groups, posing with groups of children and senior citizens in the metropolitan area. He was down to one more photo opportunity with the Hispanic League of Voters and after that a trip back to the mansion to get ready for a charity ball for the Museum of Contemporary Art.

It was at this point that events took another turn south. Cray broke the news, as always claiming for himself the role of bearer of bad tidings.

'Sir, we have a situation back at the compound,' he declared, poking his head into the back of the limousine.

Bryce looked wearily at the man. Wilder's brow was furrowed. He had his finger pressed to his earpiece, no doubt soaking in the radio chatter as he spoke. The man lived for moments like these. Every problem was a situation and, at times like these, he never failed to employ as much jargon as he could from his days in the Special Forces.

'It's the First Lady, sir. Household staff is requesting reinforcements.'

Wonderful. Lydia was throwing another tantrum.

'Get her on the phone, I'll see if I can get her calmed till I get back.'

Wilder pressed his lips together, focusing on the voices in his head. It was true, the man might be overly serious at times, but, if there were any real trouble, this was the one man in the world Bryce would want protecting him. And his wife, too. Besides, Cray looked the other way when Bryce needed women and you couldn't put a price tag on that.

'Negative on that, sir. It appears you are the . . . uh, source of her anger at the moment.'

He rolled his eyes. 'Did I roll up the toothpaste wrong again?'

It was an unfair jibe at the woman. For all her histrionics and her recent drinking habits, she'd certainly been suffering, quietly, for a very long time. He really doubted he would have lasted eight months with a spouse who cheated as much as he did, let alone eight years. Then again, she was a Davenport woman, raised to suffer in silence, keep a stiff upper lip.

Wilder's scowl deepened. The furrows reached the depths of craters. 'Sir, we need to abort this current mission and return to base. We have escalation in hostilities. It seems the First Lady has gotten hold of our copy of the tape.'

Bryce's heart sank. Son of a bitch. This was the one thing in the world he wanted to avoid. Lydia was prone enough to hysteria without seeing actual footage of his infidelities. Blast it, he was so furious with Queenie. What had possessed Abigail? Why would she want to ruin him like this? There had to be something else going on, he was sure of it. Maybe Cassie could get to the bottom of it.

Good old Cassie, loyal to the end. Was he just using her? No more than he had any other woman. He wasn't a perfect man, but he tried his best to do good for others. Could he help it if that list included the whole damned state – and they all wanted different things?

'Turn the car round,' the Governor ordered. 'Ron, get a substitute to talk to the Hispanics. Extend my apologies.'

Never enough of those to go around, he thought glumly.

'Yes, sir,' the Press Secretary replied with a nod.

They returned to the mansion in silence. It was pre-combat time and they all knew it. Lydia could be hell on wheels on a good day. And this, without a doubt, was not a good day.

Cassie hit the rewind button on the remote for the sixth time. She was on her bed, propped up against the headboard, having come home directly from the Governor's office. Legs wide apart, pussy wide open and throbbing, she readied herself for yet another orgasm. It was a pretty shameless thing to do, getting off on the Governor's sex tape, but the way she saw it the man owed her. Besides, if she was really to wrap her head around this assignment, she needed to be deeply imbedded in its elements.

The thing that struck her most, watching Bryce interact with the curvaceous redhead dominatrix, was how much he was enjoying himself in the submissive role. This was a side of the man she'd never seen. Who knew that a man who gravitated so much towards power would want to give it up so completely in sex? Then again, maybe that was the point. He was obtaining some kind of release from all that stress he bore day to day. There was also that element of worship. Bryce Clarkson had always been a romantic, a man fascinated by the feminine mystique.

That was his real secret with women. He respected them completely, even as he blatantly used them for sex. It was a complicated formula. He would lift you to the heavens, but only for a night or, in her case, a few precious, misguided months. What wouldn't a woman give up for such an experience? What wouldn't Bryce himself give up to offer it? He'd certainly given up a lot by going to that motel room. He had to know the dangers. It was almost as if he were asking for it.

Damn it, the man looked good though, all tied down like that, straining against the bonds, his face so expressive and lust-filled behind that blindfold. His body hadn't suffered at all during the time she'd been apart from him. It was true what they said about all the exercise he got. The man treated himself as a temple.

Even if he did walk all over his marriage vows in a very unholy way.

Could she do what this Queenie Amazon was doing? Could she wear latex and high heels, wielding a whip to make the chief executive crawl? Could she believe that much in her sexual mystique – enough to turn the tables on this notorious womaniser? He'd gone to her willingly too, that was the rub.

Cassie stroked her dripping pussy, feeling a pang of jealousy. She wanted to be in that picture. She wanted Bryce ... again.

She knew this was not good. Not good at all. Lifting her hips, she tried to think of someone else, anyone else, as she built herself to what she vowed would be her last orgasm of the day. She needed to get back to work. She needed to call her office, find out what was going on, then call Queenie, whose real name was Abigail Auvignon.

First, though, she needed to get off, and for that she needed a male image. There had certainly been enough hot bodies to stimulate her libido today, but whom would she settle on, other than Bryce? The rap star? The trooper? The security chief? In the end she chose Jones, driving with him in her imagination to that remote spot he'd wanted so badly to take her to.

It's a dirt road, deep in the woods. He has her in the back seat, her hands cuffed behind her. He is looking in the rear-view mirror, reading her rights.

'You have the right to be fucked,' he tells her. 'The right to spread yourself for me. You have the right to squeal when I give it to you and the right to beg me to stop when I spank your tight little ass. You have the right to come. And come. And come.'

He hauls her out of the back seat and lays a deep kiss on her pliant lips. She leans against the side of the patrol car to keep her balance. She's still wearing the blouse and skirt from before, though this time he has no qualms about ruining them.

'Got any concealed weapons?' he asks with a grin, tearing open her blouse. She is helpless to stop him as he pushes the bra down out of the way of his greedy hands.

'Only these two, officer,' she says demurely.

Trooper Jones handles her breasts, squeezing them the way a real man does, one who wears a badge and puts his life on the line. He holds them as if there might not be a tomorrow, and right now, in her daydream, she doesn't care if there isn't.

'You did a lot of teasing this morning,' he reminds her. 'What do you think we should do about that?'

Her nipples are rubbery as he rolls them between his fingers. 'I should be punished,' she whispers hotly.

'Yes, you should,' he agrees. 'And first we need to get you nice and hot for it.' He sinks to the ground on one knee, lifting her skirt and pulling down her panties just enough to get at her snatch. His tongue is strong and masterful, snaking its way into all the right crevices. She cries out as he finds her clit and sucks on it till it is swollen and tight. She wants to come so bad, but she knows he will make her wait.

Pulling her panties back up and rising to his feet, Trooper Jones puts his hands on her shoulders. It is time for her to go down on her knees in the dirt. She is starving for his cock, desperate to please him. He opens his khaki trousers, pulling out a beautiful, thickly veined shaft, which she immediately sets to worshipping. The man is at least five years younger than her, and she can scarcely believe the power he has over her. It's the uniform, of course, and his body. The thick biceps and the barrel chest. He is all man and will accept her as nothing less than all woman.

'I'm gonna give you a good spanking,' he tells her. 'Then we will get down to business.'

She sucks him enthusiastically in response. She is his prisoner, wrists still cuffed, and she wants him to know she is going to be cooperative. Obedient.

'That's enough.' He snakes his hand in her loose, sweat-soaked hair. 'Time for your sentence.'

She feels the tug on her scalp. It is a delicious pressure that passes right down to her burning pussy. She wants it rough. She wants the young cop in charge.

'You'll feel the metal on your bare tits,' he explains, making sure her bra and shirt are out of the way as he pushes her down onto the hood of his vehicle. The engine is still warm and her nipples respond helplessly to the smooth metal.

'Is this what you were hoping for,' he asks, tearing away her skirt, 'when you cock-teased my partner and me today?'

'N – no, sir,' she croaks.

The officer's hand falls across her panty-clad ass. 'What did you say?'

'Ouch,' she cries, her distress disturbingly erotic. 'All right, yes, this is what I wanted.'

'I thought so.' Trooper Jones shreds the panties like

paper, exposing her ass and pussy. 'That lie will cost you,' he says.

She moans as he delivers ten more smacks, heating her flesh to incendiary temperatures. She squirms, pulling her wrists against the cuffs.

'Have you learned your lesson?'

'Oh, sir, yes, sir, I have.'

'We'll see,' he growls and, next thing she knows, his cock is at the entrance to her sex, wanting, demanding entrance. She is wet and ready to receive him, as open as she's ever been in her life.

'You will not come until I tell you.'

'Oh, sir,' she cries. 'Oh, yes . . .'

He slides his pole to the hilt then begins to create a steady, rhythmic thrusting that will bring them both off, fast.

Cassie holds out as long as she must until at last she yields at his command to a gut-wrenching orgasm. The man matches her, filling her with a copious load, warm and heaven-sent. On and on it goes.

Cassie sighed as the dream faded, her orgasm secure. Sated, she pulled her fingers from her centre. Mission accomplished, she thought with a smile. Now to earn her fee. How odd, she reflected, they never even mentioned whether they would pay me or not. At this point she supposed it would depend on the outcome. A bad result would leave none of them worth a plug nickel.

Her included.

In that case, they could all go work for Killer Vice. He'd have a whole lot of Plug Nickels then, wouldn't he?

Bryce rapped lightly on the door at first, on the off chance Lydia had gone to sleep, or passed out, as was the case more often than not these days. 'Lyd, are you awake? It's me. Can I come in?'

Lydia Davenport Clarkson responded in typical fashion, throwing something breakable against the closed door. The sound of crashing glass gave him all the answer he needed. His wife was awake, and still very pissed off.

'Go to hell, Bryce! I never want to see you as long as I live!'

He'd heard that one before, though admittedly she'd never actually seen him tied down on a strange bed before, with a strange woman riding his cock like there was no tomorrow. Yes, this was going to require an extra-sensitive touch on his part. Still, she'd come around in the end. She always did.

'Sweetheart, let's be reasonable and settle this like adults.' He opened the door a crack just in time to have a vase flung at his head.

'Fuck you,' she exclaimed. 'And that fucking self-righteous attitude you rode in here on, too.'

Bryce deflected the crystal vase, cursing himself for neglecting to have her room swept for potential weapons this month, as usual. 'I've made a mistake, Lydia. I freely admit that. I'm here to apologise.'

'Apologise?' His wife laughed at him from the crouching position she'd assumed on her king-size four-poster bed. She really was fucking beautiful like this, her hair a tangled mess, her eyes bloodshot, her chest heaving, barely covered by a short spaghetti-strap nightie. 'What the fuck would you apologise for? You're not sorry. This is your whole way of life. Winning votes. One fuck at a time.'

He noted the empty vodka bottle on the floor. 'You're drunk, Lydia. You don't know what you're saying.'

'Oh, I know plenty fine, you just don't like hearing it is all.'

This was not the conversation he wanted to be having at this moment, not by a long shot. Still, he needed to get the woman under control. 'Let's get you laid down.' He put his hand on her shoulder. 'A little nap and you'll feel worlds better.'

'Let go of me.' She shrugged him off. 'You don't have the right to touch me.'

He reached for her again and this time she smacked him, taking him by surprise with a blow to his famously squared jaw. 'Son-of-a-bitch!' He grabbed his chin.

Lydia backed away, her eyes full of fury, her teeth gritted. Hell hath no fury, he thought grimly, like a Davenport woman scorned. 'You are going to lie down,' he said firmly. 'And that is that.'

'What, am I supposed to be scared of you?' she spat. 'According to that tape, all I have to do is crack my whip and you'll come crawling. Isn't that how you like it, Bryce? On your hands and knees? Tied down on your back?'

Bryce frowned. He was not at all happy about having his sexual proclivities ridiculed, least of all by his singularly unavailable and uptight wife. 'At least I like sex, Lydia, which is more than we can say for you.'

The remark was ill-advised, especially given her inebriation. The half-naked, barefoot heiress, still extraordinarily youthful and fit at thirty-seven, flew at him, all claws and teeth. She got in a couple of good swipes at his face before he managed to pin her down on the bed.

'Go ahead,' she panted, her wrists secured by his hands. 'Do it to me. Rape me. You know you want to.'

Bryce's cock swelled inside his pants. 'I don't want to rape you, Lydia, and you don't want that either.'

'How the hell would you know what I want?'

'I have no idea,' he admitted. 'It's been too long. Way too long.'

She avoided his eyes, scared as always of the emotion they might contain. All of Richard Davenport's children had this trait. It was the natural result of growing up with a tyrant.

'Look at me, Lydia.'

'No. I hate you, Bryce. Just get out. Please.'

Bryce kissed his wife, capturing her swollen lips. Even without lipstick, they were blood-red, luscious and sensuous beyond belief. It was her lips he'd noticed first upon being introduced to her by a mutual acquaintance. Always he'd tried to keep such personal things about her in the forefront of his mind, especially when weighing the obvious political gains that came from her bank account and connections.

It was hard to love a rich woman. And harder still for a rich woman to feel loved in return. What if Lydia were poor? He'd often wondered this. Would he have picked her from a crowd? Would he have seduced her – for that excellent body of hers, and for those lips and long, raven-black hair? Seduction, yes, but marriage, that was another question entirely. He'd never really seen himself married to anyone before he met her. The concept held little meaning for him.

Except with Cassie. In the depths of her eyes, in the warm, conspiratorial comfort he felt when the two of them would talk politics long into the night, sometimes to the detriment of the sex. He'd never had that with any other woman before or after – enjoying her company so much that he forgot, for a little while, about bedding her.

Although there was another – a woman he was trying his best to block from his mind at the moment. A woman by the name of Abigail, who had fractured his trust and maybe, just maybe, broken his heart into the bargain.

Lydia kissed him in return, moaning her protests. It was a kiss of spite, a cold locking of lips, a cruel engagement, teeth to teeth. The problem with any strong emotion, however, was that it too easily turned into its opposite. In this case, overwhelming, unquenchable lust. In no time at all, her mouth was opening, her tongue reaching for his. Arching her back, she pressed her peaked nipples to his chest.

This was how it worked between them, the few times that it had over the years, and it was the only way he'd ever known his wife to be capable of passion. Sex after battle, in the wake of harshly spilt words and deep, ingrained contempt. That's what made her wet, that's what turned her on.

'You're an adulterous bastard,' she hissed in his ear the moment he released her. 'You make a mockery of our wedding bed. You sleep with fucking whores. Whores who make perverted tapes to humiliate me. Tapes of you tied like an animal. Jeezus, Bryce, can't you even have decent normal sex, at least?'

'You wouldn't know the meaning of the word.' Grasping her small wrists in one hand, he used the other to feel between her legs. 'What kind of normal wife gets horny watching her husband cheat on her?'

'I didn't get horny from that disgusting tape,' she said, squirming. 'I got horny thinking about you finally ending up in jail where you belong, a couple of nice big muscle men greasing you up and making you beg for it in the ass. You like that idea, Bryce? You ready to be someone's prison bitch?'

Bryce manipulated his wife's pussy, inducing a deep moan. He'd always known how to touch her, how to make her body function in counterpoint to her attitude. 'What are you babbling about prison for?' he demanded. 'I've done nothing wrong.'

She smiled darkly, her hips undulating in time to his masturbating hand. 'Oh, no? What about Landview?'

Bryce might as well have been punched in the solar plexus by a champion prizefighter. Landview was a development project, and not just any project, either. Over the course of the next three years it would bring billions into the state economy, as well as create thousands of new jobs and an entirely new community where there was nothing but swamp. He'd signed off on everything up to now, but in recent weeks he'd been hearing disturbing reports that some of the backers might have ties to organised crime. A full investigation was being planned. Lydia's father Richard Davenport, one of the biggest investors, had urged him to keep things on track, but if need be Bryce would stop it altogether till the charges were sorted out. No amount of money was worth it if it came from drug dealers and pimps and murderers.

'What about Landview?' Bryce demanded. 'Who have you been talking to? Your pill-popping mother? I've already been over this with your father – he gave me his full assurance everything was above board.'

Lydia feigned shock at his outburst. 'Is the big, powerful Governor reduced to asking his feather-brained socialite wife for help?' she taunted. 'For shame, Bryce Clarkson. For shame.'

Bryce had had enough politics for the day.

'Enough talking, Lydia. It's time for you to perform

your wifely duties.' Bryce tore the nightie from the neckline, ripping it clean in half.

'Does that make you feel like a big man?' she wanted to know.

His hand returned to her sex. She was sopping wet, more than ready for penetration. He decided to make her suffer a little first. 'No. I think I need some more affirmation.'

'Well, there isn't very much I can do, is there?' observed his pinned-down wife. She was pretending displeasure, but he could tell from the flush in her cheeks and the excitement in her eyes that he was reaching her, at a visceral level far below the morass of words and innuendoes that usually flowed between them. If only this kind of heat could be sustained outside the bedroom, or even within it, they would be an inseparable team, unbeatable. For some strange reason, it always came down to the right balance of power – her willingness to submit and his to dominate.

He played with her nipples, making her shiver. 'I would like you to say how sorry you are for throwing a vase at me.'

'At least it wasn't an axe,' she replied defiantly.

Bryce pinched the vulnerable flesh, inducing an instant attitude change.

'I'm sorry.' She winced. 'I shouldn't have thrown it.'

'And I shouldn't have slept with another woman,' he replied.

She looked at him, her eyes liquid. She was as alive as he'd seen her in years. 'Why?' she asked, the sheer heartfelt simplicity of the question undoing him completely. 'Why do you do it?'

His own eyes watered, too. 'I wish to God I knew, Lyd.'

The beautiful Lydia took a deep breath, closing her eyes. She was about to restore her dignity, the way she always did. The slate was about to be wiped clean, as it had been a hundred times before.

'Let me be what you need,' she whispered. 'Let me be your slut.'

These were all the words he needed to hear. 'Lydia,' he breathed into her neck. 'I love you. I always have.'

It was true, in a strange sort of way. From the moment he'd taken his vows and been given charge of her life, he'd felt that affection. Bryce Clarkson was not a faithful man, but he was a loyal man. He stood by people. And he took responsibilities to heart. From the kittens he'd been given as a boy, after successfully begging his father not to drown them, to his own grandfather, whom he visited twice a day, before and after school, fixing him meals and keeping up his house, giving him the illusion of self-sufficiency long after he should have gone to a nursing home, Bryce had been there. It was his deepest drive in life.

It was why he'd chosen politics. And it was why he would be leaving it, too, as soon as he convinced the venerable Cowell to let him resign.

'Just ... fuck me,' his wife hissed, her nails digging into his shoulder blades.

One stop first. Something overdue. Something owed from long ago. Something from the lips to ease, if not counter, the treachery. She gasped in surprise as he kissed between her legs. She was a beautiful woman here, too, a lady, an angel. Nuzzling her, he coaxed the lips apart. A woman should never be trifled with. By God, why didn't he do this more often with Lydia ... really love her?

He was rewarded with deep sighs as he dabbed his tongue. She was sweet on his lips, pure as only a woman faithful to her husband could be. He suckled the sex lips, then plunged deeper, his tongue a miniature cock to give a foreshadowing of ecstasy to come.

She tensed as he found the clit. She was close already. He could make her explode this way or give it to her in the way that would fulfil them both at once.

He opted for the latter, shedding his clothes, baring his naked body to the one woman who was supposed to see it like this: erect, nipples stiff, skin flushed and ready for love. There was no need to hold Lydia's hands down now. She was open, legs spread, reaching for him, in fact. This was no millionaire's daughter he was dealing with now, but a hungry female, earthy and horny. He wasted no time sinking his cock between the folds of her swollen outer lips. She groaned as the friction built along her clit. Gone was his ice goddess, gone his paragon of cynical indifference. Feverishly, he clung to her, his mouth devouring one small, rounded breast and then the other. He'd had this on his mind from the moment he'd seen her, hellfire in her eyes, rage on her tongue. God help him, he would probably cheat again just to get her back to this point.

'Fuck,' she cried. 'Oh, my God.' Lydia's strong legs, well exercised by years of tap dance and jazz through college, wrapped around his ass. Her French-manicured nails raked his back, in all likelihood drawing blood, though at the moment he felt nothing. All the better. He wanted the marker, wanted the pain and afterwards the memory. Who knew how long it would be till their lives coincided like this again.

Bryce's cock swelled fiercely inside her. They were still a damned good fit. The first time they'd made love, she'd screamed like a banshee. What a pleasant shock for both of them as they tangled on the thick carpeting, wet from the Jacuzzi and drunk from champagne in a hotel suite overlooking the Grand Canal in Venice.

She'd looked so incredible asleep afterwards. He watched her for a while, unable to sleep. He told himself it was because he felt unworthy of her that he snuck downstairs to fuck one of the maids, but that seemed rather self-serving in retrospect. He was simply establishing the precedent of being a cheating prick, that was all.

'Give it to me,' she groaned. 'You bastard ... screw me.'

There was more than a little irony in that request. Bryce did his best to comply, working to a furious pace, slamming his cock home over and over, pile-driving her small frame deep into the underutilised mattress. She clung to him the whole time, along for the ride, encouraging, giving back as good as she got.

'Gonna ... fucking ... come,' he announced, the declaration coming in three distinct blasts of air from his flaring nostrils.

'Oh, Jeezus,' she cried, as if she was about to behold a sacred mystery. 'Oh, my God.'

It wasn't particularly religious, though, it was animal. Two bodies, locked limb to limb, coated in sweat, with a long complicated history that only ever seemed to work itself out this way. They were fucking because otherwise they'd probably end up killing each other.

Bryce came with all the vigour of a twenty-year-old. The woman, his wife, accepted it with all the wonder, heat and mystery of a virgin. This, too, was fortunate, as he could never become bored with her in bed, or she with him. Her spasming sex encouraged his own final pushes, calling on him to squeeze out every drop. Chest to chest, lips locked once more, they enjoyed the final moments of the act, knowing all too soon it would end, engendering once again the inevitable recriminations and awkwardness.

She clung to him a little longer than usual and he did his best to stay inside her. At last, however, his organ shrivelling, he was obliged to remove himself. Rolling onto his back, he covered his eyes with the back of his arm. Seconds ticked by, with neither of them speaking, no signs of affection passed between their tingling bodies. His fingers were so close to hers, but they were like lead, immovable. He couldn't bring himself to close that gap between them and hold hands, and neither could she.

They were back to square one.

She broke the silence at last. 'Well, I suppose that's that.'

He had no answer for this and so it became a self-fulfilling prophecy. Rising from the bed, he looked for his clothes and put them on in record time. At the last second he remembered the charity ball.

'I'll be ready,' she said robotically, sounding too tired to fight.

'Good,' he said with a nod, though at the moment it was anything but good.

Closing the door behind him, he heard her quietly begin to sob. He wanted more than anything to go back and hold her, but, as she'd said in the beginning, he had no right. No jurisdiction. Quietly, the chief executive went to his own bedroom, feeling utterly powerless. It was a sensation he did not relish at all, but one he would have to get used to, sooner rather than later.

5

Cassie double-checked the name and address of the club she'd scribbled on the back of one of her old grocery lists. Leather Love, 1401 East 30th Street. This was the place, all right. Finding a spot for her convertible a block or so up, she ventured onto the dimly lit, litter-strewn sidewalk.

Thirtieth Street was in the old warehouse district. They'd done a lot of refurbishing in recent years, turning many of the dilapidated old structures into bars and nightclubs. The places had themes, from cowboys to motorcycles, though mostly it was about getting drunk and throwing bottles without having to worry about damaging nearby homes or stores.

Cassie had been to several of these places before, though she'd never ventured inside the Leather Love. It was considered a hardcore establishment, catering to sadomasochistic types. Hopefully her all-purpose black cocktail dress and pearls would pass muster with the bouncers.

She'd called earlier, looking for Queenie. A rough-sounding man with a New Jersey accent had answered.

'I was given this number,' she told him, 'by a mutual friend . . . in a very high place.'

'Be here at ten,' he told her, catching her meaning. 'She'll be here.'

She'd pressed for further information, to which he replied with a resounding click, terminating the call.

There wasn't anything in this to make her feel better, that was for sure. Why the hell was she even doing this? With the passage of each hour, it made less and less sense for her to be trying to get in the middle of something she didn't understand. There was some kind of bad blood here, and Bryce needed to be facing up to it.

That was the trouble with the world. Men were always making messes, and women were forever rushing in to clean them up. Even if those very same men had already hurt them with their carelessness. She'd believed in this particular man long ago and would have done almost anything for him, but could she really say she knew the Bryce Clarkson who sat behind that big desk today? Had she seen even a glimmer of the bright, funny young man she once knew? The man who wasn't afraid to frolic barefoot in the grass or dance in the moonlight with his sweetheart in his arms?

The thing that really got her today was his eyes. She'd never seen the man look so beaten. Not in all these years of watching his career, and certainly not in all the times she'd been intimate with him. The Bryce Clarkson she knew literally laughed at adversity, considering it a personal challenge to work twice as hard and be twice as good.

What had changed? What was fundamentally different in this situation? It was something she was determined to sort out. Whatever the answer, it began with this Queenie person, this dominatrix who was paid to do things that even swingers and nymphomaniacs balked at.

The club was a block long, two storeys high and made of black steel. There were no windows in the façade, just a single door, which was locked. She knocked, it opened and at once her senses were assailed with purple light, colours pouring out along with a cacophony of industrial music, half singing, half shrieking and a lot of mechanical mayhem to hold it together.

'You got an invitation?' The question came from a huge man in a black tank top, bald and pot-bellied but with enough meat on his arms to knock down a gorilla.

'I was told to be here,' she said, trying to keep from sounding like a total newbie. 'At ten.'

He looked her up and down with small, beady eyes. From his pushed-back nose she took him to be a boxer, probably not a very successful one. 'Did Ian call you?'

She debated dropping the name of the Governor, though the man probably wouldn't know who he was.

'I don't know any Ian. I'm here for Queenie Amazon,' she replied, cutting to the chase. 'Is she here or not?

'Room 21,' he growled, pointing over his shoulder with a beefy thumb.

She nodded. 'Thank you.'

Was it appropriate to tip a living relative of King Kong?

The Leather Love was indeed a Mecca of alternative sexuality. Everywhere Cassie's eyes travelled, she saw men and women living fantasies most people dared not conceive, even in the privacy of their own thoughts. The club had three main levels, the top two with balconies overlooking the first floor. To her immediate left was a bar, tended by a woman in a silver spike-tipped brassiere. Her hair was blue and her nails were bright pink. She was mixing coloured liquids from two U-shaped bottles in a thick test tube for a huge bearded man in a long fur robe and boots. At his feet, on her hands and knees, he had a woman, absolutely hairless, lean and young. She wore a collar and leash, the end of which he held in his hand.

A little further down a plump woman in a red sequined dress, barely four foot high, was standing on the back of a naked man on all fours. The man wore a leather hood which left an opening for his mouth and nose but not his eyes. His ass was bright red and welted from some kind of whipping. Beyond this, milling about, were some more normally attired people, such as you might find at any black-tie affair. There were some motorcycle types, too, sitting at a little round table. A naked girl with ringed nipples was serving them drinks. They amused themselves by tugging on the gold rings, trying to make her spill the contents of the glasses. More tables ringed a central pit in which she could make out two women, covered in mud, wrestling with each other. People from the upper levels were watching, cheering as they leaned over the balconies to observe the spectacle.

The most intriguing thing, from Cassie's point of view, was the whipping on the second floor. The victims were a naked man and woman, chained to crosses, side by side. The woman had her backside exposed, the man his cock and stomach. A masked man, bare-chested and wearing tight leather pants, was administering the corporal punishment using a variety of devices. In one hand he had a small riding crop and in the other a long, multi-braided flogger. At present he was employing the crop on the female's ass, leaving pretty little red patches with each blow. She was moaning intensely and writhing, though clearly not from pain. From the way she was moving her pelvis, it seemed likely she was being penetrated by some kind of dildo. Her alabaster flesh mesmerised

Cassie as it twitched in complicated pleasure. Meanwhile, beside her, the male was enduring his own agonies. As the man paddled his nipples, a heavy blonde girl was on her knees kissing his scrotum, teasing. His head was bobbing to and fro in helpless need.

Cassie felt twinging heat between her thighs. The last thing she needed on her mind right now was sex, but this scene was just too goddamn hot to ignore. She was on the verge of finding herself a play partner, or ditching into a stall in the bathroom to play with herself, when she felt a tap on her shoulder.

'Ma'am, may I show you to Room 21?'

She regarded the thin, pale young man in the leather harness and collar. 'Yes, that would be very kind of you.'

The young man led her through a doorway just around the corner from the bar. She followed his naked ass willingly, enjoying the bounce of his baby-soft cheeks. He had no whip marks, though, from the collar about his neck, she gathered he was some kind of submissive or slave.

The rooms were numbered on either side of the hallway in the back, odds on one side, evens on the other. There were tiny windows in each of the red doors and Cassie was quite tempted to look inside. Finally she heard a faint moaning and could hold back no longer. Moving as lightly as she could, she snuck a peek into Room Eleven. A muscular man wearing nothing but a pair of cowboy boots was masturbating over a young woman serenely posed on her back. Behind the man was a second woman in a latex body suit with a strap-on dildo that she was using to fuck the man in the ass. He was trying to come, but the bugger was making him wait.

'Miss, are you coming?'

Not yet, thought the overheated Cassie, but I'm getting there. More noises were coming from the adjoining Room Thirteen, so she decided to commit a second peccadillo. 'I'll be right there,' she assured the fine-assed young man. 'I'm just ... doing research.'

Room Thirteen had two occupants, a man and a woman. The woman was dressed as a typical schoolgirl, with a very short plaid skirt, white socks and blouse and black patent leather shoes. Her long brown hair was tied back in a bow. She was long and lean, with the body of a dancer. Nervously, she stood before the man, who was sitting in a plain wooden chair. He was dressed as a schoolmaster, complete with a black robe, and in his hands he held a long, nasty wooden cane. His face was pudgy and pink as he pointed the rod at the lovely young woman. He was telling her something, something that was making her blush.

But what was it he'd said? Cassie would give anything to find out.

'If you wish,' said her escort, coming up behind her and startling her, 'you may hear what they are saying.'

'It makes no difference to me,' Cassie replied, trying to keep her cool. 'Though I suppose it might be amusing.'

She watched him flip a switch on the wall. At once her ears were treated to the naughty dialogue coming from Room Thirteen.

'And where did you let your boyfriend touch you?' the man was asking.

'I ... I let him touch my privates, sir,' the pretend schoolgirl said.

'Be specific. Did he touch your titties?'

She swallowed hard, displaying all the terror a real student might in her place. 'Yes, sir ... he did.'

'Show me,' he said with a scowl. 'Exactly how.'

Torment filled her face. 'Oh, sir, please don't make me do that.'

The pretend schoolmaster whistled the cane through the air, landing it with a seductive thwack on her naked thigh. The girl whimpered. 'I'm sorry, sir, for being disobedient. He touched me . . . this way.'

She put her fingertips to the middle of her breasts, massaging her tight nipples through the blouse. The schoolmaster watched, his pink cock rising to poke its head out from among the folds of his black robe.

'And did you enjoy this, you little slut of a girl?'

'Oh, no, not at all,' she said, shaking her head vehemently.

He raised the cane as if to strike her once again and immediately she changed her tune. 'I did enjoy it, sir. Please forgive me.'

'Come closer,' he ordered. 'Closer still.'

She moved right between his legs, her straining breasts at eye level.

'It is your fault this happened.' He ran the cane up and down the side of her leg. 'You tempted him.'

'Yes, sir,' she said miserably.

He tapped authoritatively. 'You may unbutton your blouse.'

The girl complied quickly.

'Take it off and put your hands behind your head.'

A moment later she stood before him stripped to her white cotton bra, breasts thrust out, eyes staring straight ahead.

'A girl such as yourself needs discipline,' the man lectured. 'She requires sexual control so as not to be a distraction to the men and boys around her. You are a slut, my dear, and must be treated as such.'

'Yes, sir,' she rasped, not daring to look at him.

'What must be done with sluts?' he inquired.

'They must be humiliated, sir. And punished.'

Cassie pressed her tits to the door, wishing she were in the girl's place, receiving all that energy, living in that sexual tension.

'Are you a slut?' he continued, clearly getting off on the word.

'Yes, sir,' said the pretty, bright-eyed actress. 'I'm a slut.'

'Legs apart.' He ran the cane along the inside of her thigh, up to the juncture. 'Are you wet right now?'

The girl trembled very slightly. She was more than an actress appeasing this man, Cassie decided. She was a genuine player. 'Sir, forgive me, I am ... aroused,' she confessed.

'You would like a cock, then, wouldn't you?'

Her chest began to rise and fall with remarkable rapidity. 'Yes, sir.'

'Any cock ... my little slut?'

'Oh, yes ... any cock.'

'Even mine?' He ran the cane up her belly, pushing it into her smooth white flesh.

'Oh, sir,' she moaned as he toyed with her bra-covered nipples, making her writhe against the cane. 'Yes, please.'

Cassie leaned harder against the door in response, this time kissing the glass window with her lips.

'This give you any ideas?' the young man in the leather straps inquired. He was groping her, his body pressed in close from behind.

'For starters, you could fuck me,' Cassie said, pulling mindlessly at the back of her dress.

The young man helped her, lifting her dress to her waist and pulling down her panties. A moment later he was inside her, impaling her with a long, thin cock, alive and pulsing. With fresh eyes, her pussy clamping down in a pulsing rhythm, she turned her attention back to the room.

'Take down your panties,' the schoolmaster commanded, 'and give them to me.'

The girl pulled up her skirt and did as she was told.

'These are sopping,' the man said disapprovingly, holding them at arm's length.

The young woman, stripped now to shoes, socks, skirt and bra, lowered her eyes. 'I am a bad girl, sir.'

He parted his robe exposing a nude body and a thick, stubby member. It was red and hard, with purplish veins. 'Bad girls don't get to go to recess,' he declared. 'They have to be punished. Like the little sluts they are.'

She looked in mock terror at his cock. 'Please, sir, don't make me –'

'But you will,' he thundered. 'On your knees, now!'

Cassie pushed her ass back against the young man, filling herself with his anonymous member. This was just the stimulation she needed to accompany the little show.

The girl student kneeled down, ready to take the schoolmaster's dick in her mouth. 'Do I have to swallow this time, sir?' she asked with a pout.

'Every drop,' he insisted, stroking himself hard. 'And you'll get a good caning thrown in.'

'Yes, sir.' She crawled to him, putting her hands on his lap. He promptly entwined his fingers in her hair and pushed her onto his erection. The pretty brown-haired woman bobbed her head enthusiastically.

'That's it,' he said approvingly. 'Show me what a little slut you are.'

She moaned as he extended his arm to whack her with the cane through her skirt. She jolted slightly with the blow to her ass, but did not slow the progress of her work. In all he gave her five, meanwhile insisting that she run her lips and tongue up and down him like a good little vacuum cleaner.

At last he started spasming and dropped the cane. He was going to come. Grasping her shoulders with both hands for support, he drove himself deep, with animal grunts. She took it all without complaint, even when his eyes rolled back in his head and he called out the name of someone else – a man called Giovanni. The girl was actively swallowing now, gulping come.

Cassie reached back to caress her lover's face. 'You come, too,' she said.

But the young man had no opportunity to finish, for no sooner had she spoken than a pair of strong men in leather vests rudely pulled him out of her.

'Where in blazes have you been, boy?' asked one, a bald man with a goatee.

'I was showing the lady to her room,' he said.

'Well, unless her room's at the frigging North Pole,' said the other, a tall blond with a ponytail and a large chest, 'you been dicking around on us.'

'I'd say that's literal,' the bald man commented, looking at the young man's glistening, rapidly shrinking cock.

The white-assed young man sank to his knees and embraced the bald man. 'I beg you to punish me. I'm a bad boy.'

'Don't worry,' he laughed, low and rough. 'That won't be a problem.'

'You know where you're supposed to be?' The blond turned to Cassie, who was busy pulling her panties back up over her tingling posterior.

'Yes, sir,' she replied, caught up in the submissive spirit of the place. 'I was told to report to Room 21. I'll show myself the way.' She took off hastily down the hall.

Here goes nothing, she thought as she turned the knob on the door of Room 21. My own heaven or my own hell.

Or maybe both.

Bryce spotted the woman as soon as he and Lydia walked in. She stood dead centre under the rotunda of the museum's main hall, converted for the night into a grand ballroom, complete with a thousand champagne flutes and a twenty-piece orchestra. He had an eye for this type of female. Lonely, beautiful, passions wilting on the vine, sorely neglected by whatever male dolt held sway over her life.

Lydia saw the woman, too, and, as soon as she realised that her husband was going to make a play for her, she disappeared into an alcove, no doubt to hole up with one of the waiters bringing trays of sparkling alcohol. How quickly they slipped back into their routines, he noted sardonically.

'The one in the red with the short blonde hair,' he said, nodding discreetly, bringing the woman to Ron's attention. 'She's new to the herd.'

'The herd' was his nickname for the entire upper crust, male and female alike, who grazed at functions like this: the same dull faces and dull minds at event after event. A thousand dollars a plate here, five hundred there, till you could almost kill for a hamburger and fries, to be eaten in greasy take-away containers in front of a television set.

'That's the new Mrs Payton Willoughby. Number four, I believe.'

'She can't be more than twenty-two,' he said, shaking his head. 'And yet she's already completely disillusioned with life.'

'If you say so,' said Ron. 'Just don't let Cowell catch you sniffing around her. He'll have your hide. Or Willoughby, either. He's always been a jealous son-of-a-bitch.'

'Don't worry,' the tuxedo-clad Governor assured him, even as he began to run over schemes in his mind to bed the pretty little straw-haired woman. 'I've learned my lesson.'

The lesson being, don't go anywhere you can be taped. Do it more creatively, in a place no one expects. Right here, for instance, under her husband's very nose with hundreds of potential witnesses. How about that for some fucked-up kamikaze logic?

He plucked a glass of champagne from a passing tray. Whatever it was going on in his head right now, a little alcohol couldn't hurt. He had the waiter stay there while he drank two glasses. One woman who really used to love champagne was Cassandra. She would just go wild for the stuff. Once they'd stolen a bottle from a fundraiser and drunk it under the stars, barefoot, lying on their backs in the grass, he in a tuxedo, she in a gown. It was one of those nights they'd actually forgotten to fuck, so wrapped up were they in conversation. He remembered giggling a lot, and wishing on stars. There must have been a million of them out that night, and they hadn't skipped one.

Fuck it. Is that what all this was about? A lot of sentimental drivel over Cassie? I must be losing it, he thought. No wonder Queenie betrayed me. She sniffed out my weakness and struck like the proverbial black widow.

Maybe the hardest part of seeing Cassie was sensing

the hidden condemnation in her eyes. He was no longer the Bryce of long ago. Where was his idealism, his ethics? Was he thinking of anything but getting elected any more? That and getting fucked?

What if something was wrong with Landview? Worse still, what if it was too late to stop it, and he would have to live with the knowledge that it was his fault for being blind in the first place, because all he'd seen was the dollar signs, never once thinking where the money came from?

'I don't believe I've had the honour.' He presented himself to Lindsay Willoughby, trying to drive all unpleasant thoughts out of his mind.

The young woman went starry-eyed as he took her white-gloved hand. 'Governor Clarkson, I'm the one who's honoured, trust me.'

'Not at all,' he insisted. 'I'm just a washed-up politician, but you ... you are the light of the future, not to mention the belle of this ball.'

Now she was blushing redder than her off-the-shoulder velvet gown. There was no question he had her, it was simply a matter of evading all the prying eyes long enough to find some dark out-of-the-way corner to take proper advantage.

'Me? A belle?' She nearly giggled, belying her recent graduation from teenagerhood. 'I hardly think so.'

'Dance with me,' he said, challenging her, 'and I'll prove it to you.'

She sucked in her lower lip, looking adorable as she considered the possibility. 'But ... my husband ...'

The Governor laughed dismissively. 'That old codger? Why, he'll be honoured to have you shown off as the beauty you are.' Flashing a charming, disarming smile, he extended an arm. 'I'll issue an executive order if I have to,' he said. 'This is your last warning.'

Lindsay grinned happily, melting against his side. There was no substitute for the touch of a younger woman, the freshness and the eagerness. Nothing could restore his own youth more quickly or more joyously.

The fourth Mrs Willoughby proved to be an excellent ballroom dancer. She had finesse and skill and an obvious love of life. What a waste of her spirit to be tied to an old sack of wind like Payton. It was at times like these that Bryce cursed the power of money. To buy up beauty and creativity and even love, as it so often did, was a true crime against nature. Then again, whom had *he* injured over the years in order to have power?

This poor child would be a whore in many people's eyes for marrying a billionaire forty years her senior, but they had no right to judge, none of them. Only a worse sinner, such as himself, could say a word, and, as his hand slipped down her back, as he felt her smooth curves, as he gazed into her lovely bright eyes and clasped her rosy palm, he saw nothing but innocence and truth.

'You are superb,' he told her when they'd had their fill of waltzes.

'My father was a dance teacher,' she explained. 'And I was, too. That's where I met my husband.'

He looked at her intently. 'I wasn't referring simply to your dancing.'

She lowered her gaze, taking his meaning at once.

'Come with me,' he said, striking while the iron was hot. 'We'll sip champagne while we explore. This museum has one of the finest collections of Morel sculptures in the world.'

Before she could raise an objection, Lindsay was being ushered from the main hall towards the museum proper. Two of Bryce's security people were following at a discreet distance. He gave the nod to Cray, indicating he was about to go on reconnaissance, the term they employed to describe his little clandestine operations. Wilder would cover his rear, preventing anyone from getting too nosy.

The long, high hallway was dimly lit, which suited the horny Governor very well. Truth be told, he couldn't tell a Morel sculpture from a Michelangelo, but he did appreciate the value of darkness where seduction was concerned.

'Are you sure this part of the museum is open tonight?' she asked.

'Well, they'd hardly want to hide the Morels,' he observed.

'You must be quite an art enthusiast, Governor Clarkson.'

'Please, call me Bryce.'

They walked down the hallway a little further, heels clicking on the marble floor. 'Tell me, Bryce,' she asked, 'do you prefer the early work of Morel or the later period, just prior to his death?'

Bryce continued to scout for a room with some sort of couch. 'I think the later period,' he said absently.

She stopped in her tracks and raised a mischievous eyebrow. 'Is that right? I find that interesting, considering the man is still alive.'

The Governor frowned. Obviously he'd underestimated her. 'Congratulations,' he said. 'You've just succeeded where an army of reporters and nearly two dozen political opponents have failed over the years. You have caught me out in a bold-faced lie.'

Lindsay Willoughby laughed and grabbed his hand. 'Come on. I know what it is you're looking for.'

He nearly had to run to keep up with her. Wherever they were headed, she knew where she was going.

Scooting through a display of calcified food products that passed for contemporary sculpture, she brought them to a small circular chamber with large futons all over the floor.

'It's the film viewing room,' she explained. 'It's where all the college kids come to make out.'

Bryce pulled her into his arms. 'You little vixen,' he said. 'You actually had me thinking I was hoodwinking you into this.'

She pulled his jacket off his shoulders. 'I knew I would fuck you the moment you walked in the door. I willed you to come over and talk to me.'

'Is my reputation really that bad?'

Lindsay was working on his shirt, baring his chest as quickly as possible. 'Nope. You're just hot. A woman would have to be deaf, dumb and blind not to see that.'

He released a contented sigh as she fell to his nipples, kissing them. 'You kids today take all the fun out of seduction, you know that?'

'Uh huh.' She was yanking open his pants, pulling them down over his hips. 'Tell me you hate it.'

'I hate it,' he breathed.

Lindsay dug her nails into his pecs, dragging them down his torso as she lowered herself to her knees. 'Liar.'

He put his hands on her shoulders for support as she absorbed his cock. Lindsay was one hungry little lady, that was for sure. Not at all the lonely, shrinking violet he'd expected.

'Whoa, honey,' he said warningly, 'I won't be able to hold out long at this rate.'

'I don't want you to,' she replied, coming up for air.

'But what about your pleasure?'

'I'm blowing the Governor of the state. My pleasure will be to tell my grandchildren.'

She put her mouth back before he could come up with any more objections. The only option now was to enjoy. 'Lindsay, you're good, you know that?'

She bobbed her head affirmatively. Her self-confidence made him laugh. 'Maybe there really is hope for the future,' he mused aloud.

So long as she didn't let herself be disillusioned by someone like him. The way Cassie was disillusioned. It had broken his heart to see the change in her after he'd let her go. She never did see it as an act of liberation on his part. Something inside her seemed to have died. The young woman who wished on stars and wrinkled her nose over champagne bubbles was no more. The woman who took her place was certainly a worthy successor, a force to be reckoned with, but he alone knew what had been lost to the world.

'Lindsay,' he whispered, being very careful to get her name right, 'dear, sweet Lindsay ... you've no idea ... what this means.'

She probably did, though. So far she'd been ten steps ahead of him. Hopefully she was that many ahead of Willoughby, too. He'd bet his bottom dollar she was. In the end, this perky, bob-tailed blonde would have the last laugh. She deserved it, too, for putting up with assholes like her husband and his snob friends. And, to some extent, Bryce himself, and all the other men who made the world what it was – a place so unsympathetic to women.

All men were of the same ilk, after all: composing their backroom deals, smoking cigars, cooking up schemes. Like Landview, which, the more he thought of it, had the makings of one of the biggest scandals of the decade. Did he dare look into this thing any further and blow the whistle? If he did, he would run foul of the most powerful men in the state – and, if the allegations were true, a whole bunch of gangsters too. Compared to what they would do to him, the public humiliation ensuing from a released videotape was a stroll in the park.

Bryce tried to clear his mind for the moment. Young Lindsay wanted her fifteen minutes of fame. Rearing back his head, he made one final push, thrusting his aching cock deep into her warm, silky mouth. She took him tenderly, respectfully, but also with incredible passion. It did indeed make him feel young again.

He groaned his appreciation, pumping his life fluid, releasing the accumulated tension that sex with his wife had not managed to sap. Lindsay absorbed it all, swallowing it whole. He was still shuddering slightly when she let him go and stood back up.

'Thank you,' he murmured, caressing her cheek.

'Oh, no.' She delivered a peck on the cheek. 'Thank you. I won't forget you ... ever.'

'No,' he agreed, 'you won't. Because we're not done yet.'

She flashed a questioning glance, to which he replied with a wink, helping her back onto one of the futons. Her pussy was more than ready beneath her lace panties. She had luscious lips and a beautifully shaved mound. If anything, she was more fresh and lovely down here than on the rest of her body.

'You are a very bad girl for trying to keep this from me.'

'I didn't want to be presumptuous.'

He spread her legs wide, making sure she was comfortably nestled. Tossing aside the panties he'd removed, he ran his finger up and down her crack and was rewarded with tiny droplets, signs of her passion.

'Oh, I think in your case you can presume all you like.' The Governor went straight for paydirt, using his silver tongue to part her. She grabbed at his hair, bucking beneath him at once.

'Oh, fuck . . . oh, sir, fuck . . .'

The girl was irrepressible. He worked at her clit, building her steadily, gauging by her breathing and her sighs how to apply himself. It was a lot of time to give, he knew, but he owed it to her. Hell, he owed so many things to so many different women, by now he'd lost count. At least here, for once, he could exceed expectations.

She had to put her hand over her mouth. Writhing beneath him, holding his head tight just where she wanted it, she exploded, filling his mouth with a sweet emission. Damn, she was a squirter too.

'Oh, Governor,' she murmured, kissing him afterwards. 'Are you sure you don't want to marry me?'

'Can't,' he said with a rakish smile. 'We both have spouses already.'

'I'll try and remember,' she said. 'As soon as I can remember my own name again.'

Five minutes later, they were back in the main room, back to their separate friends, their separate lives. Such was politics. Such was life.

'Sir?' It was Cray, looking for a status report.

Bryce gave him an affirmative nod. 'Mission accomplished,' he assured the man.

Cray pursed his lips. 'She looks like she'd be quite a pistol,' he observed.

'You don't know the half of it.'

Cray knew enough not to pursue the matter. If there was one thing you could say about Governor Bryce Clarkson, for all his carryings on, he did not ever kiss and tell.

If only the rest of the world could be so discreet.

6

Cassie moved unsteadily but deliberately down the hall to Room 21. Behind her she could hear the young man with the leather straps and his handlers.

'We'll show you not to keep us waiting,' the blond was saying. 'Kneel down and open wide.'

Chains jingled as the white-assed young man sank to his knees before his handler. Moans followed and the distinctive sound of lips slurping over a cock. Her insides tingled with unmet need, ever-mounting and ever-pressing. Whatever was in that room, it had better get her off quick.

It was not locked. Turning the handle, she opened the door into near-darkness.

'Hello?' she called out cautiously, poking her head inside.

She heard nothing. Had there been some mistake in sending her here? She was about to close it again and go back to the main area when she felt the brush of latex on her cheek. It was a human hand, gloved.

'Come in, my sweet,' said a voice, deceptively soft and feminine.

Cassie felt a chill down her spine. She knew at once, instinctively, that it was the woman from the videotape. 'You're her,' she announced. 'The one with Bryce.'

The gloved fingers curled around her own, tugging her fully inside. 'Very perceptive,' the woman said. 'Now let's see how much more you can figure out.'

From the tape Cassie knew that the woman was

shorter than her, but she must have had heels on, because their lips met perfectly. 'I'm Queenie,' the woman said.

Cassie's breathing quickened under the influence of the light, thirsty little presses to her mouth. They were designed to tease and entice, not satisfy. 'I'm Cassie Dane,' she managed to reply. 'I was told to meet you here at ten.'

Queenie's hand played over Cassie's bosom, fingertips electric-quick over the fabric of the thin party dress. 'And so you did. Do you always follow instructions that well?'

Cassie arched her back, her nipples begging to come out and play. 'It all depends,' she said with a sigh.

'Yes,' said Queenie drily as she ran her hands over Cassie's lean hips. 'I'd forgotten. You're the media consultant. You're paid not to give straight answers.'

Cassie strained to see the woman's face in the dim light. She was beautiful, she knew that much. 'And what are you paid for?'

Queenie's hand slid beneath the hem of Cassie's dress. 'You tell me,' she said, moving immediately for the sweet spot between Cassie's legs.

Fuck. Cassie wasn't going to be able to keep up the role of razor-sharp interlocutor at this rate. 'I'd say,' Cassie declared, trying not to react to the odd, wicked feel of a rubberised index finger in her pussy, 'that you were paid to give men what they want and are afraid to ask for.'

'How diplomatic of you.' Queenie touched her clit, making Cassie spasm. 'And what about women? Do you suppose I do anything for them?'

'I'll have to excuse myself from testifying,' she gasped. 'Nothing personal ... it's just a conflict of interest.'

Queenie laughed, a light, endearing sound, with just the tiniest edge of menace. 'Take off your clothes,' she said, 'and we'll see if we can't realign your interests.'

'I – I don't think that's a very good idea.'

'Neither is disobeying me.' Queenie pushed her fingers deeper, simulating the shape of a strong and possessive male organ. 'Is it?'

Cassie groaned softly, impaled. 'No,' she concurred. 'I suppose not.'

The fingers angled higher, forcing Cassie onto tiptoes. 'You suppose not, *ma'am*.'

Cassie repeated the phrase, granting the dominatrix her title. She was so wet now she was sure her panties were saturated.

'Come,' commanded Queenie. 'Come on my hand.'

'Y–yes, ma–am.' Cassie gritted her teeth, willingly fucking the woman's fingers. Queenie knew what she was doing and in a matter of seconds she had her victim crying out in orgasm, her head thrashing to and fro, her sex clenching and unclenching wildly, her body pushing and straining against the confines of her clothing.

Queenie brought her down expertly, maintaining complete control. 'Lick,' she commanded, putting the come-soaked glove to Cassie's mouth.

Weak, helpless and still very much aroused, Cassandra sucked her own fluids from the woman's fingers, taking them one by one between her lips like miniature cocks. Queenie made her take her time, ensuring that by the time she was done she was fully aroused again. Not to mention fully frustrated. When the last finger was popped from her mouth, Cassie moaned impotently.

'Strip,' Queenie ordered her again.

This time Cassie could not obey fast enough.

Fumbling in the dark, she unzipped the dress first, pulled it over her head and let it fall to the floor. She felt wicked as hell. The bra was next and finally the panties.

'Leave the shoes,' said the dominatrix.

Cassie stood at attention, suddenly alone. Queenie was no longer touching her, no longer within range of her limited senses. If that was meant to intimate her, it was working. With every heartbeat she ached to feel something, anything. Even pain would have done, so long as this sudden terrible isolation were put to an end.

'Hands at your sides.'

Cassie removed her crossed palms from in front of her pussy. Again her world was plunged into the almost palpable emptiness of waiting. She nearly leapt out of her skin when the end of the whip grazed her thigh, slithering like a snake.

'You think you're up for this?' Queenie asked, directing the words into her ear as she nibbled at the lobe. 'You think you can play with the big dogs?'

Cassie arched her neck. This felt good – way too good. 'I am just trying to do my job,' she insisted.

Queenie snapped the whip across Cassie's ass cheeks.

'Fuck,' Cassie yelped. 'That hurt.'

Truthfully, it wasn't that bad. She'd kind of liked it actually, but this woman didn't need to know that.

'Then tell me to stop. Tell me you can't take it and I'll let you go . . . little girl.'

Cassie thrust her ass out brazenly. 'I can take it just fine. Better than you can dish it out.'

Queenie whacked her three more times. It stung like hell, but the glow was incredible. Unable to resist, she felt her cheeks. They were hot.

'You play with fire, you get burned,' said Queenie. 'You ought to know that from dealing with Bryce.'

Cassie felt a new kind of heat, this time the fire of betrayal. 'You know about that? About us?'

'He told me himself.'

She felt a rush of anger mixed with a strange new kind of weakness. 'He had no right.'

Queenie took her hand. 'Follow me.'

The dominatrix knew her way in the dark. She took Cassie to the bed, which was large and soft. 'Lie down,' said Queenie. 'You're way too tense.'

Cassie reclined, her body sweetly absorbed by the mattress. It was nice, very nice. She could almost fall asleep, in fact, but she had to find out what he'd told Queenie. 'What did Bryce say?' Cassie asked. 'About me, I mean.'

Queenie crawled next to her on all fours, kissing each of her nipples lightly. 'Do you really need me to tell you that, honey? To him you're the one that got away. You always will be.'

Cassie shook her head, resisting both the kisses and the information. 'That isn't possible. I never meant anything to the man. He made that abundantly clear.'

Queenie's flesh pressed against her, belly to belly. Magically, she was naked, too. 'A man like Bryce never speaks his real mind,' she said. 'You ought to know that.'

Cassie yielded her mouth to a deep female kiss. Queenie's fingers were creeping to her sex again and there was going to be no denying the lovemaking. Yet, her brain was screaming out a different denial. It couldn't be. He'd made her this big speech. He'd married another woman, for God's sake.

Anyhow, all this was a decade ago. Ancient history. They'd both moved on with their lives. Hadn't they?

'When?' Cassie gasped even as Queenie mounted her, connecting their pelvises tight and hard. 'When did he tell you this?'

'No more talking,' Queenie ordered. 'Only fucking.'

Cassie grabbed the woman's hips. 'Yes, ma'am.'

Queenie inserted a finger to wag Cassie's clitoris. 'I want to hear you scream. Scream for me, Cassandra.'

Cassie inhaled a ragged breath. It was a sweet assault, devilish and merciless. With greedy hands she reached for her lover's tits, wanting to feel the luxurious, vibrant mounds for herself. Queenie made no objection, indicating her pleasure with a delighted moan. Cassie tried to imagine just how she'd look in the light. It was more exciting this way, not knowing for sure the physical details of the one taking her.

What she did know was the *why* of what was happening. This was about power. It was about that tape and about Bryce Clarkson's career. A man who, if this woman were right, had been nurturing some kind of feelings for her all along. The one that got away. Too incredible to believe. But she'd seen stranger things in her time, hadn't she?

'I need to come,' Cassie pleaded. 'Please, ma'am, may I?'

'No,' said Queenie. 'Not yet.'

Cassie whimpered as the woman climbed off her. A moment later she was back, but this time in a sixty-nine position. Eagerly Cassie plunged her tongue into Queenie's tight wet hole, even as she herself was devoured.

The woman's taste was sweet and succulent. Cassie did her best to pleasure her, licking round her clit and taking in whatever juices spilled into her mouth. Queenie was undulating pleasantly, her rocking hips adding to the rhythm of her pussy-licking. This in turn drove Cassie to new heights of pleasure-giving. It was a spiral of sweet woman-to-woman love, uninterrupted by male energy.

Cassie knew precisely when her partner would come, just as she knew when she herself would. It would be mutual, and spectacular, too. They held tightly to each other's bodies, rolling and twisting in a forbidden horizontal dance, pure instinct, pure, primal creation energy. Breasts swollen, nipples electrified, hearts thrumming against one another, bellies sealed and rippling, faces fitted perfectly to the task, upper and lower lips connected inviolably, they fulfilled their expectations, then shattered them. Sweet sweat intermingled, limbs entwined they reached the pinnacle and then plunged.

All the way down to a green valley below, pristine and untrodden by human feet. Eden reborn. For an aeon they lay like this, lovers and soul sisters in the perpetual night of Room 21. Eventually – a minute, an hour, maybe two hours of earth time later – Cassie tried to remember her identity, her mission and her purpose.

'The tape,' she murmured.

Queenie put a finger over Cassie's lips. 'That's not important. It's a diversion. There's a man you need to find. He'll help you get what you need.'

'A man?'

Queenie propped herself on her elbow and brushed damp strands of hair from Cassie's face. Strangely, they could see each other now, even if only as faintly outlined shadows. 'His name is Jake. Jake Andrews. Find him and ask him about Landview Development.'

Cassie committed the name to memory. She didn't expect any more details from Queenie. If she'd learned anything else on this assignment, it was to anticipate the element of surprise. After one day, she'd certainly had her fill of that. She could hardly imagine what tomorrow might bring. Especially if this Jake Andrews proved half as interesting as the people she'd dealt with so far.

Or half as sexy.

It was two in the morning by the time Bryce made it to the gym. Having his own personal workout area was one of the perks of being Governor, though, at times like these, he considered the stress relief to be a necessity, not a luxury. He began with the bench press, setting the bar at two-twenty-five. He could go as high as two-fifty, assuming the adrenaline was pumping fast enough.

Tonight it was a headache he was trying to get rid of, a knot that began in the base of his skull and went all the way down his spine. Pulling off his shirt to bare his smooth, carefully sculpted chest, he laid himself down on the bench. He was about to heave the bar when he heard a familiar recriminating voice.

'You shouldn't be doing this without a spotter, sir.'

It was Cray, appearing as usual out of thin air.

'Damn it, man, you're going to give me a heart attack one of these days.'

Cray positioned himself directly behind the bench, his hands under the bar. 'Give me four reps,' he said.

Bryce stopped at three. 'I'm getting too fucking old,' he said breathing heavily.

'Wait till you're my age,' Cray replied with a grin.

The Governor rose from the seat, a fine sheen of sweat on his skin. 'Don't give me that crap.' He set the bar for three hundred, anticipating Cray's lift. 'You're twice the man I am and you know it.'

It was a routine between them, one repeated several

times a week, unless Bryce was particularly agitated, like now and tried to exercise alone.

'Hardly,' Cray said as he lay down. This time the Governor put his hands under the bar, though there wasn't much need. Effortlessly, his security chief lifted the three hundred pounds, locked his elbows and lowered the bar back into place. 'I can pump iron,' he told his boss, 'but that doesn't make me a leader.'

'Neither does sticking your dick in everything that moves.'

They went to the body bag next. Cray hugged it from behind while Bryce pounded the living daylights out of the four-foot hanging sandbag. For every punch he tried to take back one fuck. The betrayal of his wife. Of his constituents.

'The way I see it,' said the former Special Forces sergeant and three-time Purple Heart recipient, 'men have needs, and the more powerful the man, the greater the needs. It's nature. Look at your primitive societies. The women went to the ones with the biggest clubs.'

Bryce grimaced, leaning into his work with a ferocity that defied ordinary niceties. 'When you say clubs, do you mean wood ones . . . or flesh ones?'

'Either one. Women want to be conquered by the strong. Sultans have harems, emperors have concubines, presidents have mistresses. Hell, in France it's public knowledge. About the only thing they do right over there, if you ask me.'

As always, Cray's opinion left something to be desired in the political correctness department. He'd known lots of capable, brave Frenchmen and he was also pretty sure that most women had higher ambitions than to be a notch on some man's belt, even a powerful one.

In his own way, though, he was trying, making a genuine effort to get Bryce to feel better about himself. Truth be told, Cray Wilder had never cheated on a woman in his life and never would.

'If only the world were as forgiving as you, Cray, I'd have a future yet.'

'Are you kidding?' The man's eyes were fierce and black behind the bag. 'There's no way I'll accept our defeat. We will win this. I'll be damned if you're going to resign over this, either, sir.'

Bryce let down his arms, heavy as lead from the exertion. 'I have to do what's best for the people.'

Cray frowned, looking about as emotional as the Governor had ever seen him. 'Put up your fists,' he declared.

'It's a little late at night for sparring, Cray.'

It wasn't sparring he had in mind, though. 'Hit me,' he said, holding his palms out as targets. 'Sir.'

Bryce sighed, relenting. The first few times he merely tapped the man's hands, but as Cray put up more resistance, pushing back, Bryce started hitting harder.

'Is that all you have?' Cray taunted. 'My grandmother could do better than that.'

Bryce slammed his fist hard. Cray absorbed the blow and immediately looked for another. They went on like this for several minutes, the Governor escalating to full force.

'This is combat, Governor.' Cray moved about in a circle, leading his swinging opponent. 'Single-minded focus. Man against man. This is life. You live it or you lie down and die. That's the choice, every morning you wake up. Every time you take a breath. You choose.'

Bryce knew he would never be able to knock the man down. The point was to expend himself in the effort. It was like the sexual act, a release of every bit of oneself, a coil unspringing, a gun firing. How many lessons had there been so far in the four years that Cray had been with him? In the past, in addition to boxing, there had been karate, barefoot kicks and wooden fighting sticks. Once they'd even done a little fencing.

Both men were fiercely competitive and highly motivated to excel over the rest of the men in their circle. They also happened to share a high interest in sex. Cray's tastes ran more towards oriental women, quiet, respectful and docile creatures. He'd actually ordered a couple of brides from the Philippines, though both those situations had ended in disaster. Cray, it seemed, expected the girls to be like the two-dimensional pictures in the magazine, without the complications of real feelings and real human needs.

He wasn't a tyrannical or insensitive man, but he was hardly flexible, either. And when it came to dealing with the rebellions against authority that his wives made when they'd tasted American life, he was thoroughly ill-equipped. He'd divorced them both, leaving them with healthy settlements. Since then his tastes had run to whores. The way he looked at it, with a prostitute you knew up front what you were going to have to pay and you could be sure to get your money's worth.

He'd told some stories of his days in the service – those parts of his classified work he was allowed to share – and they were enough to make Bryce's toes curl. When it came to exotic situations, including sex in a parachute drop over the Andes and on the floor of a burnt-out government building in the middle of a raging civil war, Cray had him beat. Though the prize for sheer numbers still went to the Governor.

'Enough.' Bryce lowered his hands to his knees at last, stooping in utter exhaustion.

Cray slapped him on the back. 'That's the kind of stuff it takes to stay in the game ... all the way to the presidency, sir. Trust me.'

Bryce wasn't so sure. One thing he did know, if he ever got the job he'd have to find ex-sergeant Wilder a new position, something to keep him busy and out of the hair of the Secret Service whose job it would then be to guard him. In the meantime, Cray was his front-line defence, and his rear-line as well.

'I want you to do something for me, Cray,' he said, employing a tone he reserved only for the gravest operations.

Cray's eyes focused like an eagle's as he awaited the Governor's orders. Bryce knew he could ask anything, up to and including the man's immediate suicide, and it would be done. Fortunately, he had no desire to give any eulogies in the near future.

'I'm worried about Cassie being out there all alone. Until we know for sure what we're dealing with and what Queenie's up to.'

Cray studied him, looking for the underlying thoughts and motivations of his superior. 'I can put a man on her, sir.'

Bryce nodded. 'I would feel better if you did, yes.'

'I'll make it the best one I've got. She won't be able to powder her nose without your knowing about it.'

'Not a spy, Cray. Just a ... guardian. Someone to bail her out if she runs into any unsavoury characters.'

Cray was silent for a moment. Bryce braced himself

for what he knew was going to be a personal question. 'You have feelings for her, don't you?'

'The Cassie Dane who walked into my office today was a stranger,' he said honestly. 'The girl I knew is long gone. I have a responsibility to protect people I put in harm's way, that's all. Especially people I put there without their consent.'

Cray's lips furrowed. 'She is pretty extraordinary, though, isn't she?'

'I think I've said all I want on the subject,' Bryce replied with uncharacteristic curtness. 'Now . . . or ever.'

Cray inclined his head. 'Yes, sir.'

Bryce left without another word. Up to bed for what was sure to be a sleepless night. He didn't even bother turning down the covers. Collapsing in the easy chair, he flipped on the television, picking up some droning diet pill infomercial with a young hard-body brunette. She looked familiar. Hadn't she been a finalist in some beauty pageant he'd judged? She'd lost, but he'd fucked her, anyway.

Fifty years from now he'd still be doing this, he thought ruefully. Sitting around in some nursing home, telling a lot of other old geezers about women he'd slept with in the days of the dinosaurs.

Closing his eyes, he let the sound of happy diet pill converts dull his over-stimulated ears. What a way to live. He could hardly wait to be president.

His last coherent thoughts as he slipped towards unconsciousness were of Cassie. Was she lonely, too? She didn't wear a ring and the rumour was that she didn't make time for relationships. Busy career women were frigid in most people's eyes. He did see a coldness there and a part of him had wondered what was behind it. Was it sex she hated, or just love?

What he wouldn't give for a little time alone with her. What would they do now after all these years? Box each other like he and Cray? Fall all over each other, ripping at clothes? Or would they start in to talking, filling each other's souls with champagne bubbles and giggles, forgetting all about the sex?

Bryce forced his mind to go cold and blank. There were places a man didn't let himself go and this was one of them. For his sake, and for hers, he renewed the vow he'd been periodically making and remaking for a decade.

No more Cassie Dane.

Not now. Not ever.

7

This was starting to feel more like a wild-goose chase with every move Cassie made. Did Queenie have any idea just how many Jake Andrews there were in the metropolitan area? Was she expected to personally interview 57 different men to find one with information about the Governor's sex life? Using the computer, she was able to do some cross-referencing. There had to be something special about this particular Jake Andrews. One was a retired firefighter, another an insurance salesman. Two were still in elementary school, which definitely ruled them out. She did find one who'd been a policeman, but it turned out he'd died the previous winter. She was about to give up when she came across a writer, a freelance investigative journalist with the byline of Jason Andrews. Reading a few of his stories from the city paper, where he'd been a stringer at one point, Cassie began to see a possible connection.

This Jake Andrews liked to go after men in high places. Politicians and business executives. Seemed he'd helped to expose a cover-up in the metro police department in which three off-duty officers had been caught at a local strip club shaking down the owner.

The final article was dated June of last year. Why had he stopped writing? Had he left the area? There was still a local address, though the phone number was disconnected. Maybe he'd moved.

Having nothing else to go on, Cassie decided to

check it out. She left the office around noon, putting Stephanie in charge. Since she didn't have any appointments for the rest of the day, she figured she'd just head home early after exposing this obvious false lead, or maybe catch a movie.

To her surprise, though, the unshaven, shirtless man at the door of the shabby apartment actually acknowledged himself as Jason Andrews the writer. Well, at least he didn't deny it right off.

'What are you supposed to be?' He looked the crisply suited Cassie up and down. 'A door-to-door flight attendant? Or a grown-up Girl Scout?'

Cassie did a little looking of her own, namely at the nice package under his tight, ripped jeans and the medium-sized, firm muscles on his arms. 'I'd hardly call myself a Girl Scout,' she quipped.

'In that case,' he said, 'you can come in.'

The apartment was littered with papers, wrappers and other debris. She also noted a few empty liquor bottles. Scotch – the bane of many a writer.

'Make yourself at home.' He padded to the refrigerator. 'Beer?'

She watched his ass under the denim. He was barefoot and tanned. His sandy brown hair, uncombed, hung midway down his back. He had the look of a lion, tawny and lazy. Lions had claws, though, and they were also carnivores. This man certainly had his bestial side, going after the most powerful men in the city with apparent fearlessness.

'I prefer not to drink before happy hour,' she said.

'And I prefer not to drink alone.' He tossed her a can of cheap domestic beer, apparently unwilling to take no for an answer.

She popped it open and the contents fountained.

'Your floor,' she said apologetically, looking at the foamy cascade.

'Leave it.' He stood there, barefoot on the linoleum, draining the contents of his own can. She watched, bedazzled as the liquid disappeared down his throat. He had such a nice tapered waist, such a perfectly formed arm. Pure aerodynamics. A study in bodily perfection, masculine style. Most men could work out for a lifetime and never achieve a body this hot.

Jake Andrews crumpled the finished can and tossed it into the sink. 'Sit,' he said, pointing to a green plaid sofa half buried in newspapers.

'What am I?' Cassie rebelled. 'A Cocker spaniel?'

He grabbed another beer and shook his head. 'Nope. I don't allow dogs on my sofa.'

Cassie clutched her purse, wanting this little interview to end as quickly as possible. 'I really don't intend to take up much of your time,' she began.

He guzzled half the second can. 'Makes no difference to me. I can sleep just fine whether you're here or not.'

She frowned, trying to keep her temper. He was obviously one of these confirmed bachelor types who thought he could get away with anything just because he was good-looking. 'Oh, good,' she said sarcastically. 'I'd hate to think I was interrupting your beauty rest with my annoying questions.'

Andrews drained the second can, tossed it and licked his lips. The move made her heart quicken. With his chiselled cheeks and classically oval face he could be on TV. Even his three-day beard and lack of hair grooming only made him look better.

'How do I know your questions are going to annoy me,' he asked, 'until I've heard them?'

The man had a point.

'All right, try this on for size. Does the name Queenie Amazon ring a bell?'

He shook his head. 'That's strike one.'

'How about a big fat guy who likes to make his own dirty movies . . . using very special stars?'

Jake stared at her, his movie-star face locked in an expression of complete uninterest. 'Strike two,' he droned.

Cassie tried to hold her temper. 'What about Landview Development, then?'

For a moment she thought she spied something in his golden-brown eyes, but when he opened his mouth it was more of the same. 'That would be strike three,' he told her. 'I guess you're right. You are annoying after all.'

'What the fuck is your problem?' Cassie wanted to know. 'It's pretty obvious you're not exactly overworked, so why won't you give me the time of day?'

He polished off another beer. 'Because you're a rank amateur and you're meddling with things you couldn't possibly understand.'

'Maybe so,' she snapped. 'But what does that make you? At least I'm out there trying to find something out about the world. What the hell are you going to find, staring at the bottom of a beer-can all day?'

'Peace and quiet,' said Jake Andrews. 'The door is over there.' He inclined his head. 'You'll find it works both ways.'

She flipped him the bird. 'And this is my middle finger. You'll find it works just one way.'

'If you're trying to get me riled up, it won't work. I passed that point a long time ago.'

Cassie looked around for something to vandalise. She had no idea why, but it had suddenly become crucial to her to do just as he'd said: rile the man, in a major way. 'In that case,' she said, marching to a bookshelf against the wall and clearing a thick stack of newspaper clippings with a wave of her hand, 'you won't mind if I help you redecorate a little.'

'You're a pretty good decorator,' he said when the paper storm had finally settled. 'Want to work on the bedroom next?'

'Thank you, no,' she replied haughtily. 'The last place on earth I need to be doing anything in is your bedroom.'

The innuendo was unintentional on her part, at least consciously. Naturally, he picked up on it immediately.

'Why's that? Afraid you'd get in over your head?'

'Hardly.' She found herself forced to rise to the challenge. 'I just don't care to swim in the swamp, that's all.'

His eyes flashed. It might have been playful but then a lion played with its prey before devouring it. 'It's all right, you're not my taste at all.'

Cassie tried not to fall for the bait. 'Oh? And exactly what kind of woman do you manage to lure to this fabulous bachelor pad of yours, pray tell?'

He gave her a slanted smile, enough to undercut her knee strength by a good seventy-five per cent. 'They aren't nosy little Girl Scouts who throw temper tantrums, that's for sure.'

Ooh . . . was this man ever pissing her off.

'No, I'd imagine you prefer silicone-breasted bimbos who swoon at your beer-can-crushing ability and beg to sit on your smelly old sofa.'

'I'll tell you what,' he offered in reply. 'I'll help you with whatever harebrained investigation you've got going on in exchange for your help on a project I've been working on here.'

She regarded him suspiciously. 'And what project is that?'

'My cock.' He massaged his crotch shamelessly. 'It hasn't seen decent pussy action in two months. I'd be perfectly happy to jerk off after you leave, but I'm afraid if I don't get some sack time in soon I'll forget how.'

Cassie's mouth dropped open. 'You can't be serious? You actually expect me to ... sleep with you before you'll cooperate?'

'There's no sleeping involved,' he said. 'I'll expect you to be fully awake and participating. In fact, I will expect you to be at least as good as any of those twenty-dollar hookers down the street I could call up here to do this in your place.'

Cassie had never been so insulted. Or so aroused. 'Why don't I save you the trouble?' She fished a twenty-dollar bill from her purse and tossed it in his direction. 'Have yourself a wonderful time ... asshole.'

She slammed the door behind her, letting him know just how totally unacceptable his offer was. It wasn't till she was halfway down the hall that she considered the other aspects of the situation. There was her responsibility to Bryce with regard to the tape and, on top of that, this whole new mystery about Landview, which according to her research was a super-huge development deal. And then there was her own reputation as a problem-fixer, a political magician. Coming up dry on this would kill her chance of working on a lot of other attractive things down the line.

Finally, there was the nagging feeling that this bastard had just gotten the better of her. Cassie Dane had never backed down from a sexual challenge in her life. So what if this guy made Brad Pitt look like Frankenstein's monster? Why should she be intimidated? She was perfectly capable of satisfying him, thank you very much. In fact, she could make a man like that beg for her least little touch. Just like Queenie Amazon.

Not only will I go back, she decided, I will make mincemeat of this man, turning him into a pliant little puppy, eager and willing to help in my investigation any way he can.

He didn't bother to answer when she knocked the second time. She was sure he could hear her, too. Knowing it was all part of the game, she opened the door on her own.

'I'm back,' she announced.

Jake was lying on the couch, hands behind his neck, eyes closed as if he'd been in this position all day. 'It's too late,' he said, not bothering to look at her. 'The offer's been rescinded.'

Cassie stood frozen in the middle of the living room. Now what? Her plan hadn't covered this. He was supposed to run into her arms smothering her with grateful kisses, not playing harder to get than a subway car without graffiti.

'But I just left a minute ago,' she said.

'The point is you left at all.'

'No,' she said huskily. 'The point is you're about to throw away the best blowjob of your life.'

Jake Andrews sat up. 'Well, well, seems our Girl Scout is away for the afternoon.'

'I'm here to take her place.' Cassie moved forward boldly and stood between his spread legs. 'If that's a problem, you can always throw me out again.'

'I'll take the blowjob first.'

'When I'm done, you'll owe me information,' she reminded him, leaning forward and resting her hands on his thighs.

His hands moved to his zipper. 'I told you, I want more than your mouth for that.'

She felt a hot surge in her pussy. 'Yes,' she said drily. 'I have to spread my legs. Who could forget that?'

'You plan on talking all day?' he wanted to know. 'Or are we going to get down to business?'

Cassie lowered herself to her knees. His cock was huge, curved and uncircumcised. She took it between her hands and ran it softly over her cheeks. 'Does that answer your question?'

'You're still talking,' he observed.

She put her lips to the tip of him, letting him know what else they were good for. Gently, reverently, she kissed the penis of Jake Andrews, one-time investigative journalist and all-round smartass.

'Mmm,' he moaned softly. 'Now I think we're onto something.'

Feeling encouraged and very, very female, Cassie applied light touches up and down the length of him, extending the range of her cock worship. He groaned more deeply as she blew on the inflamed skin, following each motion of her finger with a tantalising brush of her mouth. By the time she began licking in earnest, she had him in the palm of her hand – in every sense.

Cassie knew her way round a cock and she considered it a personal point of honour to exceed and shatter this man's expectations. In a way, all men were alike. All one had to do was slow down and work on the sweet spots. Like the thick vein on the underside of the shaft, where much of the sensation is located. And the base, too, just in front of the scrotum. Squeezing that, just so, could send a man into orbit, almost as though he were already coming.

Jake Andrews was no exception. In fact, he was the rule. The very kind of arrogant, macho fool who could be demolished most easily by feminine charm. And feminine tongue power. His head was back on the couch and his hands palm up by the time she was ready to suck his organ for real. Like stealing candy from a baby, she thought. Jake put his cock between her lips, smooth as silk. Silk over steel, that is.

Cassie felt a rush of sheer joy. There was nothing like this first moment of possession, taking a new shaft inside you this way, feeling the simultaneous pulse between your legs as you imagine it ... and him down there as well.

All in due course, though. For now she must complete this opening act of lovemaking, bringing his cock to its fullest level of readiness without pushing him over the edge. She counted on his age to keep him from spurting down her throat. He was probably 35 or so and by then a man ought to have some self-control.

It was a good thing there was a bed nearby, because she wasn't doing so hot in the area of willpower. She wanted this shaft where nature had intended it to go and she wanted him taking charge of this, and of her. That wasn't exactly a thing a girl could demand, though, was it?

Then again this was the twenty-first century. 'Fuck me,' she exclaimed, pulling her mouth away from his cock.

Jake put one of his large, capable hands in her hair, twisting it sensuously. She followed the irresistible pull, her lips magnetising to his, her body falling forward against his. He could taste his own cock now, and the thought gave her a thoroughly wicked thrill.

Reaching for her, he lamented her current state of dress.

'Too many fucking clothes,' he breathed.

Cassie kept her lips right where he'd put them even

as she went to work feverishly on her jacket and blouse. He had his hands on her tits before she could manage to undo the silk bra. There was no more delicacy now. He wanted her naked globes and he was prepared to tear the bra away to do it. Happily, the straps fell down over her shoulders, giving him full access. He kneaded the flesh roughly, demonstrating his intention to use her without mercy. Not about to hold anything back, she wriggled against him, straddling his lap to treat him to an intimate feel of silk-covered snatch.

'Oh, yeah,' he told her, his eyes lit with lust. 'That's what I want. Get on that hard cock, sweetheart, ride it till you fucking explode, right here and now.'

That sounded like a plan to Cassie. Lifting her ass, she tried to yank down her panties. Realising how impossible this was in her current position, she decided to rip them instead. It was a desperate act, but she wanted him inside her so bad, and he was close.

Finally, she made it. They were one and now the rest would follow, like water cascading over the edge of a fall.

'That's it,' he said, gritting his teeth, lifting her hips to get her moving. 'Fuck me now, fuck me hard.'

Cassie bounced with all her might, inducing a cavernous groan of pleasure. The next bounce was twice as hard, and twice as appreciated.

'More,' he cried. 'Faster, come on, you glorious bitch!'

Yes ... that was exactly how she felt, too, like a queen of bitches, a goddess of sex, able to drive this man fucking crazy, able to suck his cock inside her, above and below.

'My tits,' she hissed. 'Maul my tits.'

Jake punished them hard, pinching her nipples till she started to come. Her own fingers dug into his chest as she begged for his semen. 'Fill me, you mother-fucker. Do it to me with that great big dick.'

His body went ramrod straight. His cock threatened to push right through her body and out through her spine. She was trembling like mad, the original orgasm opening into a bigger one and then a bigger one still. They were beyond talking now, just grinding, groaning, seizing, flesh gripping flesh, neither able to let go for dear life.

His sperm flowed endlessly. It felt as if he was pumping at a million miles an hour. It went on and on and, even after they'd both climaxed, neither wanted to stop the sexual escapade. They'd simply gotten themselves too worked up for just one orgasm.

'Get on the floor,' he rasped. 'I'm going to eat out your pussy.'

She flooded all over again in response to his words. Lying with her feet on the floor, her knees bent and her legs spread, she opened herself to his tongue. Jake came to her on all fours, kissing and nibbling at her kneecaps. She tried to grab his head, but he was not about to be rushed. He wanted to work her slowly to the verge of uncontrollable, so that she was ready at a touch to give of her deepest animal self.

'Jake ... Jake ...' She said his name over and over. 'Please, don't make me wait.'

He skipped her pussy altogether on his first pass, instead working on her breasts. The gentle pressure of his lips that might have thrilled her earlier now only served to frustrate. 'Oh, God, I need to ...'

'Hands down,' he warned.

Whimpering, Cassie put her arms back over her head. 'If you could just touch me,' she pleaded pathetically, 'even for a second.'

'Try to touch my hand,' he teased.

Cassie contorted her spine, trying to lift her pussy up to his dangling fingers. She was so goddamned horny. 'Can't reach,' she cried.

'Too bad.' He yanked back his hand. 'Lay still, then. Totally still, or I'll leave you like this all afternoon.'

Cassie lay like a statue. 'You can't come till I tell you,' he said, licking up the length of her thighs.

She clenched her fists impotently. It was a good helplessness, though, the kind that made her feel wholly sexual, wholly desirable. As if she was the queen of the universe and no man could keep his hands off her.

'I won't,' she promised.

Could she keep her end of the bargain, though? Especially when things started really heating up?

Jake lingered at the border, just grazing the swollen edges of her labia. Her pussy pulsed, desperately trying to draw him in. It took all her energy to be obedient, not move, not seek her own pleasure. She was tempted push her hand down there, to flick her clitoris just right and send herself off into that place of private delights. But she was not alone and she was not at liberty. She was on this infernal journey, originally sponsored by Bryce Clarkson and entailing, as it were, a trip from one lover to another, each sexier and more dangerous than the last.

At last his tongue ventured into the holy of holies. The very act of restraining herself from moving in response nearly put her into orgasm. This was what she needed, to be completely vulnerable, at a man's mercy, protected and loved and teased all at once.

What she was wanting, as she thought about it, was a sexual version of her father, steady and true. But with a spirit of adventure, too. In short, an impossible man, one who could never exist in reality.

Jake knew how to make love with his tongue. It was like a perfect little cock, a guided heat-seeking missile designed to skirt every crevice and cranny and reach the places of deepest need. 'Oh, baby,' she gasped. 'That's it, that's the place.'

He dabbed with typical male satisfaction at having found her magic button. She heaped more praise, combined with healthy begging. In response he reached up to manipulate her nipples, doubling the sweet torment.

'Please,' she stammered, 'can I . . . come?'

His head shook no, but what the hell was she supposed to do about it? And who was he to stop her in the first place?

'N – now,' she gasped. 'Got to be . . . now.'

Jake denied her his tongue immediately, cutting her off. It was only the first of several punishments for disregarding his instructions. The second was to keep her from pushing her fingers into the desperately needy hole he'd vacated.

'Fuck!' she screamed. 'I'm right there!'

'Not till I say,' he told her calmly, rolling her with diabolical ease onto her belly.

'No,' she cried. 'Take your hands off me.'

'Is that what you really want?'

Her teeth chattered. She was face-down on the rug, her belly and breasts rubbing against the carpet fibres. 'No, I . . . I want you. I want you, Jake.'

'What you'll get,' he informed her, 'is a spanking.'

His hand followed immediately, hot and hard on her vulnerable ass cheeks. She tried to wriggle free, but he held her fast.

'Moving around will only prolong this. Now, are you going to take your punishment like a good girl or not?'

'Not!' She tried to sound grown-up about it, though

at the moment she was feeling completely bratty, not to mention out of her mind with sexual need.

'Fine. I'm a patient man.' Jake smacked her pert bottom five more times in succession. Each stroke pushed her pelvis down, pressing her crotch agonisingly into the floor. If he'd just let her alone, she could fucking climax and be done with it. Then again, she was getting a little bit used to this punishment thing, too. There was a rhythm to it, a deep, intimate connection of punisher and victim, a wild, kinky game involving hot sensations you couldn't feel with sex alone. She thought of the naughty schoolgirl she'd spied on at the club yielding to the robed schoolmaster, and of her own fantasies about Trooper Jones. Two authority figures, having their way with randy girls who loved paying the price for their indiscretions.

'Had enough?' he asked after the fifth blow.

'What do you think?' she spat. 'I was over it before you even started.'

Jake Andrews laughed. 'I think your mouth and your body need to get on the same page, that's what I think.'

Cassie noted her position. To her distinct embarrassment, she realised she was raising her ass off the carpet, unconsciously begging for more. 'You don't fight fair, Jake Andrews.'

'All's fair,' he reminded her, hooking a finger in her pussy, 'in love and war . . . and lust.'

Cassie moaned, the largest exhalation so far. 'In that case . . . I surrender.'

'Come,' said Jake Andrews, man of words and other skills to boot. 'Come on my finger. Now.'

It was an order Cassie could happily obey. 'Yyyess,' she groaned, straining with every muscle to impale herself on his finger. Pressing her palms and knees into the carpet, she lifted herself up, a levitation of lust designed to sink him all the way. She was rutting and sweating, a sleek little animal on display, her every need out in the open, for his visual and tactile pleasure. It was her element. Sheer and complete naughtiness. Totally unredeemed hedonism. No apologies. All about Cassandra and Cassandra's carnal consummation.

'You are so fucking incredible,' Jake was growling.

The orgasm was racking her body by now, not just her cunt but every fibre of her being, every nerve-ending, the centre of her brain lit up like a Christmas tree. 'No,' she cried, her head thrashing. 'Don't tell me that. Tell me I'm a bitch, a slut ... talk dirty.'

'You're a slut,' he agreed, smacking her ass with his other hand. 'You're a dirty girl. You like to come on the floor, fucking a man's hand, a man you don't even know. A total fucking stranger, that's what I am. And you spread for me at the drop of a hat. You took my cock in your mouth and you don't know the first fucking thing about me. You rode my dick like a twenty-dollar whore and I'm not even gonna pay you that much. You hear me? You're gonna walk out of here with nothing but a red ass.'

'Oh God, oh God, oh God ...' The convulsions were on her. Another climax with the first one barely past. If the last was a raging torrent, this one was the collapse of the dam. No restraint, no dignity. She'd come to this man's place, liked how he looked and fucked him. She was a scandal, a disgrace. She deserved this spanking. She deserved a caning, too, like the sweet but whorish schoolgirl in the sex club. And she deserved Trooper Jones' shackles and the discipline of his dick, teaching her what it meant to be held in place by a real man.

But Jones wasn't here. Or the larger-than-life Governor, for that matter. Just this man, Jake Andrews, the cock of the moment. 'P–put it in me,' she pleaded, contorting her body like the first snake. 'Put in dick . . . before . . . too late.'

Jake flipped her and threw himself between her legs. He hit her mid-orgasm, master of timing that he was. She was afraid the shock of her convulsions might kill him, but he was a big boy. A hard boy, too, even harder than the first time, if that was possible.

He wasn't talking dirty now. He'd done enough of that to work them both up for a year. She could hardly make out the colour of his eyes as he pounded at her. A lesser woman would have screamed for mercy. Cassie, on the other hand, had asked for it and was getting it.

'Go, go, go,' she chanted, exhaling with every word. 'Fuck . . . fuck . . . fuck.'

On the floor, this was the place for dirty sex, amidst the newspapers and wrappers and God knew what else. She bit into his neck. The sinews tasted delicious. Most women would die to get at a body and a face this good. And his attitude, that was all sex, too. He even had the smell of a rebel, a rough musk that wouldn't cut it in the halls of power.

Some called men like Jake Andrews pesky flies that buzzed round the ears of the powerful, or, worse still, jackals that picked at the corpses of misery. But she knew he was the lion, ever stalking the self-satisfied, plump gazelles and wildebeest that ground and chewed the grass of the people. Why had he given up, though? If he could still fuck like this, there were no limits to what he could do to corrupt politicians.

Was Bryce one of them? Was he mixed up in something with Landview that wasn't kosher? Is that what

Queenie was trying to do, reawaken Jake's soul so he'd go after the Governor? But why bother? She already had him dead to rights if all she wanted was to destroy him. Cassie clutched her lover even more tightly. Always so many questions, so much responsibility. This was the problem of mixing sex and politics. You had to love the rush, but there was always fallout. She ought to spend more time with rap stars, she mused, arcing into yet another whistling, sky-rocketing rainbow of pleasure with the burnt-out reporter.

Yeah, this Jake Andrews was good. And if he was this good on the floor, how good would he be in an actual bed?

He rolled onto his back afterwards, letting her rest her head on his chest. She liked the feel of her body next to his, hip to hip. There weren't many men whose company she could tolerate after the sex. Mostly she couldn't wait to get away, if not the first time then certainly by the second or third. Generally there wasn't much more to know about a man once you'd seen how he fucked. They weren't all that interesting otherwise.

And yet they all tended to think so highly of themselves. Didn't matter if they were contractors or senators or singers, they had their little formula, the same formula by which they judged the world, carefully excluding anything and everything that challenged their way of thinking. That was why they never even asked if you were satisfied, because their egos required that you had to be, and, if somehow you'd missed their glorious orgasm train, well, it was your problem, wasn't it?

But this Jake Andrews with his silver tongue, she was curious about him. There were layers to him she hadn't begun to explore. Pains she hadn't begun to expose. Was this what it felt like to start a relationship with someone? She didn't have much experience to go on. Looking back on it, she supposed she and Bryce had had something of a relationship, though they never made a conscious effort. That's probably why it worked between them. They hadn't fucked it up with real dates. Just talks, honest sharing and no bullshit. They were friends. That was the key.

So maybe he'd done her a favour after all. You don't fall in love with your friends, do you? And you sure as hell don't marry them. You marry people like Lydia Davenport, who can do something useful for you. Cassie had hated Lydia for a long time. Lydia was an airhead. She was spoiled. Had she worked a day in her life, this daughter of a multi-generational financial empire? Had she ever faced a single hard decision? So Richard Davenport was supposedly a hard father to have, never around, aloof, impossible to please. Well, Cassie's family had troubles, too, and there'd been no money to smooth the way.

But all that was water under the bridge. Cassie was never cut out to be a politician's wife, anyway. She'd have had too many opinions. She'd have spoken out and actually tried to make a difference. That didn't go over big in the United States of America, even in this day and age. There were still limits for women, places they could go and places they couldn't. It was all hypocrisy, of course. Since time immemorial, females have ruled from the bedroom, making or breaking the men of their day. And no man has ever objected, either, so long as he got his rocks off regularly.

'You gave me a run for my money,' Cassie murmured, running her hand over his lightly haired chest and resting it possessively over his spent cock. 'For a minute I thought I'd have to throw in the towel.'

He grabbed her wrist and brought it to his mouth. 'Who says you didn't?' He nibbled playfully at her fingers.

She sighed, nestling even closer. 'You know, it's not just anybody I'd give it up for on an unvacuumed rug.'

'I'm flattered.' He released her fingers, reaching for her ass cheeks instead. 'And now that you mention it, I think I'll have you vacuum first next time.'

She squirmed, the heat of the spanking still very real. 'What makes you think there will be a next time?'

'Because the information I have is worth more than one fuck, that's why.'

She slapped at his stomach. 'That's cheating. We had a deal.'

'Deals were made to be broken. Haven't you been in politics long enough to know that?'

Cassie pinched his nipple, intending to deliver just a little payback for all the punishment she'd received. 'If you welch on me, I'll expose you to the press.'

'I think you've exposed me plenty, thank you very much.' He pinched her clit, just hard enough to re-establish supremacy.

'Ow,' she said, laughing. 'Now that *is* dirty politics.'

'So is using this fine little body of yours to drag me out of a perfectly good drunken stupor.'

She climbed on top of him, feeling more playful than she had in years. 'You loved it,' she said, grinning and pinning his wrists over his head. 'And you know it.'

He feigned a growl, though of course he was allowing all this, especially her show of physical dominance. 'What I would have loved was about four more beers.'

She lowered her lips to his, giving him reason to expect he might collect on all the future fucks he required as payment for his services. 'I'm better than beer,' she crooned. 'My highs are higher and there's no hangovers afterwards.'

The erstwhile reporter with the physique to die for rolled Cassie back over. 'That remains to be seen.' He pinned her for real.

Jeezus, he was getting hard again. Exactly how long had it been since he'd had a woman, anyway?

'Careful, there, big guy. As keeper of this little sex tavern, I am here to inform you that if you don't start showing a little moderation, I will have to cut you off.'

His hand slid across her hip, as if she was personal property. 'And what if I become addicted?'

Cassie arched her back, proffering her re-aroused nipples. 'In that case, here's to co-dependency.'

'Touché,' he said with a grin. 'You're a woman after my own heart.'

A minute later he was lifting her up, carrying her to the bed, their talk about the sex tape and Landview delayed yet again. Though there was no serious objection – from either party.

8

Ian showed up on Queenie's doorstep at the ungodly hour of eight in the morning.

'Are you trying to piss me off?' the wild-haired dominatrix asked, standing there with her curvaceous body barely covered by a short silk robe.

The portly Ian leered, reaching for a tit. 'If it gets me laid, sure.'

She slapped his hand away. 'Don't fuck with me, Ian. I'm not in the mood.'

'Hey, save the attitude for your clients, will ya? I'm supposed to be a colleague.'

Queenie locked the door behind him, wishing like hell he was still on the other side of it. How much longer would she have to put up with him and his bosses? Hadn't she given them enough already? When would they leave her – and Bryce – alone?

'The only colleagues you can claim live under the rocks in my garden. Now how about you relaying whatever message it is you've been sent here to bring and we can both get back to our wonderful little lives.'

'How do you know I don't speak for myself?' Ian made a second play for her creamy flesh, his own obese body overflowing in turtleneck and jeans.

For Queenie, once was enough. 'Because,' she answered, popping him in the solar plexus and doubling him over, 'you are nothing but a lackey. You were born a lackey and you will die a lackey.'

He made it back to an upright position, just barely.

'See,' he said, grinning masochistically and holding his midsection, 'that's what I like about you, you're a gal who speaks her mind.'

'If I had the time or inclination,' she informed him. 'I would tie you down to a table, shave every square inch of body hair and drip hot wax on you for about twelve hours straight.'

He licked his lips. 'Promises, promises.'

Queenie shed her robe, baring the curvy body men spent up to a thousand dollars an hour worshipping. 'You see this? Get a nice look and get it out of your system, 'cause it's something you'll never get as long as you live.'

'Maybe not,' he agreed. 'But what if the bosses want some?'

Queenie tried to imagine Ian's criminal employers with their shiny cars and pinstriped suits putting their hands on her. She'd sooner die than succumb to such a fate.

She didn't know any of them by name, but it was clear enough they represented heavy elements of organised crime. It was they who wanted this tape made, and the truth was, it had as much to do with sex as she did with the Methodist Women's Club. In reality, it was all about Landview. The project's mob backers and their money-laundering bankers were getting nervous about leaks, and they were even more nervous that Bryce might take them seriously enough to stop the project, thereby leaving them all in the lurch – or in jail.

The Governor, as they saw it, needed to be removed from the picture.

Of the methods at their disposal, blackmailing him into resigning was the easiest. They'd approached Queenie in Paris, making it clear they were willing to employ harsher methods against Bryce if she did not help them make the tape. Queenie knew the man would hate her forever for tricking him, but at least he would be alive.

Would it really end so smoothly, though? Bryce might yet refuse to resign, and, even if he did, the mob might still want to eliminate him in a more permanent way. Hence her appeal to Jake Andrews, the crack investigative reporter, through the pretty consultant Cassie. If the pert blonde could convince Jake to look into the matter, they might find a way to expose the truth, saving Bryce's life and his reputation while putting the criminals in jail.

'If your bosses want me,' she replied defiantly, 'then tell them to come and get me.'

Ian unzipped his pants, pulling out a long soft cock. 'That's the problem with you hookers,' he said, wrapping his hand around the meat and stroking it. 'You never see the big picture. Just remember, we're all expendable, sweetheart. So how about you get over here on your knees and start showing me how sorry you are for treating me so bad ... before I go giving you a bad report card to the bosses?'

Queenie Amazon went to him, though not with obedience on her mind. She was after revenge, beginning with this man and working her way up. People would pay, at the highest levels if need be, and in the end Bryce Clarkson would be vindicated. For the time being, she would have some fun with the poor fool in front of her.

Sidling up close, she nuzzled his neck. 'I have something better in mind.'

He wrapped his arms around her and glommed her ass cheeks. 'Oh, yeah, and what's that?'

Queenie took hold of his rod, letting it stiffen. 'Well,'

she said, smiling with deceptive sweetness, 'I was thinking about having you take off all your clothes and get down on the floor on all fours so you can bark like a dog.'

Ian tried to free himself in vain. She held him all the tighter, employing her nails. 'You know it's what you've wanted,' she said teasingly, pushing her naked tits against his puffy chest. 'You've been begging for it all along, without even realising it.'

Ian was on the verge of panting already. 'You're a crazy bitch. You don't know what you're talking about. The only thing I want is to see you crawling around a roomful of gangsters, servicing their cocks.'

'You're the one who's gonna crawl, Ian. And we won't have to wait to see that, will we?'

'F–fucking bitch,' he hissed.

It was already too late for him, though. He was pushing his pelvis against her, giving in to the sensations of what her hand was doing, making himself vulnerable, dependent.

'You think I haven't had you figured out from the start, Ian?' She was unbuttoning his pants with her free hand, and meeting no resistance. 'All that needling you gave me? You're a submissive man. You need to be humiliated and controlled by a strong, dominant female. You need to be reduced.'

He swallowed hard, watching paralysed as she pulled his belt from the loops of his jeans. 'That's for later.' She wrapped it around her neck like a snake. 'For now, let's get this shirt off.'

Ian, a look of complete bewilderment on his face, stood there unmoving as she removed the turtleneck.

'See?' She ran her fingertips over his belly at will. 'That wasn't so bad, was it? Just keep thinking of yourself as my property and we'll get along fine.'

Sweat was already trickling down his forehead. His skin was flushed. His eyes were wide. His arousal was ill-disguised.

'Take off the rest of your clothes,' she instructed.

Ian stumbled twice, trying to pull off his sneakers, socks and jeans. When he'd finally stepped out of his boxers, she ordered him to stand in front of her, hands at his sides, back straight.

'This is mine.' She poked her fingertip at his cock. 'And so are these.' He released a small moan as she caressed his balls.

'You may call me Mistress,' she informed him.

'Yes, Mistress.' The word rolled off his tongue well. There was no doubt it suited him.

'So.' She traced a sharp line along the underside of his balls with her index finger. 'Back to the matter of crawling. What have you to say now ... slave?'

'I beg to crawl for you,' he croaked. 'I beg to go on all fours ... and crawl and ... bark like a dog.'

'Very good, slave. Extra credit for your good memory.'

He dropped to the floor. There would be no way to explain to a non-submissive male the thrill she was engendering in him by agreeing to dominate him. He would bark for her for hours, and he'd crawl, beg and squirm too. Though it was Queenie's business occupation, she got a personal thrill from bossing men around and watching them humiliate themselves for their own subversive enjoyment. It was all about the pleasure, albeit an offbeat one the rest of the world could not easily understand.

Ian made a passable dog, though he was howling more than barking.

'You're pathetic,' she said, condemning his effort, giving him precisely the negative reaction he wanted.

It was especially ironic in a situation like this, where she didn't like the man all that much. If she really wanted to punish him, she'd deny him the abuse, not heap it on.

What Ian the lackey did not realise, however, was that he was about to make himself Queenie's pawn. Not too long from now it wouldn't just be sex he'd be begging for but a chance to serve her every whim. Through him she would begin to find out what she needed about his superiors, up to and including the big bosses.

'Forgive me for being so pathetic, Mistress.'

'Were you given permission to speak, dog?' she demanded.

The man-dog hung his shaggy head, shaking a no.

'Turn about,' she commanded. 'Let's see if we can change the colour of that ass for you.'

Ian whimpered but did as he was told. She intended to beat him with his own belt and it was obvious he knew exactly what was coming.

'You may thank me in advance for whipping you, slave.'

'Thank you, Mistress, for whipping my ass.'

She taunted him with the end of the belt, letting the leather trail over his quivering flesh. 'Afterwards you'll take a dildo from behind. You may thank me for that, too.'

He drew a ragged, anticipatory breath. 'Thank you, Mistress, for fucking me in the ass.'

'Such a pretty slave.' She took him down a notch further in humiliation. 'Such a pretty, submissive little man.'

Ian was shivering, aching with the need to be purified and touched and hurt. 'Oh, God,' he groaned. 'Please, please punish me.'

The belt sailed through the air, a thing of beauty, whistling as it found its way to the target. The leather made a sensuous cracking noise against the generous cheeks, the impact more than willingly absorbed.

'You may keep count,' she commanded imperiously. 'In addition, you may thank me each time I deign to kiss you with the belt.'

'Y–yes, Mistress,' he cried, immediately bringing himself up to speed. 'That was one. Thank you.'

Number two was administered just as strictly. He gave a pleasurable howl, followed by a fresh thank you.

'Touch your dick,' she said now. 'As I am whipping you.'

The slave was made to play with himself during his own punishment. The intense feelings of humiliation were making him crave the leather all the more. She caught him pushing up his ass for more and, when she got to five, he whimpered for her to go on.

'Take your hand away,' she chided. 'Stop behaving like such a little slut.'

His body jazzed with obvious pleasure at being called a dirty name, especially one so often reserved for females.

'You are a naughty little beast,' she persisted. 'You don't deserve pleasure, do you?'

'No, Mistress.'

'You deserve the dildo, don't you?'

'Yes, ma'am. I deserve to be fucked in my ass.'

'You'll squeal for me, won't you?'

'Yes, ma'am.'

'While I'm going to get the dildo, you will repeat the following phrase, over and over. "I am a little slut, Mistress. I like it in the ass." Think you can handle that?'

'Yes, Mistress.'

She heard him say the words, once, twice and again, as she went to her bedroom to break into her toybox. She kept a special, choice supply of domination devices in here. The rest were in the back room, which she had converted into a fully functioning dungeon. She had her doubts the man could handle anything that intense, so she'd opted to subject him to some easier play. Granted, an eight-inch rubber penis attached to her crotch might seem heavy duty to some, but in her business this was child's play. She'd seen dominatrixes use far bigger, not to mention the natural organs gay men used on each other all the time. There was no telling what experience Ian had, so she had to be cautious. To that end she also made sure to give him a safe word.

'If you can't handle any of this,' she declared, 'I want you to say Rumpelstiltskin. Do you understand me?'

He interrupted his recitation long enough to answer. 'Yes, Mistress.'

Queenie rubbed the lotion on the plastic cock she was now sporting. It would go in easier with lubrication, and deeper too. 'Your ass looks good all nice and red. You should see it,' she told him.

'Yes, Mistress.'

'I want you to go over to that table.' She pointed to the dining room. 'Bend over it, face down.'

'Yes, Mistress.' Ian promptly placed his naked self in the required position, rendering his ass fully fuckable.

She slapped him lightly. 'Are you a virgin back here?'

'No,' he confessed.

'No, Mistress,' she corrected him with a harder slap. 'Was it a real cock?'

'Yes, Mistress. There were others, too. I am ... bisexual.'

The information was important. It meant she could use him all the harder.

'You'll take me deep, slave. I expect absolute and total submission.'

'My ass is yours, Mistress.'

She placed the tip of the lubricated plastic penis between his ass cheeks. 'We'll see.'

Ian sighed deeply, feeling the pressure on the cavity of his anus as she pushed down into him.

'You weren't lying.' She injected an inch deep between his cheeks, and then another for good measure. 'You really are a little ass slut, aren't you?'

'Yes, Mistress. Oh, God, yes.'

'Beg for it, then.' She smacked his behind. 'Let me hear you.'

'P–please,' he groaned pathetically. 'Use me. Make me your ass slut.'

'You already are.' She went in another inch. 'You're my property, remember?'

He pressed his cheek to the table, vanquished. 'Forgive me, Mistress. This slut begs your pardon.'

Queenie smiled, knowing it was time to begin pressing her advantage. 'That isn't good enough, slave. You'll have to do better.'

'Anything, Mistress, please, just don't be angry with me.'

She withdrew the tiniest bit. 'If I feel I can't trust you, I won't play with you any more,' she warned him.

'Trust me, trust me, Mistress.' He was audibly aching from the potential absence of her.

'Tell me about the bosses, then. I want to know all about them.'

He gasped, as if he'd been stabbed. Trapped again,

she thought laughing inwardly. 'I can't do that ... please, don't make me.'

'Go home.' The shaft was gone from his anus. 'Don't waste my time ever again.'

'All right, I'll tell you,' he wailed. 'But it's not much. There are six bosses in all. I answer to one of them, the head boss.'

'And where does he live?'

'Just outside the city. Real upper-crust area.'

'Tell me how they function.'

'It's all one syndicate, Mistress. One organisation, like an umbrella corporation, formed to work projects like Landview.'

'What about the legitimate partners? Who are they?'

'Everybody,' he groaned. 'It's everybody.'

'And how many know about the mob being involved?'

'Enough of them,' he whimpered. 'More than enough.'

Such a tangled web, Queenie thought, one strand leading to another, all the strands interconnecting. She wasn't sure what led her to ask the next question, but ask it she did.

'What about the Governor's father-in-law, Richard Davenport?'

Her suspicions were not entirely unreasonable. Not only was the man's bank the major co-signatory for Landview, he was also the father of Lydia, a cold and heartless woman whom Queenie hated with a passion for all the hurt she'd caused Bryce over the years.

'I–I've seen him at a couple of meetings. He and my boss are tight. That's all I know, I swear!'

Queenie, the one-time Abigail Auvignon, felt a chill down her spine. If Lydia's father were in on this, then Bryce would never be safe. He might spare Bryce's life for his daughter's sake at first, but in the long run he would kill him, she was sure of it. After all, who but a total monster would mix up his own family in the mafia in order to make a few extra dollars he clearly didn't need?

There was no doubt Bryce was in danger. He wouldn't listen to her, though, not after what had happened in the motel. There was only one person Queenie could get a message to in time and that was Cassie Dane. All this was very clear. The only real question was whether Queenie could get to Cassandra Dane in time to save the man they both loved.

Jake Andrews woke up to a world of trouble in his bed. And it wasn't just the hot little blonde, either. Though she was certainly enough all by herself. What the hell was her name? Had she even told him? Jeezus, he'd fucked a nameless woman who'd shown up on his doorstep. Talk about a low point in judgement.

He pulled the sheet off her sleeping form for a closer look. OK, so she'd been worth the ride. Perfect curves, nicely sized breasts, not too large, not too small. She was that really fuckable kind of blonde, too, the kind with the scrumptious hair, layered, not just yellow but shaded with gold and wheat and gritty flecks of sand. She was a down-and-dirty blonde, not quite dishwater, but not platinum high society either.

Certainly she knew how to screw. He hadn't been ridden like that in ages. She must have been as starved for love as he was. How many times did they do it in all? Four? And he'd been able to keep going even after he was sober, too. The last time he'd fucked a girl sober was – hell, come to think of it, that was a first for him.

Looking at her now he just wanted to nibble on her precious little ear lobes and then work his way down to those prize-winning nipples, and below that her concave belly, like a sweet valley teasing the eye even further down to her sweetly lipped pussy. What a package. Subtle, classy, but sexy as all get-out.

Damn. He was getting hard again. He was going to have to fuck her one more time for the road. Then it would be goodbye.

Jake Andrews hated goodbyes. It was the women who made it so tough. No woman ever says goodbye without leaving her hooks in. No matter how much she might tell you ahead of time that there'll be no strings attached, she'll still have those stars in her eyes by the end. Visions of a white dress and a long petal-covered aisle. It was a genetic thing. A huntress thing. Bagging male prey, dragging it home and binding it to an easy chair, remote control stuck in its mouth as a pacifier.

Well, Jake wasn't about to fall for any traps. One more nice little scene with this woman, and adios ... don't let the door hit you on the way out.

Hold on, though, why was it she had come here, exactly? Certainly not for the ambience. Landview, that was it. She'd come to pick his brain about the project and he'd agreed to in exchange for sex.

Fuck. How had a nice girl like this gotten mixed up with a cesspool like Landview Development? Landview was a mob slush fund, a huge swamp of black commerce where monies merged from a thousand crooked sources, tributaries pouring into a great sewer that fed the entire system. Such was the life-blood of the legitimate economy, of course, though people liked to pretend there was such a thing as real morality. In reality, everyone sucked from the trough, including the corporate executives.

It was only on television dramas and in campaign

speeches that there were clean lines drawn, black and white, right and wrong. Criminal activity versus honest business practice, and men of courage to detect and enforce the difference. Police and prosecutors. And newspaper men. Carriers of the torch. Lights in the darkness. Once upon a time there was a man named Jake Andrews who'd thought such battles worth fighting. He'd worn his colours bravely and won ... absolutely nothing.

There was no way out, he'd learned, no high road to take. The game was fixed, rigged from the start. Everyone was in on it. Everyone who'd ever touched, coveted or hoarded a dollar, probably right back to the Garden of Eden when the currency was leaves.

Suicide was the answer. Slow or fast. He'd picked a bottle, which was slow. This curvy little angel beside him had decided to go snooping around in the business of the Syndicate, which was a fast way to die. A very fast way. Shit, now he needed a beer. On top of that, he'd lost his hard-on.

'Honey, you need to wake up.' He tapped her shoulder, inducing her to reach out for him, eyes still closed.

'Take me,' she murmured, back arched in her sleep.

'Baby, we're not fucking any more, we need to talk.'

She pressed her lips up to his, making little mewling noises. After a few seconds, her eyes popped open, the dream giving way to what was probably an unpleasant reality for her.

'Omigod,' she said, rolling across the bed away from him. 'Did we ...?'

'Yeah,' he quipped, 'I'm pretty sure we did. Unless we had some stand-ins I don't know about.'

She blinked, her beautiful blue eyes bright as crystal. 'This shouldn't have happened.'

He laughed drily. 'Why not? Are you a lesbian or something? Because if you are, you sure could have fooled me.'

She pulled the sheet up around her body defensively. 'You don't even know my name.'

'Would you feel better if you told me now?'

'No. Absolutely not.'

'Fine.' He shrugged. 'I'll look in your wallet and find out for myself.'

'Hey, you can't do that!' she protested.

'I'll make something up then. Hilda? Erica? Cecilia? Am I getting close?'

'I'm Cassie, damn it!'

He stuck out his hand. 'Nice to meet you, Cassie Dammit.'

'Screw you,' she replied.

'Already did. Four times, unless I miss my count.'

'Which means you owe me a hell of a lot of information, buster, and you better start spilling.'

Jake barely suppressed a smirk. What was it about seeing a little creature like this so fired up that made a man just want to mess with her so mercilessly?

'How about you give me my sheet back first?' said the naked man, in an attempt to talk her out of her only covering. 'So we can be on more equal footing. Conversation-wise.'

Cassie Dammit was not fooled by his platonic pretence. Cassie Dammit was seeing his cock, slowly moving up from half-mast to full attention. 'No more bullshit, Andrews. You will tell me about Landview, and you will tell me now.'

Jake puckered up. 'How about a kiss first?'

'How about I cut your balls off with a rusty knife?'

He thought for a moment. 'I'm not sure I have one

of those in the kitchen. Then again, it has been a while since I've looked in my silverware drawer.'

'That's all right.' She edged forward on her knees, trying to threaten him with one hand while holding the sheet with the other. 'I can use my nails.'

Jake waited till she was close enough then yanked away the sheet. Cassie shrieked and tried to cover herself.

'You're interfering with my view,' he drawled. 'Do you need another spanking?'

Much to his surprise, she put her arms down, though she carried on complaining. 'If this is your idea of wooing a woman, Andrews, you have a hell of a lot to learn.'

He regarded her, crouching, her pendulous breasts displayed to complete advantage. She wanted him to come after her. That was obvious. He'd have to talk quick, before their hormones got the better of them yet again.

'One doesn't woo you, my dear, one uses tranquilliser darts.'

'Say what you want,' she replied airily. 'You're the one with the hard dick and no hope of relief.'

'Open your legs, Cassie. Play with yourself for me.'

She spread wide, her ass back on her heels. 'Suit yourself, cowboy.'

It was a posture of submission, though she was trying her best to put a different spin on it. 'Now you tell me about Landview, if you can keep your concentration.'

'I'm fine,' he assured her. 'Knees a little farther apart, please.'

She gave him a dirty look, quickly suppressed. Clearly she did not wish him to know that his dominance was having any effect on her, though there was no denying the glistening liquid at the folds of her sex. Or the faint, quintessentially female aroma that went with it.

'Happy now, Andrews?'

He watched her finger rhythmically caressing. It was rather comical as she tried her hardest not to react to what he was making her do. 'Not really. I can't honestly say I've been happy since my chocolate milk days at Emerson Elementary. But I probably wasn't *really* happy then, either. I've just forgotten the bad parts, like everybody else. I will tell you, though, that I would be a hell of a lot less unhappy if you would drop this unsavoury interest in real estate you've developed.'

Her breathing was already quickening. With each intake, her flat, delectable tummy recessed, forming a smooth depression. The action only reinforced the beauty of her breasts. 'I can't. It concerns a client. I'm bound to pursue this.'

'Don't tell me, you have a nice little code of ethics, don't you? On the wall of your office, in a heart-shaped frame above your desk.'

'Are you always such a cynical bastard?' asked the masturbating woman, her nipples full and ripe.

'Only when I am trying to save someone's life,' he said, though he knew this wasn't exactly true. 'Look, I'll cut to the chase. Landview is the biggest real-estate deal this region has ever seen. It will change the face of the state. Something like that attracts attention, some of it good, some of it bad. People want pieces of the pie. And they are not all the kind you'd take home to meet mommy and daddy.'

'You mean the mob.'

He watched her swollen clit, as she tickled it to and

fro. How was she keeping track of what he was saying when he could barely do so himself? 'Yes,' he confirmed, trying to give her the not entirely cynical version of what was going on. 'The mob.'

'I wonder what that has to do with Queenie and her tape,' said Cassie, thinking out loud.

'Excuse me?'

He listened to the wild story about the sex tape and her mysterious meeting with a dominatrix named Queenie. A dominatrix who'd sent her here to ask about Landview. Something stank here, and it wasn't the six months of laundry lying around.

'She said the tape was a ... diversion,' Cassie supplied. 'I think that's the word she used.'

'So the Governor must be involved in Landview and someone wants him out,' Jake reasoned, employing his rusty but not entirely decayed reporter's intuition.

He saw the light flash in Cassie's eyes. 'The bastard – he set me up. He sent me out there to talk to Queenie, knowing full well what this was really all about.'

'We don't want to jump to conclusions, Cassie.'

'But you said yourself Bryce had to be involved.'

'Yes, there has to be a connection,' he confirmed. 'But for all we know he is trying to stop Landview and the mob is trying to force him to resign and using Queenie in the process.'

She cocked her head. 'So you're telling me you believe in the possibility of an honest politician? Tell me, Mr Reporter, what are the odds of that?

'They're small,' he admitted. 'I think you better let me look into this, Cassie. In the meantime, I want you to promise me you will do no more snooping around on your own.'

Her eyes lit up with mischief. Sex-fired mischief. 'No. I don't have to promise you anything.'

That was a cue if ever he'd seen one. 'How about if we see about a little friendly persuasion, shall we?'

'Best keep your distance,' she warned. 'I bite.'

'I suppose I needn't ask where,' he smirked.

'Anywhere I like,' she crooned.

A minute later they were wrestling, rolling over and over on the bed, giggling and laughing like a couple of college kids. It had been years since he'd had companionship this good. If he didn't know himself better, and if he hadn't already been convinced of the falsity of such emotions, he might actually believe himself to be falling head over heels in love with this Cassie Dammit.

Quickly, very quickly, he moved to turn things sexual once again. Lust was what he needed. Lust was what he understood. A bright, bright flare to light up the heavens and then to fall. Safe. Predictable. And terminal. A fuck and nothing more. His cock in her pussy, anonymous, lots of grunting, nameless, biting, clawing even, so long as it was back to normal afterwards. Back to man and woman, staring at each other across the great divide.

She cried out as he took her, the heat almost molten. Closing his eyes he gave in at once to the orgasm. No time to react, to plan or to play. Just like that, they were one.

9

It was the last straw. Lydia Clarkson was finally going to strike back. She was going to commit adultery, for the first time ever, by fucking her personal trainer, right there in the gym of the executive mansion.

Lydia had made the decision as she breakfasted alone on poached eggs and dry toast, washed down with a cup of black coffee spiked with vodka. The chief executive, or, as she preferred to call him, the chief copulator, was off already doing God knows what on the taxpayer's dollar.

Last night at the museum ball he'd been doing a blonde tart young enough to be his daughter. Assuming they'd ever gotten around to having any children. Eight years, and nothing to show for the effort. Maybe if they did the deed more than once a year? One of them might well be sterile; that was possible, too. Or else the fates had just been kind. What the hell would either of them have done with a child? In this house, no less?

The pundits had hinted more than once that children were worth votes, and some of his new handlers at the national level were actually looking at her as some kind of party backstabber for not providing Bryce with strapping sons. Oh, they were out there, she was tempted to tell them, they just weren't hers. But who didn't know that already? Lydia Clarkson's place as a female version of a cuckold was already fixed in state annals and soon, thanks to her husband's ambitions, it would be known all across this great nation as well.

But wait. Hold the presses. Now his enemies had a tape. An actual honest-to-goodness stag film. That was a little harder to spin out of existence, wasn't it? Maybe she wouldn't have to worry about picking out drapes for the White House after all.

Bryce wouldn't give up, though. Oh, no. He'd go down swinging. Make that fucking. That's right. Hold the presses again, because who had he hired as his supposed consultant and go-between? That little bitch Cassandra Dane. The prototypical blonde slut. The one he'd left behind to marry Lydia. Like that was some big fucking favour he'd done her, Lydia thought.

Three guesses what kind of consulting they'd be doing. Don't forget to pack the camera, dear. Ta ta!

Fucking shit-for-brains asshole. Had he ever once asked her what she might have liked out of their life together before he flushed it all to hell? But, hey, maybe she shouldn't be so hard on the man. After all, he'd just wanted a piece of the big slime pie her father and his cronies had been hoarding for years.

So Bryce was waking up to the fact that something was wrong with Landview? Talk about a naïve sorry-ass bastard. Or had he just inhaled enough of his own bullshit over the years to believe it himself? Where did the man think all that Davenport money had come from? From illegal speakeasies and rum-running and, before that, slave-trading. Richard Davenport was a money launderer *par excellence*, the ideal middleman between the back-lot scoundrels and the upfront pretty faces like Bryce.

Daddy had chosen Bryce. Didn't he realise that? Bryce Clarkson was a puppet on a string from day one. And, like every puppet, he'd serve till his time was up and no longer. Was there any point in telling him? No. The man hadn't listened to her once, not ever in all the years they'd been together.

He was getting what he deserved, as far as she was concerned. The tape, the loss of his career, the impending blow-up over Landview – it was all coming his way. And pretty soon he'd be getting another little surprise. From her divorce attorney.

But first there was the matter of Jean Paul, the workout instructor. He was waiting for her when she arrived in the gym. Flashing him a big smile, she did her best to put a little sashay in her step. Apparently she tried a little too hard because she tripped over a ten-pound barbell on the floor.

The first lady of the state cursed herself under her breath. Nice going, Lyd. Maybe a little less vodka in that coffee next time. As luck would have it, though, Jean Paul was there personally to intercept her destabilised person. See? Things were looking up already.

'Are you quite all right, Madame?' queried the very French and very hunky trainer as he helped her straighten up.

'I'm better,' she drawled, with a flip of her auburn hair. 'Now.'

Jean Paul smiled politely as she clung to him a bit longer than necessary. She had dressed as suggestively as possible today in tiny Spandex shorts and a crop top. In combination with lots of perfume, it made for a deadly package. Though he was fifteen years her junior, there was no way the aquiline-nosed, hazel-eyed paragon of fitness could remain oblivious to her charms. Even without trying, in the three weeks she'd had this particular instructor, she'd been able to give him hard-ons. Was there any limit to what she might accomplish today?

'Shall we begin with a warm-up?' he suggested, sounding like a young Maurice Chevalier.

'Oh, definitely.' She moved back, but not particularly far. 'You know, Jean Paul, I've been having this problem with a tight muscle.'

'You have, Madame?'

She nodded, sultry-eyed. 'Uh huh.'

'And which muscle would that be?

'Can I show you instead?' The first lady turned around and backed her ass up against the trainer's crotch. 'Here, give me your hand.'

She placed his palm against her nude belly, the fingers widely splayed. 'There,' she sighed, craning her neck. 'That's the one.'

Jean Paul swelled against her, his manhood eagerly pressing against the Spandex. 'Madame Clarkson, I don't think this is a very good idea.'

She smiled at his attempt to maintain professional decorum. 'You don't? But I thought you were French. Wouldn't this be completely normal where you come from? Why, even your president has a mistress.'

'That is true,' he acknowledged. 'But things are not the same, so to speak, for the gander as for the goose, if you take my meaning.'

'You mean you have a double standard, too?' She turned back round and flung her arms around his neck. 'Well, you needn't worry about this little gander. She has her goose in the pressure cooker. One false move and he can kiss my daddy's money goodbye.'

Lydia could hardly believe she was talking like this. Something must have snapped inside her. Yes, Bryce had gone too far this time, and his slapdash, fraudulent attempt to win back her affections yesterday afternoon had only solidified things in her mind. It was time to take care of herself for a change, giving hubby a taste of his own medicine.

'Tell me you wouldn't like to make love to me, Jean Paul.'

'Of course I would. But the time, the place,' he insisted. 'These are hardly conducive.'

'Well, it will have to do.' She pulled his T-shirt from the waistband of his shorts. 'Unless you can think of a way to squeeze you and me and half a dozen nosy security men onto a hotel-room bed somewhere.'

'But surely we are being watched now.' He scanned the perimeter of the gymnasium nervously.

'Oh, I hope we are,' she muttered. 'I really do.'

'What did you say?'

'Nothing, Jean Paul. I was just saying I'd really like to see your triceps. Lift your arms, will you?'

Jean Paul raised his hands in surrender.

'Mm,' she murmured, running her hands over his bare chest. 'Now this is what I call a national treasure. Tell me again what we had to give your government in exchange for you?'

Jean Paul missed the joke entirely. 'What do you mean by "exchange", Madame? Do you refer to presents, as during Christmas?'

Lovely as sin and thick as a brick, she sighed. Just what the doctor ordered.

The first lady moved on to the next act, putting her hand down the trainer's pants. 'Yes, that's it exactly, darling. Let's just see what Father Christmas has in the stocking for little Lydia this year, shall we? She's been such a good girl. Too good, really.'

Jean Paul was huge to the touch. Eager to confirm this with her other senses, she fell to her knees on the exercise mat and yanked down his shorts. A massive one-eyed wonder swung immediately within range of her mouth.

'May I?' She didn't wait for an answer before running her tongue along the length of him, top and bottom.

Releasing an oath in French, he put his hands on her shoulders for support.

'I can hardly believe that beautiful thing is going to be inside me,' she exclaimed. 'And I bet you'd give me a baby, too, won't you? First time out of the gate. Wouldn't that be the irony of the century?'

'*Sacré bleu*,' he was saying now, trying to push her head onto him.

'You said it, brother.' Lydia took him into her mouth, taking an inch or so of the trainer's cock toward the back of her throat. He rewarded her with further exclamations in his own language. She hoped she was doing this well. Judging by the grunts accompanying the words, she assumed so. Either that or he was in horrible moral anguish. Fuck it, she was having fun, though. Cheating on her husband. And under the hawk-eye of the cameras, too. She wondered if he'd be watching right now – Cray, the den mother, the silent, complicated one, the only one of Bryce's entire inner circle she might ever actually like to sit down and talk to, one on one.

Everyone said he was a Neanderthal. No sympathy at all for the position of the neglected wife. But she thought there was more to the man. He'd been married, twice, and both times it was he who'd been cheated on, not the spouses. He must have a heart of gold in there, under the military exterior. Clearly he had the devotion of a saint, the way he kept on loving her husband, believing in him when even she herself had given up.

She'd always meant to thank him for that. Maybe one day she'd buy him a drink, let him cry over it with her. Lydia Davenport always did have a thing for rough-and-ready men: military types, cops, firemen. If she hadn't been prevented from finding her own spouse by her family position, there was no telling what kind of man she'd have chosen.

It wouldn't have been a politician. It wouldn't have been Bryce. That was the one thing she couldn't fault Bryce for: not being someone else. And she couldn't hold him responsible for her father's boundless ambitions, either. Eight years ago he'd seen in Bryce a man who could be President, and he'd wanted his family on that wagon train. Richard always blamed his worst deeds on loyalty to his wife and daughter. What was it about blood ties that could bring out such darkness? Cray was like family to Bryce, and look at the things he'd done, procuring hookers, helping him philander right and left. She knew that Cray carried that guilt; she could see it in his eyes. If she could, she would tell him she bore no grudge, that she forgave him.

'Madame,' cried her instructor. 'I am going to explode . . .'

Jean Paul, it seemed, was having a little too much fun. 'Don't you dare,' she snapped. 'I want those spectacular little beret-wearing seeds inside my cunt, do you hear?'

She had to drag him to the gymnastics horse. It was perfect for a woman to lean on while being fucked from behind. Now there was something you didn't learn in gym class, that was for sure. Jean Paul didn't have any problem getting the message about the type of exercise she wanted to work on next. Returning the favour and pulling down her pants, he eagerly pushed his rod between her buttock cheeks, filling her wet canal.

Lydia was more than ready to receive him. This was an act years in the making. She might have known this man only a matter of weeks, but she'd dreamed of someone just like him to break her vows with and break open her prison cell of a life. For this wasn't just sex, it was an act of liberation, a declaration of freedom. And videotaped by the mansion security cameras, no less. How was that for irony? Let him put this in his video player and smoke it. Maybe she'd have copies made. Now there was a thought. She could come up with her own blackmail demands. But what would she want from him in exchange for not revealing her ass all over the media? Sensitivity? Companionship? Fidelity?

That was a laugh. She might as well ask him to cure cancer or tack up a rainbow on the back gate. No, it would be enough to make him feel just a little of the shame and humiliation she'd been feeling for eight long years.

In the meantime, she had her masterpiece to finish, starring herself and the handsome Frenchman who, at this very moment, had a load of semen to deposit in her womb. What more fun could a woman have, short of another shot of vodka and a killer divorce settlement?

Lydia closed her eyes, taking him deep, breathing in the air of sex, the smell of adultery, so very French, so very ripe. It wasn't half bad, this sin business. You could almost see why Bryce did it so often. Probably should have taken this up years ago myself, she thought.

'Jean Paul,' she moaned. 'Do it . . . make me come.'

Jean Paul obliged, more than earning his hourly fee

in one fell swoop. It was a molten orgasm, purely physical, mutually satisfying and without any higher redeeming value. When it was done, Lydia Davenport Clarkson kissed and thanked her lover, put her Spandex on and walked away, without the least bit of remorse.

Vive la différence, she mused, pausing to blow a kiss to the surveillance camera on the way out.

Cray knew he had a situation on his hands unlike any other. There were about a hundred decisions to make all at once, not least how to handle the principal parties involved, the first couple and the so-called fitness instructor whose nationality ought to have surprised no one. It was a temptation to pick up Mr Jean Claude Van Dork, or whatever he called himself, and detain him on some sort of assault and battery charge. Unfortunately, the First Lady had been a more than willing partner. In fact, if anyone had a case for assault, it would be the Frenchman.

What he could do was run the clown's records, check his immigration status and so on and maybe get his over-polished posterior bounced back to Charles de Gaulle Airport on the next red-eye. He put a man on the case, and instructed another to escort Jean Paul's sorry ass off state property. Then he turned his attention to Mrs Clarkson.

He'd been acquainted with Lydia long enough to know not to confront her directly. A lot of others made that mistake and, frankly, they hadn't lasted. No matter how beloved one might be by the Governor, Bryce would only put up with so much carping from his wife before turning his displeasure on the third party.

It was strange, when you looked at it, how little Cray ever talked to the woman directly. It was almost as if they avoided each other. Cray would never be rude, but something inside him warned him to keep away. What could he be afraid of? She wasn't about to strong-arm him, as his position with the Governor was unshakable.

Was it her beauty? Yes, she was extraordinarily attractive to him and there were times Cray caught himself wondering how a man like Bryce could be so foolish as to ignore her the way he did. But that was the Governor's business. You didn't meddle in another man's affairs. Except to encourage him in his manliness. Cray never had any support in his own marriages. He'd known what it was like to be betrayed by women. Then again, he'd made mistakes, too, by being emotionally unavailable. All in all, he'd had his shot at matrimony, twice over, and now he'd have to get by with call girls the rest of his life.

It was ridiculous to think he had any feelings for Lydia Clarkson. Sure, he'd wanted to tear the Frenchman's head off when he saw that cock of his dipping between her pretty lips, and he'd been unable to avoid thinking of himself in the man's place when he was fucking her, but that was a normal reaction, a basic biological thing, purely male and generic. It certainly wasn't emotional.

He was just a little overwrought because of this business with the sex tape and Bryce's talk of quitting. Hell, they were all shell-shocked. When your commander-in-chief threatens to surrender, it's bound to hit the men in the trenches too.

And things were going to get worse now, in a hurry. Bryce was liable to go nuts. And Lydia would only dig in deeper. Hell, they could end up going to the press themselves, denouncing each other, never mind any sex tapes. Speaking of which, he needed to confiscate this particular tape right now and swear to secrecy the agent who'd been monitoring at the time.

Pulling the black cassette from the machine, he found himself fighting a strong urge to go and watch it, and maybe even play with himself at the same time. When was the last time he'd done anything like that? Not since high school. What was it about Lydia that brought this out in him?

He had no answers. Not for anything, least of all how he was going to word this thing when he talked to Bryce in the next five minutes.

Cassie was still tingling all over when she left Jake's apartment. A quick shower beforehand and a change into fresh panties (stowed in her trunk for emergencies) did little to calm her down. The man was conniving, but he'd sure given her a healthy share of orgasms. All in all, it was the kind of manipulation a woman didn't mind. She'd have happily lent her body to the man for another two weeks straight in exchange for information, but he'd already given her more than she needed.

So Landview was backed by the mob. Why should she not be surprised? Bryce had come a long way all right, clear down into the scum. Congratulations were probably in order. He was a true politician now. No more staring at stars and giggling over champagne bottles with interns. Although he did keep his interns, didn't he? Right where he wanted them, between his legs.

Jake had advised her to consider the possibility that Bryce was innocent, but she didn't believe it for a second. If he were, he'd have told her everything from the start.

To say the man had nerve getting her involved in

this mess was an understatement. She wasn't sure whether to laugh or cry or simply drive her car into his nearest highway campaign sign, pulverising his face. How many billboards would it take to appease her? They couldn't make enough, actually. The worst part, other than being made a fool of and sent in potential harm's way, was the fact that Bryce Clarkson had just sat there yesterday like some paragon of virtue, acting as if he didn't know what was really going on.

Fucking asshole. He could lie to the whole world if he wanted. But not to her. That made it personal. That made it fodder for some serious payback.

Cassie's thoughts of slow, mediaeval revenge were shelved, however, by a more pressing problem. There was a grey sedan behind her, which had made two turns following her. Should she be paranoid? On a whim she made a quick right onto a side street. The car went right past. There. She'd been seeing things. This was real life, not some spy movie.

Panic gripped her a few minutes later. The car had magically reappeared behind her, two vehicles back. Was she really being followed or could she be confusing two cars? There was a driver and no passengers in this one. He was a young man, clean-cut. He looked like a cop, but he could be anybody. Even a mobster.

She nearly leapt out of her skin when the cell phone went off. According to caller ID, it was an unavailable number. Normally she ignored these, but these were not normal times.

'Hello?' she ventured cautiously.

'I need you to listen closely,' crooned a female voice. 'I can't talk long. This call could be traced. You have to warn Bryce. About the mob, and Landview, and especially about Richard Davenport.'

Christ, it was Queenie Amazon. Of all times for her to play Deep Throat in some cheesy remake of *All The President's Men*. 'You're too late, sweetie, I followed your little lead, and I found out Bryce is already in the mob's pocket. If he has anyone to fear right now, it's me.'

'But you don't understand—'

Cassie broke the connection. The sedan was on her like glue. Should she call for help? Whom could she trust at this point? Bryce had set her up and she really did not want to go crying to Jake with every little thing. On a whim she called the state police office. Trooper Jones was off today but she got his voicemail. Thankfully he had left a pager number. She left him a message after the beep: 'It's me, the VIP from yesterday with the legs. I need help.'

He called her back in less than a minute. 'Where are you?' he said, wanting to meet her.

She gave him the nearest intersection.

'There's a coffee shop a block up on the left,' the trooper instructed. 'Wait for me there.'

He hung up before she could even begin to describe her problem. It was probably overreaction on her part, and she did feel a little embarrassed that he was coming all the way over here for her. For some reason, though, she felt safer already, just knowing he was on the way. She also liked how he'd sounded so concerned, almost as if he cared personally.

Feeling more than a little jittery, she parked by the coffee shop, walked in and ordered a triple latte. Caffeine was the last thing she needed, which is why she got it. Finding a small round table in the corner, she waited for her knight with shining steel badge.

He showed up on a motorcycle, sleek and black. Cassie licked her lips; she always did have a thing for the sleek, two-wheeled machines, and all that chrome firepower between a man's legs, spewing fumes and burning rubber.

The officer's personal appearance made her lick her lips, too. He was wearing a sweatshirt and jeans, both tight, revealing a full set of muscles. His boots were black and he had the look of a man who was ready to kick ass first and ask questions later.

'I'm really sorry, I know it's nothing,' she began apologetically.

Jones treated her to a cop frown. 'I'll be the judge of that.' He sat down across from her, worry written all over his face. 'How about you fill me in?'

She watched the flex of his biceps, natural and menacing. 'I think I'm being followed by a man,' she said, getting right to the point.

The frown deepened. 'Is the guy here now?'

Trooper Jones' eyes were scanning the room, lightning-quick, checking the six available male candidates. The guy following her was lucky he wasn't among them, Cassie knew that much.

'No. He was driving a silverish grey car. Every time I looked in the mirror, he was there. But always two or three cars back. Does that make any sense?'

'It does if you're trying to track someone without their knowing you're there.'

'Well, he gave me the creeps,' she admitted, feeling the tension drain just from his presence. 'I'm glad you're here.' She touched his hand. 'Thank you.'

There was a small spark between them, but Jones had other things in mind than holding hands. 'I want you to sit tight while I go check round outside. You see anything suspicious, I want you to call 911 and then my pager, in that order. You got it?'

She nodded.

'Good.' To her amazement he leant forward and gave her a peck on the cheek. 'I'll be back.'

Stunned, though not unpleasantly so, she watched his denim-clad ass move efficiently out of view. It was kind of cute, really, though she felt a little bad, because here she was lusting after his bottom and he was out there prepared to risk his life. Unless she missed her guess, though, the young cop had a crush on her, too. That was flattering, even if she was a little old to be passing notes back and forth in geometry class. What she needed to do was keep him focused on sex and not genuine affection, she thought, as she braced herself with more of the warm, rich coffee. Otherwise, he might get hurt. And maybe, her too, odd as that sounded.

Bryce was in his motorcade, on the way to pick up a Japanese trade delegation at the airport, when he got the call from Cray. His security chief identified the matter as code one, highest priority. Quickly ruling out any terrorist attacks, civil disasters or political melt-downs, he was on the verge of being annoyed with his long-time deputy.

'What the hell is important enough to risk pissing off a planeful of Tokyo billionaires itching to dump their yen into the nearest tipped hat?'

Cray cleared his throat. 'It's the First Lady, sir.'

He felt a rising panic. 'Is she hurt? Tell me she's all right.'

'She's ... uh ... fine.'

Bryce was going to lose it, he really was. 'Cray, have you been drinking?'

'No, sir. Lydia made a little tape of her own, sir, that's what's going on.'

Bryce felt the blood drain from his face. 'A tape? What kind of tape?'

'It's X-rated, sir . . . her and the . . . fitness instructor.'

Fuck. And double fuck. The woman had come unhinged. Finally. After all these years. He should have seen it coming.

'Don't let her leave the house, Cray, whatever you do.'

'I'm on it, sir. What's your ETA?'

The Governor exhaled deeply. His first impulse was to run straight home, but the damage was clearly done by now. Besides, he needed time to cool off. Spur-of-the-moment anger would help nothing. 'I'll be back as soon as I finish with the Japanese,' he decided.

There was a pause, indicating the man had reservations.

'What is it, Cray?'

'Permission to speak freely, sir?'

'As always.'

'The woman needs comfort, sir. If she doesn't get it, there's no telling what she'll do.'

'You take care of her, Cray.' Bryce surprised himself with his own indifference. 'You know her as well as I do by now.'

More silence, though this time the Governor did not intervene.

'Yes, sir,' his security chief said at last.

'Keep me posted.' Bryce broke the connection, ending what was about to become an extremely awkward conversation. Why exactly had he just told another man to give comfort to his own wife? Was he that dissatisfied with her? Certainly it didn't help matters right now that she was the daughter of the man who'd single-handedly sold him on Landview Development, only to go strangely absent now that he had questions.

Twice he'd left messages for Richard Davenport, increasingly urgent in tone. He'd been told the man was on a tour of the Brazilian rain forest, but no one could be that out of touch these days. Even jungles had fax machines, and what the fuck was wrong with his cellphone? The man had become more elusive than a UFO.

All Bryce was looking for was some added reassurance: that the accusations he was hearing about Landview were wrong, that what Lydia was saying was just a scare tactic and, above all, that Richard would stand beside him as his father-in-law through these difficult days ahead, with respect to the tape.

Damn it, he hated being this helpless. But what more could he do? Not one of his legitimate contacts was saying a word. The ones that answered his calls were spouting mumbo-jumbo, nothing more. There were obviously people that might know something, but they weren't the types to contact a state Governor, were they?

On the other hand, what if he were to reach out to them? What if he were to bypass the legitimate businessmen, the men at the top, and go through back channels? It could spell political suicide, whether or not Landview was crooked, but at this point what did he have to lose? And what if there were someone out there willing to talk, willing to lay all the cards on the table in exchange for immunity? The whole house of cards would come down then, wouldn't it? It was a hell of a gamble. He could turn up dead. But a win could turn everything around, make it all come out right in the end.

It was a good theory. The only problem was finding a flesh-and-blood person who'd talk to him. He didn't exactly have an address book filled with Vito Corleone types. Not that they were all Italian – organised crime came in all shapes and colours nowadays. What he needed was someone with enough guts and brains, someone with experience, who knew the ropes.

Only one name came to mind. Jake Andrews, the reporter. Jake was hell on politicians, him included, but he was smart and he knew everyone. If anyone could steer him in the right direction it would be Andrews. He only hoped the man was still around. The rumour was that he'd fallen off the wagon and given up journalism.

That didn't make him a very strong ally, but Bryce had no choice. Hitting the speed dial, he called his personal secretary. 'I need you to track somebody down for me. Give it the highest priority.'

'Yes, sir,' said Shirley Wilson, yet another of his trusted aides. 'Shall we send a car to pick him up?'

'Assuming you locate him, no, I'll want to handle this personally.'

'Yes, sir.'

It was personal, all right, as personal as it got. Putting on his game face, Bryce readied himself for the Japanese delegates. With all this going on, he thought, my marriage dissolving, my career shot, my very life at stake, I still have to try and earn the state a hundred million dollars before lunch.

Only in America, he mused.

10

Cray Wilder was the only person in the world Lydia would even consider talking to right now. 'I'll let you in,' she told him, standing in her bedroom doorway, 'if you can promise me you are here to speak for yourself and no one else.'

The stone-faced old soldier did not answer right off. He was thinking the same things she was: about the conflict of interest between his position as Bryce's underling and his feelings about the Governor's wife. Bryce did this a lot, playing people off against each other for his own benefit. It wasn't even conscious. That's what made him such a natural politician.

'I will speak for myself,' he said at last.

She took him at his word, because that's what you did with Cray Wilder. 'But Bryce did send you, didn't he?'

'He asked me to look after you, Mrs Clarkson. He cares for you a great deal.'

She smiled, thinking maybe the man had missed a calling as a diplomat. 'Oh, I'm sure he does. In his own way.'

The eagle eyes of the security chief flicked momentarily to the half-filled suitcase on her bed. 'You're leaving,' he observed.

'I am. And if anyone tries to stop me, I will fight them for everything I'm worth.'

His lips angled upward, hinting sympathy. 'I am sure you would give my men a run for their money,

Mrs Clarkson. You have my word that they will not attempt to do so, however. I will try and persuade you to stay, but I would never use force.'

'Why do you do that?' she asked compulsively.

'Do what, Mrs Clarkson?'

'There – you just did it again. After all this time you still call me Mrs Clarkson. Why won't you ever call me by my given name?'

'It's not my place,' he replied, still trying to ignore the fact that she was fresh from the shower and dressed only in a bathrobe.

'So what is your place, Cray? Kowtowing to Bryce your whole life? Pimping whores for him night and day?'

His face betrayed no emotion. She imagined he'd endured far worse attacks in his day. 'I do my duty as best I can.'

'I'm sorry.' She recanted at once. 'That was a cheap shot. You don't deserve to be treated poorly.'

'Neither do you,' he said.

Lydia decided to let it all hang out. 'But you do help Bryce against me, don't you? You and he have this ... this code thing, when he sees a woman he wants. You may not intend it, but you encourage him. And he looks up to you. Did you know that?'

Lydia read the man's love for the Governor, revealed in the tiniest twitch of his moustache. It was uncanny, thought Lydia, how well she understood Cray. Where had that ability come from? Sure, she'd spent thousands of hours with him when he was protecting her; sure, he'd always been a calm, steady presence, but that was background, not foreground.

'If that is true,' he said carefully, 'I didn't ask for it. He's the one who's supposed to be looked up to, not me.'

'*Supposed to*,' she repeated. 'Your words, not mine.'

'Whatever you're implying ... Lydia ... I am not prepared to follow this train of reasoning.'

Lydia replied with her lips.

The kiss happened too fast for either of them to stop it. By the time she realised her body was in motion, she was already glued to his lips, pressing, hungry and needful. It was the biggest leap of her life into the unknown, and she knew in her heart that if the man rejected her she would surely die.

'Lydia ...' He held her shoulders, whispering life into her name.

She looked into those deep, wounded eyes and began to weep, for both of them. 'Cray ... I'm sorry.'

His embrace was as strong as one would expect of a man like him, but it was gentle too. A woman could feel safe here, not stifled. 'You're like a dream,' he whispered fiercely. 'God help me, you are.'

'I've felt like everyone's nightmare,' she sobbed. 'My whole life. "Just stay out of the way, Lydia, don't make trouble, Lydia."'

He took her head in his hands. 'Don't say that, it's not right.'

His intensity was more than she'd ever seen in the man. Was this what he looked like in combat ... or in love? 'It *is* right, Cray. I have no place here. I never have. I've been a stranger to my own life.'

'But you're ... beautiful and smart and ...'

'And I live through the bottom of a vodka bottle. That makes me a coward and you know it.'

He continued to hold her, keeping her eyes fixed on his. 'I want you to listen to me, Lydia, very carefully. I'm fifty-two years old, though no one would guess it. When I turned eighteen we still had the draft. Two of my buddies were called up. They went into the

Marines, straight to Vietnam. I got my notice and my parents pulled strings with a congressman. I went into the Guard, spent my time in Alabama. Meanwhile one of those friends of mine had his leg blown off. The other never came back out at all. Now you tell me, who was the coward?'

'You did what you had to.' Lydia felt his pain and sorrow. 'That was such a horrible time. No one knew what was right or wrong.'

'I did,' he said. 'And I will never forgive myself.'

'But you joined the army later on. You were decorated in the Special Forces. Surely that made up for things?'

'Not enough.' He shook his head. 'You can't bring an opportunity back once it's lost.'

'And now?' she whispered, their breath intermingling. 'Is this an opportunity?'

He knew what she meant and this time it was the veteran himself who initiated the lip-lock. There was a moment here and, if they let it go, they might both regret it the rest of their lives. Then again, they might live to regret following it just as much.

'Lydia, wait . . .' Something was giving him second thoughts, something powerful enough to stop him ravishing her mouth.

'What is it, Cray?'

Now it was his turn to test motives. 'Tell me this isn't because of him. Tell me you're not just getting back at Bryce.'

The question was fair. It deserved a full and dramatic answer. Stepping back, she shed her robe. 'I want you, Cray Wilder. I want you to have my body . . . and my heart.'

Was she truly this available, this free to commit herself as she willed? Yes, in the wake of this morning, she was. In many ways she'd been ready all along, just afraid to act on her feelings.

'It's you who has kept me going here all this time,' she said, attempting to erase his scepticism. 'I never saw it because of my petty anger at Bryce. I was so busy playing the wounded socialite, I never looked to see where my true allegiance should have lain.'

'I ... I had no idea,' stammered the lion-hearted warrior. 'I assumed you took no notice.'

She touched her naked breasts to his clothed chest, interlacing their fingers. 'And what of you? What have you been hiding all this time? Aside from that erection I'm feeling?'

He flushed slightly. 'I made it a point not to feel. I kept my distance, kept your existence as abstract as possible.'

'You were afraid,' she guessed.

He nodded. It was the toughest admission of his life, but one he had to make. 'Afraid of this, yes ... and more.'

Her fingers were working on the buttons of his shirt. 'Tell me what the more is.'

'You know the answer to that perfectly well, woman.'

She smiled at his teasing. It warmed her heart and curled her toes. 'A woman likes to hear it ... at least once.'

'I'm in love with you,' he said, making it sound like an infection. 'I suppose I always have been. Wasn't something I asked for, it just happened.'

She shook her head. 'It's not something you can control. I know that kills you.'

'But you can't control it, either. It's in the hands of fate.'

Lydia pulled his shirt down over his shoulders and

arms, baring his torso as if unwrapping a Christmas gift.

'Yes, well sometimes even fate needs a little kick in the ass to get it moving in the right direction.'

It was hard not to drool over the man's marvellous body. Few thirty-year-olds kept themselves this buff, let alone a fifty-two-year old. Choosing a place at random, she began by touching his left bicep. She needed both hands to circle the hard, brown flesh.

'I'm going to worship you, Cray Wilder, you know that? Just as soon as you lock that door.'

The security chief furrowed his brow. 'There's something else you need to know, Lydia.'

'If you're going to tell me you're gay,' she quipped, feeling for his hard-on, 'can you wait till after we've fucked, at least once?'

'I'm not a homosexual,' he assured her. 'But there is something else about me. Something that makes me a minority.'

'You mean you have fetishes? All the better,' she replied. 'What are you into? Shoes? Chocolate mousse? Pin the tail on the donkey? Your wish is my command.'

He managed a smile, though his eyes were dark and brooding. 'I have to have my partners tied up, Lydia. It's the only way I can come.'

'Is that all?' She laughed with relief. 'Well, have no fear. Bondage I can handle.'

The doom-filled expression remained in place. 'It's a lot more complicated, Lydia. I need more than ropes. I need . . . to dominate.'

Lydia felt butterflies in her stomach. This was an answer to fantasies too deep to utter except in a whisper, too dark to bring into the light of day. Trying to keep the emotion from her voice as best she could, she drew him to the logical conclusion of his dilemma. 'You require a submissive woman, then.'

'Does the thought disgust you?'

Now it was her turn to blush. 'No,' she said, lowering her eyes. 'It doesn't.'

'What does it do?'

Lydia's eyes were moist, utterly naked. Could it really be that there was this much trust left in her soul for a man? 'It arouses me,' she confessed.

He studied her for a moment. 'Go and lie on the bed,' he said gently but firmly, 'and wait for me.'

Lydia's heart raced. It was her first command, the first instruction given by the man she wanted, needed so badly for her lover. Would she obey him in everything? She would certainly try. Her own bed felt like foreign territory as she crawled onto the sheets. How exactly did he want her? On all fours? On her back?

She opted for the latter, arranging herself with her head on the pillow and with one leg raised. Cray was locking the door to guarantee their privacy. She watched him, mesmerised. What exactly would this domination entail? In her midnight fantasies, masturbating to romance novels, she'd pictured pirates seizing her and ripping off her clothes, forcing her to their pleasure, taking from her as they willed. She knew there were people who played these and other games, some of them actually living out the role of master and slave around the clock. It had seemed so very odd to her, so scandalous. And yet so completely . . . sexy.

Standing at the foot of the bed, Cray removed the rest of his clothes. She wanted very much to leap up and grab hold of that delicious cock, but her job at the moment was to stay where she was. This was what he'd been talking about. Domination. Not what she wanted, but what he wanted. Paradoxically, this thwarting of her will was making her even wetter, even more ready for lovemaking.

'I've never been with you before,' he told her, 'let alone pushed you to the limits of your sexual endurance. We will have a word between us – "minesweeper" – and if I hear that word from you, I will stop whatever I am doing immediately. Otherwise, I will ignore your protests.'

Lydia felt a twinge between her legs, strange but not entirely unwelcome. She was being freed to resist him, to fight, to argue in any way she liked, knowing that he would overpower her, giving witness to male desire in its purest, hottest form. And it would all be safe, with a built-in alarm cord if things got too rough.

'Minesweeper,' Lydia quipped, feeling more comfortable by the second. 'How romantic.'

'I'll need scarves,' he pressed on. 'To tie you.'

She indicated a drawer in her dresser. Cray followed her directions and selected several scarves of various colours.

'Hands over your head,' he ordered. 'It's time we slipped you into something a little less comfortable.'

'What if I don't want to?' she asked impishly, her need to surrender suddenly balanced with a desire to taunt.

He offered up a wink even as he squared his jaw for battle. 'Try me and find out.'

She suppressed a grin. 'In that case, you may consider me officially insubordinate.'

'Suit yourself,' he growled playfully.

Lydia exclaimed in laughter as he dived forward. She rolled away and kicked at him, but he managed to seize one of her ankles in an iron grip and drag her back.

'Give up?' he asked.

'Never,' she vowed, egging him on.

Cray turned her sideways and caught hold of her other ankle.

'Unhand me, you dastardly brute!' she cried in feigned distress.

'Sorry, milady,' he said, 'but you have forced me to use my secret weapon.'

She squealed again as he dived between her legs, making a beeline for her exposed crotch. She tried to push him away, but he was already inside her, his tongue taking firm command of her pussy. Her defences collapsed at once as he worked on her clit, inducing a flood.

'Not fair,' she managed to say, though it hardly mattered now. The man intended to have his way with her, even if it meant controlling her with her own pleasure.

Talk about sleeping with the enemy. The orgasm built quickly, a mushroom cloud of pleasure swelling inside her, filling every crevice of her being, making her entire self, from the depths of her pussy all the way to her toes, hum and sing. It felt so right, as if this man and this tongue had known her forever. She wanted it never to stop and yet she knew there was so much more ahead, different things she couldn't even imagine yet.

She cried out as he let her come, the man intent on relieving enough of the pressure in her body to allow her to reach the next step.

'Lydia,' he said, releasing her pulsing pussy after she'd come back down to earth, 'I'm going to spank you. I'll be using my hand. In between spanks you'll receive pleasure, though you are forbidden to come without my permission. We'll go through this together.

At the end, when I claim you, you will be mine in a way I can't describe.'

Lydia had never seen a man more intent, more devoted in her life. If anything, she felt as if he were submitting to her needs and not the other way around. 'I love you, Cray,' she murmured, giving the only possible response.

His eyes were moist. 'I love you, too, Lydia. I want you to lie on your stomach now and put your hands together over your head.'

Lydia rolled onto her belly, overjoyed despite the butterflies in her stomach. With infinite trust she allowed him to secure her wrists together with one of the scarves. He pulled her arms taut, tying the free end of the scarf to one of the brass rails of her headboard. Tentatively she pulled at her bonds, demonstrating to herself that she was not going to be leaving this bed, or this position, without permission.

The spanking was like a dream. A wicked kissing of flesh on flesh, the bright hot sensations ten times more vital than any sex she'd ever had. It was as if he were touching a deeper place in her soul than a cock could go, or even a promise from the lips. To do this to a woman, to handle her with such ecstatic care, alternating stings of his palm with electrifying, masturbating fingertips, blood-filled and passionate between her sex lips, this was something that required more than standard-issue male equipment. It took a brain and a heart. It took life experience, too, and being wounded. You couldn't give even the mild pain of spanking in love unless you'd received it yourself; that's what made it ritual, that's what made it pure. And that's why she didn't use the safe word, even when she knew her behind was turning red, even when she felt her nerve-endings scream for release, for more smacks, more prods into her sex, more Cray, all at once and at the speed of light.

Lydia had no clue what she was calling out. She was sweating, certainly, and writhing for him. He was there, lusting and wanting, intent on her, captivated by her body and soul. No man had ever been this into her. My God, she was his whole world right now. Was this what it was like to love a soldier? A humble man who received orders more than he gave them? Not a king, not a governor. Not an industrialist like her father with a heart of stone, hidden from one and all for fear that someone, somewhere might learn his weaknesses.

In all she received only ten thwacks of his warm and capable hand, but he'd been right, she was different, and they had gone through it together. Stroking her hair, he praised her, so animated and so very, very pleased. This, too, was something that had eluded Lydia throughout her life. The men she'd known had wanted empires and then, like small boys, had thrown them away when they had them, just because they were bored. Men like Richard Davenport and Bryce Clarkson could never find the answers to their life questions in a mere woman. Not even in a million women.

But a man like Cray, well, that was all he'd ever wanted. She knew he'd poured all he had into his marriages and she had a pretty good idea now why they didn't work. Not every woman could take that much, or give that much in return. Not every woman was prepared to be that much for a single man. Maybe it was too much pressure for them, or just a matter of their vanity, but a lot of women needed something more, just like her husband and her father.

He'd probably thought brides mail-ordered from a

more male oriented culture would provide the answer. What he'd needed all along, though, was love, pure and simple. Only a woman who truly loved him and wanted to be loved in return could make him happy. Only a woman who really was capable of understanding him. Only a woman . . . like her.

'Take me,' said Lydia Davenport Clarkson, freshly spanked and on the verge of the biggest orgasm of her life. 'Please?'

It was a simple enough matter to turn her over, the scarf still binding her hands to the headboard.

'Spread your legs,' said Cray and this time she obeyed, smoothly and instantly, her face lit with an eager but serene smile.

He lowered himself majestically in a single claiming motion, his cock sinking to the hilt in her silky depths. In so many ways she felt like a virgin. So much of this was new, a revelation flooding her senses. At the same time, it was comfortable and familiar, as if her pussy was made to fit this one cock to the exclusion of all others.

With a smile lighting his face, his eyes sliding shut, he pulled himself out nearly to the tip. She cried out at the sudden vacancy, though she knew it would not last. Sure enough, a moment later he was back inside her. Twice more he repeated the motion, establishing his rhythm.

Lydia braced herself, knowing this was it. He was about to begin fucking her for real and she must be alert for his every motion, tuned in to whatever word or sign he might give to indicate it was time for her to climax.

He drew a final breath, made a small sound of pleasure and then pushed his pelvis down. It was not a mere succumbing to gravity this time, but an intentional drive on his part. This was it, all right.

'Yes,' she said. 'Let me have it.'

A pile-driver, up and down and up and down. Releasing like a piston, an unbelievable amount of force; a lifetime's worth of sperm, it felt like. Could it be he'd had to bottle this up, storing it inside for her, his one and only submissive woman he'd been waiting to find?

The sinews on his neck stood out. Lydia went totally passive, receiving his dominance. She was his vessel, his lover, his sacrificial offering. It was her place to lie beneath him and she knew it. She'd come home, at long last. No matter what happened after this, no matter what fate had in store for the two of them, she would be his. Marked. Possessed.

'Please,' she cried softly. 'May I . . .'

His answer came in the form of a single powerful release, verbal and orgasmic, physical and spiritual. 'Y–yes . . .'

His word was the trigger, a call to instant compliance. He had it. He had her. 'Oh, baby,' she moaned, pouring her own orgasm into the turgid seas of his.

Together they rushed and churned, souls dissolved into one in the circulating cataclysm, a warm sweet hurricane, a whirlpool with nothing to cling to, no way to stay above the blue, blue depths.

'Ly . . . di . . . a.' He turned her name into a thousand syllables, making up in one utterance for all the times he'd called her Mrs Clarkson.

'Oh, Cray,' she replied. 'Oh, my warrior.'

The word seemed to hold some deep meaning for him. His look into her eyes in response was both rapacious and grateful. 'Lydia, my own, my love.'

She wanted to throw her arms around his neck, but she was still bound and would stay so till he said otherwise. Doing the next best thing, she locked her legs around his ass. 'Never leave me, Cray. Promise?'

His lips went flat. A man like Cray Wilder did not make idle promises. 'I will do everything in my power,' he said, 'to stay by your side.'

'If you don't I will have no reason to live.' It was not an idle threat, but a statement of simple fact.

'Neither will I,' he replied, his expression more sober than any she'd ever seen on a man's face.

'I'm scared, Cray.'

Now he smiled, cockeyed. 'I'd be pretty damned worried if you weren't.'

'I'm married,' she reminded him. 'To the Governor.'

'That's right,' he agreed. 'And I work for him. Do you suppose that means I should get my résumé together?'

In spite of herself she smiled back. This whole thing was just so completely crazy it had to be right. 'At this point, Cray, we'd all better do that.'

11

Cassie was just starting her second triple latte when Trooper Jones returned. He had an odd look on his face as he sat down across from her, not the sort of expression she would have expected after his mission of mercy.

'Well, you weren't seeing things,' the handsome, muscular cop began. 'You were definitely being followed.'

'You saw the car?' she asked eagerly.

The odd expression deepened. 'Oh, yeah.' He arched an eyebrow. 'It was silver-grey, just like you described. I know the driver, actually.'

Her eyes widened. 'You ... know him?'

He rubbed a hand over the back of his neck. 'He's a state trooper, Cassie. Assigned to the Governor's plain-clothes security detail.'

Cassie let the information sink in. 'The son of a bitch is spying on me.' She laughed without the slightest trace of humour. 'Unfuckingbelievable.'

Jones was still doing that squinting thing, as if someone had inserted a pebble in his boot and he'd been forced to walk with it in there all day.

'Out with it,' she demanded. 'I know you know something more.'

'Well, this guy is a fellow trooper, like I said, and we were together in the same patrol troop at one point. He really wasn't supposed to tell me, but I told him it was personal, so he gave me the scoop. You're not under surveillance; you're under special protection. The orders came right from the top.'

Her heart did a small flip. 'Bullshit.' She refused to believe anything good about Bryce at this late juncture. 'The Governor could care less what happened to me.'

Trooper Jones had his hands up. 'Hey, don't shoot the messenger here. I was just trying to make sure you weren't about to be kidnapped by white slavers or something.'

Cassie bit her lip. She wasn't too proud of this side of her personality, her tendency to expect the world to orbit around her own concerns and needs. Sure, she'd been caught up in something messy under some shaky pretences, but hadn't she turned round and done the same to this police officer?

'I'm sorry,' she said sincerely. 'I can be a real bitch sometimes. I didn't even say thank you for doing all this for me. And on your day off, too.'

He smiled and winked. 'It's OK, I like my ladies bitchy.'

She could feel the heat of his eyes on her body. Damn it if she wasn't responding, too, in spite of the total disaster her life had become in the last 24 hours. 'Yeah, well, this lady bitch is sorely in need of a backrub and about three weeks straight on a beach somewhere.'

'I can't help with the beach, but I could assist with the backrub part.'

'Yes, I'll just bet you could, Trooper Jones. What is your first name, anyway? I feel like I'm in the fourth grade, calling you by your title all the time.'

'It's Travis. And I give really good backrubs.'

'Is that right? Well, why don't you give me your card? I'll see if I can scare up some business for you.'

He grinned, more than up for this little game of cat and mouse. 'Maybe if you could give me a reference I'd get even more business.'

Admittedly, the offer was tempting. Unfortunately, she was already planning on paying a little return visit to the Governor's mansion. And this time she'd be the one doing the talking – and making a few demands of her own.

'I can read palms, too.' Travis Jones appropriated her hand, which was pretty damned limp at the moment, like her backbone. 'Yours tells me a lot of interesting things.' He ran a finger down her lifeline. 'Take this, right here, for instance. This tells me you need to get laid. Bad.'

'Oh, does it now?' Her heart was palpitating from the light pressure of his finger. Wow. He was good at this stuff. The son of a bitch was going to have his way with her at this rate. 'And does it also tell you I just got laid less than two hours ago, too?'

Travis pretended to study the matter. 'Yeah, but the guy was a wimp. It doesn't count.'

She suppressed a laugh, thinking of how the macho reporter would react to being called a wimp. 'You're pretty cocky, aren't you?'

He brushed his leg along the inside of hers, the denim electrifying her bare skin. It was her fault for having a skirt on. 'Just confident about things I know,' he countered.

'And what exactly is it you know, Travis?'

'I know you want to go to bed with me, but you're fighting it because you think one more man is the last thing you need. Especially a man like me.'

Her breathing quickened as the cop's leg moved higher. 'I suppose now you want me to ask what kind of man you are exactly?'

His smile was like a whip, way too fucking fast and subtle to do anything but slash and burn. 'You already know the answer to that,' he rasped, his voice moving into this low, seductive tone that was just about as unfair as the business with her skirt and the palm-reading and all the rest of it.

'You're the kind of man who could make me do just about anything,' whispered Cassandra Dane, daring an answer.

Why had she said that? It was like waving red in front of a bull – or, more to the point, it was the equivalent of lying spreadeagled in front of one while wearing a freaking Santa suit. And since when did she get so melodramatic with the male gender, anyway? This guy was a boy toy, one in a long series. A flavour of the day she ought properly to schedule in for three weeks next Tuesday, or some equally distant date.

It was this Landview stuff, playing tricks on her mind. Not to mention the effect of dealing with the ghost of Bryce Clarkson, the treacherous, heartbreaking ghost of a man she'd once thought could do no wrong. Maybe she was turning into a ghost herself. Maybe she was sitting here trying to act like a person she hadn't been for ten years. A young, carefree woman who would go with the moment and risk fucking or even falling in love with a cop just because it seemed the thing to do. But that woman was gone. She wasn't coming back, and she needed to make sure Trooper Travis Jones got that message and pronto.

His brow arched. 'In that case,' he crooned, catching the scent of victory, 'you better hope I go easy on you.'

'Just out of curiosity, Trooper, what would you have me do ... assuming you could make me do anything?'

'Right this second, you mean?'

'Sure, why not.'

Why not, indeed? She was already playing with so much fire, what were a few thousand extra burning coals heaped on her head?

Travis had his answer at the ready. 'I'd have you take off your panties for me. Right here at the table.'

'Oh.' She tried to keep her voice steady. 'And why exactly would you want me to do that?'

'So we could both see how much it turns you on when a man makes you act like a slut in public.'

Cassie snatched back her hand. He'd scored a direct hit with that one. 'You don't talk much like a cop,' she noted.

'It's my day off.'

'But it's not mine.'

'You could call in sick,' he grinned. 'Just as soon as you ask me the next thing I'm going to make you do.'

'And this would be after the panties come off, I suppose?' Just saying the words made Cassie's pussy clench, hot and needy.

'Exactly. I won't tell you, though, till you ask me the right way.'

She felt a wave of hot weakness. She knew exactly what he meant and what he wanted. And the damnable part was that she was about to give it to him, lock, stock and barrel. 'What will you make me do?' she asked, panting softly, 'after I take off my panties?'

Oh, God, she thought. It's gone from if to when.

He smiled, noting the same change. 'Once your panties are off, you will go to that table over there.'

Cassie followed his eyes to a young man, maybe twenty, heavy-set with an unruly ponytail. He was reading two computer manuals at once. 'Yes, I see him.'

'You will go to him,' said Travis matter-of-factly. 'You will sit and flirt, generally catching his attention. Once he is interested you will offer to take him to the men's room and you will give him a blowjob that he'll be talking about with his geek friends down at the sci-fi conventions for the rest of his natural born days.'

She shut her legs tight. There was no way that was going to happen. Was there? She could never just suck off a stranger in the bathroom ... and without her underwear, to boot. But wasn't it a kinky thought, though? It wouldn't even be for the young man, as much as it would be for Travis. He'd get off watching the whole thing. And that would get her off. It was a unique opportunity, she had to admit that much. It might even gain her access to the cop's body. She would happily throw herself at him after that, licking every inch of his muscular form, pushing her soft curves into all the right places, squashing her breasts against manly pectorals, not to mention opening her sex to his manly cock.

'I'll give you till the count of ten,' he said, jolting her back to reality. 'If you haven't started doing what I want by then I am walking out. Nothing personal, but I don't like playing games.'

'Seems to me you love them,' she countered. 'Or have I missed something here?'

'This isn't a game. It's foreplay.'

The cop started his countdown. She fully intended to let him walk out, but by the time he got to five, the adrenalin was pumping too fast and there was just no turning back. Of their own accord, her own hands were creeping up her thighs, her mind working on the best way of doing this without making a complete spectacle of herself.

But that was part of the thrill, knowing that at any time someone could look over to this corner and see what she was doing. Lifting herself slightly, she slipped her hands under the hem of the skirt, working her way up to the waistband of the panties. They were sopping wet now, a good indication of just how arousing it was to be doing this. Her crotch tingled as it hit the open air. She wriggled some, manoeuvring the panties down past her skirt. It was a laborious process, with a lot of half-sitting.

Just as she had them down to her knees, a well-dressed gentleman got up and headed to the bathroom, the entrance to which was located right next to them. Cassie rushed to pull her underwear back up, but Travis spoke harshly.

'Leave them,' he said. 'Hands on the table.'

He made her sit like this while the man went by. Her skin heated as she tried to avoid eye-contact. The man was looking at her with a scowl. What must he think of her, a little hussy undressing in a coffee shop?

'You're a bastard,' Cassie muttered under her breath when the man had passed.

'Keep it up, and I'll make you take your bra off, too.'

She pictured herself trying to negotiate the removal of her bra without winding up arrested. Come to think of it, he was a cop. Wouldn't he have to do the job himself?

'You wouldn't dare,' she said.

'Try me.'

It was all voluntary, of course, but Cassie was way too caught up to back down now. Besides, she'd never give him that kind of satisfaction. 'All right, I believe you,' she conceded. 'Now can I finish taking off my underwear?'

'You may address me as sir,' he informed her.

She rolled her eyes, though secretly this new element of command thrilled her. 'May I finish taking my panties off . . . sir?'

'Put them here on the table.'

Cassie pushed her chair back and bent forward. The tiny silk garment slid down the rest of the way, over her calves and down to her ankles. Lifting one foot at a time, she stepped from them. Finally she snatched them from the floor and laid them on the smooth, smoke-coloured glass of the table. Ideally she would have preferred them stuffed in her purse or in Travis' pocket, but at least they weren't on display halfway down her legs any more.

'Move your hand,' he ordered, scuppering her attempt to keep them covered.

To her horror he picked them up conspicuously and held them to his nose, breathing the odour like a fine wine. Naturally, the man in the suit chose this very moment to come out of the bathroom again. Travis made her suffer till he was back in his seat.

'Time to meet your new friend.' He tossed the silks back on the table at last.

The pasty-faced, double-chinned young computer enthusiast. Cassie had nearly forgotten. Travis was expecting her to go and make his day, and likely his year, with some intimate attentions.

'Baby, wouldn't you rather I blow you?'

Travis was unmoved by her sultry voice and puckered lips. 'Sure, but you need a little warm-up first. My cock is a sensitive piece of equipment, after all, and it has to be handled with care.'

'That's what Lorena Bobbitt's husband said ... just before she made him a eunuch with her little old knife ... sir.'

'Do I need to start another countdown?'

'Why not?' she quipped. 'As big as your ego is, we're going to need to launch it into space.'

'One.' Trooper Jones commenced the count, unflappable as ever. 'Two. Three ...'

Cassie was on her feet, a little wobbly but vertical at least. 'For the record,' she let him know, 'I think you are a sadistic prick.'

'You'll thank me for this later,' he promised. 'They always do.'

Wonderful. So this was something he made a habit of. Just the sort of thing a woman likes to find out when she's being made to do something that's a total sexual stretch. 'Thanks, Trav.' She gave him a sarcastic thumbs-up. 'Way to make me feel real special.'

He smiled warmly. 'You don't need me to feel special, lady, and you know it. You got more on the ball than ninety-nine per cent of the chicks on the planet, so go have yourself a little fun. You know you want to.'

Damn it if he wasn't right, at least about her wanting to try something new and daring. 'You're not supposed to know more than your elders,' she chided the twentysomething.

He gave her the last word, opting to close the conversation by slurping down the remainder of her latte. Which was just fine, because it would likely be cold by the time she got back.

Bryce returned to the Governor's mansion to find Lydia and Cray waiting for him in the study. They rose together from the burgundy leather couch, holding hands. What the hell was this about? Was he seeing things? These two hardly even talked to each other and now they were standing here like ... like a pair of kids on their way to the prom. OK, they looked a little too serious for the prom, but still, this was hardly business as usual.

'We need to talk, Bryce.' This from his wife, looking better than she had in years, in a skirt and sweater, her hair tied back in a ribbon, pink to match the glow in her cheeks. Jeezus, if he didn't know better, he'd say she looked like she was in love. With Cray.

Say something witty, Clarkson. Say something authoritative. You're the fucking Governor of the state.

Nothing came to mind, so he did the next best thing, walking to his desk to stall for time. He'd counted these steps a thousand times, measuring them against dozens of crises over the years. But nothing compared to this. He knew cool heads should prevail, but he wasn't feeling very cool at the moment. 'Talk? Yes, let's do that.' He pulled a bottle brazenly from the drawer. 'Would you two care for a little whisky? Or don't you drink with men you're about to betray?'

'Bryce, please don't make this any more difficult than it already is.'

'And what exactly is *it*, Lydia? Can you tell me that, since I seem to be the only one out of the loop here?' He could feel his blood boil. So far his energy was focused primarily on his wife, but he was all too aware of his security chief beside her, standing with an ill-disguised protectiveness that went well beyond the call of duty.

'There isn't any loop, Bryce. We are three adults here. You and I both know our marriage ended a long time ago, and now Cray and I have discovered in each other a chance for a new start. We didn't plan it that way, we never meant to hurt you.'

'Oh, you never meant to hurt me.' He threw up his arms sarcastically. 'Well, that makes all the difference in the world, doesn't it?'

'There's no call to raise your voice, sir.'

The Governor was on his feet. How dare the man. After all they'd been through together. 'And there's no call for you to be ... to be doing whatever it is you have been doing behind my back!'

Cray stood his ground, expressionless. It was that accursed discipline of his. With a passion Bryce hated it. Most especially because he had almost none of his own.

'Don't talk to him that way, Bryce,' replied Lydia. 'You've no right. For your information, nothing happened between us before today. I needed someone and he was there. Turns out he's always been there.'

Bryce winced, hearing his own words come back at him. It was Cray who'd asked him to come home and give Lydia comfort. And who was it that had told the man to go to her in his place?

His own dumb-ass self, that's who.

Bryce pressed his hands into the blotter, more tired than he'd ever felt in his life. How had it come to this? The most challenging hour of his career, the make-or-break hour, and here he was standing alone. Was this what he deserved after all these years of public service? All the tireless hours of looking out for the needs of others?

Of course, all that had really been about him, hadn't it? His passion, his drive and his need for accolades. When it came right down to it, he'd never sacrificed a damned thing. Today was hardly the first time he'd asked another to fulfil his rightful duty to Lydia, after all. What made it special, apparently, was that it looked to be the last.

So here it is, he thought, my chance to be the gentleman, to bow out gracefully. Unfortunately, when you haven't done the right thing for a long time, it's hard to suddenly shift gears. 'I want you both out of my sight,' he said. 'I have nothing more to say.'

Cray looked as close to emotion as Bryce had ever seen the man. 'But, sir, if we could have a chance to explain.'

'There's nothing to explain.' Bryce was smiling, in that cold and deadly way they did on the Irish side of his family. Generally it followed the drinking of much alcohol and led to decades-long blood feuds. 'You have betrayed me and I will never trust you again. And you,' he continued, turning to his wife of eight years, 'are a fucking whore. Together, I wish you a long and prosperous life. One as far from me as you can humanly manage.'

Lydia buried her head in her hands and burst into tears. Cray held her close, trying to calm her. Bryce felt like shit already, and he knew it would only get worse. Still, there was no way to go but forward. 'Get out,' he told them. 'Before I call security.'

His former chief said nothing as he steered her towards the door. They were still huddled like that as they left, a unit. Bryce looked for the nearest thing to throw. A glass paperweight in the shape of the state bird, given him by the wildlife association. He picked it up and hurled it at the wall, shattering it into uncountable shards and fragments. There, he said to himself with bitter scorn. Feel better now?

'Sir?' His secretary called over the intercom just then, her voice portending a fresh round of doom. 'You have a visitor. Miss Cassandra Dane.'

He felt her name tear at him like a knife-blade. 'Tell her I'm not in.'

'Yet another lie, eh, Governor?' She was standing there in the doorway, in the flesh. He made a mental note to get on to his security chief about such a blatant breach, but then he remembered he no longer had a security chief.

'Cassie,' he said, making a desperate appeal to the woman's sense of mercy, 'I've had a very bad day so far. I hope you'll understand . . .'

'I'm sorry to hear that,' she replied, inviting herself in. 'Especially since it's about to get a whole lot worse for you.'

'Thanks for the warning. Would you care to sit down or do you prefer to lynch me standing up?'

Cassie's devastatingly blue eyes were like lasers. 'You set me up, Bryce. You made a fool of me. You deceived me. You have no honour and I don't even know you any more.'

What did a man say to that? Especially one about to lose his wife, his best friend and his state all in one day? Did it matter that he hadn't set out to deceive her at all, or that he himself was baffled by what was really going on?

'So . . . other than that,' he said, opting for black humour, 'you'd still vote for me?'

She didn't seem to grasp the levity. 'Fuck you, Bryce. Does that answer your question?'

Bryce pressed his fingers to his pounding forehead. 'Look, Cassie, I'm sorry you've been dragged into this. It wasn't my intention to—'

'To what? To send me out there blind into things I couldn't possibly understand? To involve me in criminal enterprises? Then again, I suppose that isn't something you trouble the fluffy little blonde with before using her, is it? How long has it been? That's all I want to know. How long since you sold your soul to the mob?'

Now it was his turn to become angry. 'I've done no such thing, Cassandra Anne Dane. And you have no proof to base such allegations on, either against me or Landview.'

'You may not use my middle name.' She pointed with a beautiful index finger. 'You lost that right. As for having proof, technically I didn't when I came in. But I do now. Your guilt is written all over your face.'

Bryce promptly called her a cunning little bitch, which did nothing to calm the atmosphere of the room. In retrospect, he might have taken this opportunity to bring her up to speed on events as he knew them but as with Lydia a few minutes ago, his stubbornness gene had kicked in, causing him to shut off his emotions and speed full steam ahead into the iceberg.

Her eyes went from blue fire to ice. 'Go to hell, Bryce.'

Bryce felt overwhelming panic. He couldn't bear to have her leave him now, not like this, not with him so entirely alone. 'Cassie, I'm sorry. Please don't go.' Gone was all pretence of decorum, his cool and aloof gubernatorial façade. Bryce could and would beg for what he needed: human contact, sympathy, a shoulder to cry on, someone to baby him and sigh over him and make him feel like a man again. 'Give me one more chance.'

Cassie shook her head, delivering her sentence on him. For a man like Bryce, there was nothing more unbearable than to be shut out by a woman. Anger, contempt, anything was preferable because those were emotions and Bryce knew how to turn them all to his advantage. But stone-cold silence – that was death to a man like him who needed to be loved and adored.

His fear gave way to desperation as she turned on her heels to walk out. He intercepted her at the door, closing it in front of her.

'Get the fuck out of my way, Bryce!'

He pulled her greedily into his arms, silencing her

with a fierce kiss. She moaned a protest for all of a second before yielding to his probing tongue. Her eyes were still furious, letting him know how much she hated him at this moment for what he could still do to her body.

There was no goodbye in her stiff nipples or in the way her crotch thrust violently against him. What these things said, in fact, was that they were going to fuck ferociously, acting out their passions in the only arena where they could manage it successfully after so many years and so much pain. He wanted her on the couch and she took his meaning, wrapping her legs around him so he could walk them backwards toward the smooth, slick leather.

The distance proved too far, however, and he ended up pinning her against the door itself. They proved a perfect team, his lips and teeth ravishing her neck as she disarmed his zipper. To his delight he found her pantyless and sopping wet. She took him easily, drawing him in to the hilt and locking him tight with her pussy muscles. She felt as good as she ever had to him, just as mind-blowing.

There wasn't going to be any holding on here. It would be fast by any standards and they both knew it. They had a small window of opportunity and, once it closed, they would likely never speak again, let alone share bodily fluids. This one was for old times' sake.

He wanted and got her mouth again on his. There were few women in his life he'd ever really been able to kiss and Cassie was one of them. Ramming his cock in and out of a pussy was one thing, but touching lips was intimate. You had to really share something there and you had to take something back, something distinctly human.

Cassie's ankles locked behind his as he pumped her.

Her wrists circled his neck, her pelvis in perfect cooperation as they moved towards the release they both craved. He could almost confuse this with trust on her part and cooperation. But it wasn't. It was fucking. Pure and simple. Like you could fuck someone in exchange for money or just because you were drunk, or maybe even for no earthly reason at all other than boredom.

Strangers fucked, after all. And enemies, too. Was that what they had become?

Bryce breathed her scent, wanting to say her name, wanting her to hear it from him, especially as he orgasmed inside her, holding her hot, lithe little body against him. How would he say goodbye to this? Really this was crueller on her part than if she'd just left in the first place.

Then again, she'd wanted to do precisely that before he stopped her.

Damn it, he hated these clothes. And he didn't want this to end either, not like this. Steeling every ounce of his resolve, he grasped her buttocks, pulling them away from the door, away from the precipice. She resisted at first, not wanting their motions to cease, but when she saw that he did not intend to take his cock from inside her but only change their venue, she simply rested her shoulder against him and let herself go limp.

Bryce felt a surge of new energy and a renewed determination to give her something more. A far, far better goodbye than she'd intended. He moved her to the front of the couch and this time he did have to disengage. She made noises of mild discontent, entirely non-verbal. It was as if she knew that a single word spoken between them would break the spell and end their fragile union. Bryce knew the chance he was taking already, but that was the kind of man he'd always been. Never satisfied, always dreaming of something more. People paid prices sometimes for those dreams, people other than himself.

Placing her gently in the middle of the sofa in a sitting position, he encouraged her to lean back and part her legs. Ultimately, he wanted that golden paradise down there, but first he unbuttoned her blouse. Kneading her full breasts through the fabric of her bra, he induced a soft, satisfied moan. As her eyes closed and her back lifted, he was filled once more with hope. He was the lover, the great communicator. Or, more aptly, the great fornicator. Leave 'em smiling. Wasn't that the old show-business dictum?

God, but this was a fantastic woman. Running his hands down her bare, smooth belly, he could feel the surging life. Why hadn't she married and made a score of babies in here? She'd be a great mother. Any man would be honoured and lucky as hell to make all the babies with her. He parted her toned thighs, allowing the heat of her healthy skin to radiate through his chilled body. If he could touch this woman, just like this, even ten minutes a day, he would live for ever.

And if he could fuck her once a day, he would rule the world.

Cassandra had the most beautiful pussy. It looked especially beautiful under moonlight. He'd always wanted to drink champagne from inside those lips, champagne under moonlight, but he'd been a little shy in those days. At least with regard to kinkiness. That was before he'd had a lot of experiences, good and bad. Before Karla and Sydney and all the rest, and, of course, before Queenie.

There was the deepest mystery: understanding Abigail. Cassie hadn't given any report to him about her, but presumably it had not gone well. He hadn't realised how much he'd missed that woman, all the time she was away, till she'd come back. And then she'd betrayed him. Was that how Cassie felt about him?

So much guilt, he thought. What he wouldn't give for a few minutes under Abigail's whip. Although it wasn't just the punishment that made him feel better, was it? It was how she talked to him and cared for him. She gave him a stability, a base no other woman ever had. Strange he'd never noticed that before.

But for now there was only Cassie, with her pink lips, irrepressible. Eternally youthful. He bent forward and bestowed a single kiss on her fragrant centre.

He was rewarded with a jolt, as if she'd received a tiny electric shock. Hungry for more response, he followed up with his finger, fascinated with his own tracing motions over the labia, delighted at the way each little motion made her body sing a different note. Her head tossed left and then right, indicating readiness for more. In a show of physical strength, she clenched her buttocks, pushing up her pelvis till it was angled sharply upwards. Nothing was more beautiful than the bow of a woman's body.

Taking hold of her hips, he showed his appreciation, burying his tongue in the ready opening. The sound Cassie made was guttural and sweet, unique to her and long buried, he now realised, in his own subconscious. All these years, without knowing it, he'd been looking for this sound again. And here it was, at the tip of his tongue, accompanied by a trickle of nectar, drops of it settling on his tongue, awakening his taste buds to a dimension of sex too often overlooked by men.

She took her hands and pressed them to his head,

fingers parting through his dark hair to reach naked scalp. Still no words; only silent directing, her appreciation revealed only in the movements of her body. Bryce was happy to be guided onto her clit, more than thrilled to know she would make use of him to achieve her pleasure. This mattered to him more than his own, and in fact, at this moment, it was the only kind of pleasure he could feel.

Was this about redemption? Was he trying to expiate with his silver tongue, putting it to slightly less orthodox uses than he usually employed on the campaign stump?

Careful, Bryce. This is still just goodbye. You're just doing it your way, that's all. Because of your stubbornness and your refusal to ever let anyone else have the last word.

Cassandra's clitoris was swelling beautifully. He worked it carefully, reverently. It was her ecstasy he wanted, the sweet release of her directly into his mouth. There was always this special thing about Cassie's pussy. Just before she came, the juices got sweeter; there was this fresh release, a washing over, and then he would know she was right there. A little extra burst from there, a tiny bit more pressure from the tip of his tongue and then boom . . . explosion time.

But Cassie didn't want to go all the way today. Not like that. Just as quickly as she'd shoved his head in, she wanted it out. Was this the end? No. She wanted his cock again, this time from behind. Placing her hands on the back of the couch, she leaned forward and spread her knees, leaving it to him to lift her skirt and get at her out-thrust ass.

It was perfect this way, even more anonymous. More private for each of them. Focusing on those rounded, smooth globes, he removed the obstacle of his pants and underwear. He wanted to be naked from the waist down, so he could slap his balls against her and feel the front of his thighs against the back of hers.

She sucked in a sharp breath, almost painful as he pushed himself into her from a standing position. She began to move at once, establishing her own rhythm. Bryce was afraid he'd be left in the cold, so he countered with a rhythm of his own. Grasping her hips, he fought to establish supremacy. It was a stalemate, predictably, neither one nor the other succumbing but each seizing their own pleasure and meting out their own small doses of revenge.

We'll never touch again, said this particular copulation. We'll never cross this way but we'll want to, we'll burn for it long into the lonely, useless night. Such perfect lovers, hand-in-glove and yet so totally wrong for one another.

Bryce pushed at her and Cassie pushed back. Bryce started to climax and Cassie counter-climaxed. Bryce locked his hands on her hips and she clutched at the couch leather. Bryce swore under his breath and she hissed back. Two keen minds, horns locked, two lean bodies with way too much history and no future, only the present.

They managed a last embrace afterwards, when they had arranged their clothes.

'Take care,' he whispered.

'You too.'

She left without another word. He was looking for more paperweights to throw when he got another buzz on the intercom. 'Sir, we've located the apartment of Jake Andrews. According to witnesses he left about an hour and a half ago.'

'Good. Was he alone?'

'Yes, although there was a woman who left a little while before him. A blonde, attractive.'

Bryce considered the odds on it being Cassie. It was a million-to-one shot. Then again, she'd had to get her information from somewhere. 'Thank you. I'll go check it out. Send a car for me, please. No driver.'

It was time, he decided, to find the truth for himself. Ugly as it might be.

Cassie had ridden to the mansion with Travis. Seeing him out there on his motorcycle, chatting away with the trooper on duty outside the front entrance, filled her with inexplicable joy. She wanted to just hop on the back of that machine and fly like the wind. He must have recognised this himself because he broke off his animated conversation after one look at her face.

'I gotta run, man,' he said to his buddy.

The uniformed officer nodded approvingly, noting the attractive blonde with the tousled hair. 'More power to you, Jonesy.'

Travis mounted the bike and kicked the starter. The engine was thrumming powerfully by the time she lifted her leg across the seat. It was all coming back to her now, everything she'd felt on the way over here, all the nasty, sexy things this man had been doing to her all day, from making her surrender her panties to forcing her to caress the computer guy, Petey, in the bathroom.

OK, so it wasn't fair to say he'd forced her to do anything. He hadn't put a gun to her head – heck, he hadn't even brought his gun with him to the café. Truth be told, she'd been so charged by the time she went over to the computer geek, it really wouldn't have mattered if Travis was there at all. Yes, it delighted her to know he was watching, but it was the act itself that fascinated her.

She was more willing to give pleasure to a stranger than she could have dreamt. And this one had seemed so worthy; a decent young man without a chance in hell of getting laid on his own. She started by feigning interest in what he was reading. He was indifferent at first and then flat-out suspicious. He must have thought she was there to tease him. Finally she asked if she could sit with him, please?

He didn't refuse and she took his shrug for affirmation. For a while she let him flip the pages, as she made small comments here and there. Eventually he was sharing quite animatedly about databases and LANs. Only ten per cent of this was even remotely comprehensible. Although she did grasp one concept that she used to advantage.

'Speaking of hardware problems,' she crooned, 'you seem to have one of your own down there.'

He turned beet-red at the mention of his erection.

'May I?' She touched him, not bothering to wait for a reply. 'Oh, yes,' she nodded. 'I would say you do have a problem. A compatibility problem.'

He cleared his throat nervously but didn't budge. 'Have you any solutions in mind?'

She smiled, knowing she had him. 'I do.' She nodded gravely. Your cock . . . in my mouth.'

The rest was history as they slipped off one at a time to the restroom. She serviced him in the men's room, on her knees while he sat in one of the stalls. He was shaking as she pulled out his turgid, stubby member.

'Relax,' she cooed, sensing it was the first time he'd ever been this close to a woman. 'Just enjoy.'

He squeezed the toilet paper for all it was worth.

She barely got a lick in before he began spasming. Just in time, she managed to bear down, pushing the end of him between her lips. He was small enough to take whole and as he began to come she managed to suck it straight out of him. He didn't exactly cry out, but he did emit some strange articulations, which he identi-fied afterwards as exclamations in the language of the Klingons.

Cassie expressed surprise that there actually was a Klingon language, given that they were a fictitious race from an old television programme. Full of new-found bravado, he proceeded to explain how some other Trekkies not unlike himself had actually devised speech patterns for the notorious killers and had even published them in a book.

Declining an invitation to go back to his apartment to see it, she left him with a peck on the cheek and returned to Travis. Petey gave the man quite a look, itself worthy of a Klingon, and stalked off. Travis proceeded to tease her about her new boyfriend. 'That's not funny,' she said, slapping his hand.

It was at this point she told Travis that she would have to put off any further hijinks till after they'd been to the mansion. His offer to take her on the motorcycle had seemed innocent enough. What he hadn't told her was that riding on such a machine with a handsome man, panty-free, especially when in an aroused state already, was like pouring gasoline on a fire.

It'll be faster on the bike than your car, he'd said.

Sure, he got her there in record time. But all she'd wanted to do was strip and screw like a bitch in heat. Hardly the right frame of mind to confront a Governor with, especially one who was a former lover. Was it any surprise Bryce ended up in her pants – or rather in the place her pants were supposed to be?

Well, at least she'd finally achieved closure. Wasn't that the big word for relationships? Hell, she was through with him. All she had to do now was go on with her life while she sat back and watched for the headlines.

Governor Goes Down. Yet Another Crooked Politician Bites The Dust.

It had happened before in history and it would happen again. There was certainly no need for her to be a part of things. He was self-destructing all on his own. You make your bed, you burn in it.

The American Way.

She clung to Travis as they picked up speed. It was time to go home. Time for a nice bubble bath and some wine. After all, he had the rest of his day off to use up and it was her intention that he fill every minute of it with her.

And maybe even a day or so after that, too.

12

'Baby, somebody at door,' said the little Philippine stripper, her accent chopping like an icepick into the back of Jake's skull. He opened his eyes to see a small pair of pierced tits leaning over him, along with an angelic, painted little face.

She was lying next to him in his bed. The girl looked dressed for the stage, or rather undressed. How exactly had she ended up here? Feeling the crunch of metal under his ass, he had his answer. The same answer as always. Beer. 'How long?' he groaned.

'How long what, baby?'

The sound at the door was getting louder.

'How long ... asleep?' He moved to sit up, every muscle screaming. Shit, what had he been doing, sparring with Mike Tyson all night? Come to think of it, was it today or still yesterday? Desperately he tried to retrace his steps. Somewhere, in the ancient past, he'd made to love to sweet Cassie Dammit, professional damsel in distress. There went the end of his peaceful, wasted life. And the beginning of yet another futile journalistic crusade, this time in search of dirt on Landview. He'd followed some of his old mob contacts here and there, not turning up a whole lot of detail for her till finally he'd run into Harry the Hat, who'd sent him on to Little Carmine and so on.

The last thing he remembered, he was at the Pink Pussy Cat talking to Tony the Jackal, not to be confused with Tony the Monk, who represented a different gang, or Tony the Tiger, who was an animated character in a cereal ad.

Remember, blast it. What did the man tell you about Landview? That was it. His boss, Big Vinny, was one of the so-called investors. There were six bosses in all, forming a syndicate. Together they were funnelling money through an offshore bank in the Cayman Islands, which was dealing stateside with First Star, the bank run by Richard Davenport. First Star, in turn, was coordinating with a dozen other financial institutions.

Davenport, it seemed, was the linchpin. But what about his son-in-law the Governor? Did Bryce form the political apex of this triangle of evil? Apparently not. According to Tony, Davenport was getting spooked that Bryce might get wise to the operation and put a stop to it. Turned out the old man was the one who'd given Big Vinny orders to set up a blackmail scheme to force the Governor's resignation. And if that didn't work, there were orders for him to end up in a nasty accident.

Wasn't that something? For the first time in his career Jake Andrews actually found himself feeling sorry for a politician.

'You pass out one hour ago.' The girl supplied the information before returning to her favourite topic. 'Baby, why you no answer door? Someone for you at door.' The stripper seemed genuinely perplexed by his lack of social graces. Apparently where she came from people still gave a fuck.

'Because the only thing worth opening a man's door for is pussy and I already have some. By the way, have we fucked yet?'

'No, you pass out first.' She was on her feet, stepping over him. 'I answer door for you.'

Her shaved pussy passed right over his head like some fabled floating wonder. Whoever was at the door interfering with his chance to get in that tight box of hers was one real inconsiderate son of a bitch in Jake's opinion.

'Whoever it is, tell them to go fuck themselves,' he called out.

The stripper's ass retreated from view, narrow but fine. Would she ride as good as Cassie?

Damn. He'd meant to call her and make sure she was all right last night. He hadn't wanted to take chances on her safety, what with Landview heating up as it was. What an irresponsible asshole he was. Could he think of no one but himself? Ever? 'Baby, man here to see you.' It was the naked stripper back in the doorway.

Shit, she had some nice tattoos. Especially that dragon on her hip, the fire of its mouth breathing onto her freshly shaved crotch. The green-and-blue-scaled snake coiled around her left breast wasn't bad either, with its eyes greedily set on her small brown nipple.

Fuck, there he went again, getting sidetracked from Cassie.

'I told you, no visitors,' he complained. 'What's your name again?

'Meea. But that not matter, baby. He big man. Need to see you now.'

Jake reached for a cigarette off the nightstand. 'Big how? Like a football player?'

'Big, like head-man.'

'Head of what?' he asked sceptically, knowing how little it took to impress foreign girls like this. More than likely it was building maintenance wanting to change the fucking air filter.

'He say he the Governor.'

OK. So maybe this one was worth getting out of bed for.

Jake lit the cigarette and took a deep drag. 'Well, aren't I the popular boy all of a sudden,' he quipped. 'First a gorgeous political consultant shows up on my doorstep and now the Governor. Who's next? The Pope? Jimmy Hoffa?'

'Why Pope come here?' Meea wanted to know. Clearly his famous sense of humour wasn't getting across.

'Never mind. Just help me find my jeans.'

Meea opened the blinds and the window, too. 'You no wear old pants,' she chided. 'You dress nice for Governor.'

He squinted under the assault of the morning light. 'Meea, you trying to kill me?' he complained.

'Light good for you,' she said maternally. 'You got bad colour for skin.'

He leaned over the windowsill and breathed the fresh air. 'Oh, do tell me it's still Christmas morning ... Tell me the spirits really did do it all in one night.'

'You a very strange man.' Meea handed him a pair of khakis from the closet.

'So I've been told.' He pulled them on without underwear.

Five minutes later Jake was entertaining the Governor of the state in his living room, being served iced tea by a stripper. Talk about something to tell the grandkids.

'I am really sorry to barge in like this,' the Governor said.

'It's no problem,' said Jake, noting that the man seemed shorter in person.

'I assure you I wouldn't do this if it weren't absolutely vital.' Clarkson seemed tired, too, with rings under his eyes. And, come to think of it, he was a little dressed down, in a zippered jacket and no tie. He'd also come alone, which was remarkable in itself. Whatever was going on, it was something he wanted kept absolutely private.

'I'll do what I can,' Jake said, meaning it. Somehow, seeing him like this, as the underdog, brought home all the things he'd heard from Tony. It really was true, then. He was one of the good guys.

'It's about Landview,' said the sombre Governor.

'I'm glad you brought it up,' said Jake. 'Otherwise I would have had to myself.'

He proceeded to tell the man everything he knew, about Big Vinny and moves in the syndicate, and most especially the part about Richard Davenport being behind it all. The Governor's face bore little expression, though there was no hiding the pain in his eyes. Could the politician really be this surprised? Had he been that naïve after all these years? It was almost enough to make Jake Andrews want to start believing in the system again.

'I have to meet this Big Vinny,' said the Governor when Jake was finished with his mini-briefing.

Jake looked for signs that the man was either joking or stark raving mad. Seeing none, he said, 'Mr. Governor with all due respect, even if such a meeting could be arranged, I hardly think it would be in your best interest.'

'Fuck my best interest,' he said, shocking the hell out of Jake. 'I've spent my career looking after my own interest, it's time to start thinking of the people.'

'That's all well and good,' Jake pointed out. 'But what good will you do the people floating face-up in the river?'

'It doesn't have to go down that way. If we play our

cards right, we can have a nice little meeting and get it all on tape. I'll wear a wire and get this Vinny character to spill the beans. We'll have them all dead to rights.'

Jake pursed his lips. It really was tempting to want to throw in his lot with a guy like this. Still, how many times had he been fooled before? 'Assuming we survived a hairbrained scheme like this – and, trust me, we won't – what difference do you think one man could really make, Governor, even you, against a system this corrupt? And don't give me any speeches, 'cause I've heard them all.'

The Governor smiled, a wicked, conspiratorial grin, totally infectious. 'Realistically? Not a damned thing. But wouldn't it be fun to try?'

The answer caught him off-guard. It was about the one thing in the world Bryce could have said to convince him. 'You're good,' said Jake, acknowledging the man's persuasive powers. 'Damned good.'

Bryce smiled slyly. 'So I take it you're in?'

Jake knew this was a mistake. He'd get burned. Middlemen like him always did. Still, there was a part of him, the journalist part, that always had to be in the thick of it. It was a drug, his real drug of choice. The vodka was a shabby substitute for the danger and always would be.

Cursing himself even as he spoke the words, he said, 'I assume you have some kind of a plan for how to get Vinny to talk?'

Bryce Clarkson grinned devilishly. 'I sure as hell do. Just get me in to see the man and I'll do the rest. When it's all done, you can have an exclusive. Win yourself a nice Pulitzer for the wall in here.'

'It will go better on my tombstone,' Jake groused.

'Which is what I'll be needing by the time you're through with me.'

Clarkson laughed, the light coming back into his face. 'Fear not, my friend. I have not yet begun to fight.'

'I know. And that's what I'm afraid of.'

Cassie was in trouble and she knew it. Trying to handcuff Travis to her bed first thing in the morning in his sleep was bound to piss him off. It was a good thing she hadn't gone the next step and written all over him in magic marker.

As it was, she was on the run, trying not to let her giggling interfere with her very serious attempt to find refuge in the bathroom. She was too slow, which meant that before she could close and lock the door he'd managed to wedge one very muscular thigh in the way. Before she knew it, he had her round the waist, off her feet, kicking helplessly in the air.

'Let go of me,' she laughed. 'You big brute.'

'Not till I've taught you a lesson,' he retorted, just as good-naturedly.

The lesson proved to be particularly devious. Since she liked the handcuffs so much, he was going to let her experience them for herself. In the shower. And so the generally happy-go-lucky blonde found herself on tiptoes, her hands secured to the showerhead.

'You better let me go,' she said, squirming, 'or I'll call a cop.'

He stood just in front of her, buck-naked, his huge, erect cock poking her in the belly as he fondled her tits. 'I am one, remember.'

'Then act like it,' she chided.

'That's a good idea.' He pushed his hand between her legs. 'I'll start with a full search of my prisoner.'

'Oh, fuck me,' she muttered in mock distress. 'Why am I always opening my big mouth?'

'Beats me,' said the trooper, whose sexy body she'd enjoyed well into the night. Having him stay over was the best thing she'd done for herself in ages. He'd worked incredible amounts of tension out of her, actually managing to douse some of the boundless fires she'd been feeling. Her only regret was that it was a new day and that soon he would have to get dressed, strap on a gun and go and protect the people.

Still, they had a little time to play. 'Now what are you doing?' she demanded as he bent down to adjust the knob to full cold.

'Preparing to interrogate my prisoner.'

'You wouldn't dare!'

'I'll have to,' he said. 'Unless you confess.'

'To what?'

The cop stood up again, his body nearly touching hers. 'To whatever I say.'

She sucked in her breath as he toyed with her nipples. 'This is police brutality.'

'Extraordinary times call for extraordinary measures.' He pinched her nipples. The brief stinging sensation brought her to focus, fast. Her pussy was wide awake now, as was her imagination. 'Please, officer,' she said, playing the role of helpless prisoner perfectly, 'don't hurt me. I'll say whatever you want.'

He worked his hand in and out between her thighs, the skin wet with her own lubrication. 'Tell me what a slut you are.'

'I'm a slut.' She moved against his hand.

'You like this, don't you?'

Like it? Her whole body came alive with his every masterful touch. It was as if he made every inch of her captured, tormented body into an extension of her sexual core. By being this confined, naked and chained, she was actually freed, in a way, to express herself more fully than she ever had before. She just wanted to let go of it all, be totally sexy and desirable to this man, even as she took pleasure for herself beyond her wildest dreams.

'Oh, please.' She pretended to be a shy, imperilled maiden. 'Don't make me say it.'

'Say it,' he insisted, pushing his fingers in deeper. 'Or face the consequences.'

Cassie moaned. 'I like it ... oh God, I do. I'm such a slut.'

'How about if I got some of my brother officers up here? I bet you'd service them all willingly, wouldn't you?' Travis's fingers went to her lips.

She sucked at them wildly, tasting herself. 'Yes,' she said, the word garbled as she licked him.

Was this all part of the game, or might he really want her to do his other officers? The handsome Mike, for example, the straight arrow with a fiancée. Or any of the others she saw in uniform on the highways every day, broad-shouldered, narrow-waisted, with badges and guns.

'Enough.' He pulled out his fingers. 'It's time to get you cleaned up.'

He turned the shower on and adjusted it to a comfortably warm temperature. The water sluiced down her body, caressing her nipples and trickling inside her folds. Very gently he worked the soap up into a lather, covering every inch of her body. Finally, he unhooked one of the handcuffs and re-secured her hands behind her back.

This allowed her to stand freely. It also allowed him the chance to access her body a little more freely. Again, he showed the utmost care, buffing and polishing the surface of her skin inch by inch as if she were a fine automobile. The trouble was, she was needing a little more action by this point; something along the lines of a fresh test-drive.

'Travis,' she sighed. 'I need you ... inside me.'

Again he adjusted the cuffs, this time attaching her hands in front of her to the towel rack on the other side of the bathroom. Now she was completely exposed from behind, flat on her feet, open to whatever he might wish to insert or impose. She expected at least a normal vaginal entry, but Trooper Jones had other ideas. Her bottom was glistening and her anus was slick with soap. It was too good to resist.

'You know what they say about prison life,' he quipped.

'Don't bend over for the soap, right?' she gasped as he pushed himself home.

He took hold of her hips, his warm, controlling touch making her glow. 'Something like that,' he grunted.

Cassie's breasts were pressed to the tile wall. The smooth, cool sensation on her bare skin made her feel that much more confined, contained and controlled. 'Please,' she begged of him. 'Play with my clit.'

He was only too happy to wriggle a finger into her wet folds as he continued his anal injection. Cassie had a feeling of total fullness now, of complete sexual surrender. She was a creature of complete, shackled freedom. A living paradox.

He had made it about half way into her when he started to groan. 'So fucking tight.'

'Oh, yeah, baby, use me. Please,' she moaned. Here she was, in her own bathroom, in full view of her duck-print towels. Wasn't that a hoot? It was certainly an experience the little guys wouldn't forget. Nor would she.

It was a race to see who could come first. Cassie was first, just under the wire. Out of her mind with the sensation, she pushed him into her ass even as he hooked his finger on her clit. 'Come,' she shouted. 'Come in my ass.'

But he didn't want it like that. Pulling himself out, leaving her to fend for herself, he began to masturbate. 'Not in it,' he said. 'On it.'

Cassie tugged at the handcuffs, knowing they would never yield. Her hands were denied her. She would stay this way as long as he wanted and she would endure what he gave her, including this promised sperm bath.

'Oh yes,' she said, accepting her fate, wanting it, for all it represented. 'Do it to me. Shoot your load on me. Show me what a slut I am.'

'Gonna do it,' he panted, one hand clenching her buttock. 'Gonna come ... all over your fine ass.'

He spurted, warm and thick, and she nearly came again from the feeling. Gobs of it splattered on her ass and back. 'Yes,' she cried out. 'Oh, yes, Travis.'

He undid the handcuffs, kissing her neck. 'You are so fucking incredible.'

'Not bad,' she giggled. 'For an old lady.'

'Come on,' he said with a grin. 'Let's try the shower again – this time with your hands free.'

'Careful,' she warned. 'These are dangerous weapons.'

'I'm counting on it.' He smacked her on the ass to move her in the right direction.

About five minutes later the doorbell rang. They were still hot and heavy under the spray of the water at the time. Cassie wanted to ignore it, but Travis told her that was rude.

'Somebody came all the way over here to see you,' he lectured. 'Don't you have any sense of manners?'

She had to laugh at him sounding so much older than her. That was the cop part in him, she supposed. She relented and put on her robe, though she was quite sure it was going to turn out to be someone selling cookies or insurance.

To her shock it was Queenie Amazon instead, trying to look incognito in dark glasses, a dark coat and kerchief. 'You haven't been returning my calls,' the woman said.

Cassie did not invite her in. 'I didn't realise we had anything left to say to one another. Was there something I missed?'

'Actually, yes,' Queenie said boldly. 'We have a friend in common. A friend who's in trouble.'

Cassie frowned. 'I'm afraid that friend you speak of is no longer mutual. I'm sorry you came all this way for nothing.'

'Who is that?' asked Travis, having come up behind them, already half-dressed in uniform trousers and T-shirt.

Cassie's heart sank. Great. He would invite her in for sure.

'I am someone in need of help,' said Queenie, knowing a saviour when she saw one. 'As is Miss Dane here, though she doesn't know it.'

Travis furrowed his brow, making his cop's assessment of the situation. 'Cassie,' he said a moment later, 'let her in. I want to hear more.'

'Yes, *sir*,' she grumbled, reluctantly stepping aside.

The next thing she knew they were in the living

room, Queenie pouring her heart out about the tape and Bryce and everything. The first thing she wanted them to know was that the Governor hadn't been aware of the presence of organised crime as a secret supporter of Landview. Cassie remained sceptical of this but, as the woman went on to divulge the details of her conversation with the cameraman Ian, she began to see things differently.

The most disturbing facet of the whole thing was the involvement of Lydia's father. If Richard Davenport was indeed behind this tape, working in cahoots with one of the mob bosses, then maybe Bryce really had been set up. If his own father-in-law was that devious and had been lying to Bryce all along, then maybe the Governor wasn't the crook she'd come to think he was.

Wouldn't it be just like Bryce, in fact, to want to believe in something so badly that he refused to see any evidence to the contrary? His stubbornness had gotten him to the highest office in the state and married him into its most powerful family. Somehow he'd seen it all as the means to an end: to making a difference, in spite of it all, for the little people, the working men and women.

'Cassie,' said Queenie, making a last desperate appeal. 'I know I will never amount to anything in your book. But I know Bryce like you do. I have a heart, believe it or not. And I'm not a total moron, either, just because I use my body to make a living. The Governor is in grave danger. And I don't know anyone else he'll listen to but you. Not anyone I can reach anyway.'

Cassie felt a stab of guilt as she thought of how her last encounter with Bryce had gone. She'd walked into his office hotheaded and horny. Talk about having a tape to replay – why hadn't she seen the look on the man's face then as she remembered it now? Why hadn't she really heard what he was trying to tell her and show her when she walked in on him?

'I'm afraid I've blown that opportunity, Queenie. Governor Clarkson and I are no longer on speaking terms.'

The eyes of the hardened dominatrix began to water. 'You were my last hope,' she said.

Cassie felt a lump in her throat. So the woman really did love him. It was a humbling thing to see, and rather sobering, because it made Cassie realise she had never managed to feel so much for another human being in her life. Not for Bryce Clarkson. Not for anyone. For all her pretensions of wanting another chance with the man, she'd never really thought of him in any terms outside her fantasies. Sure, she'd tried to help him before, but the minute there was doubt, she'd jumped ship. Love didn't do that. Love stood by. To the bitter end.

'I'm sorry, Queenie, I had no idea.'

'It's not your fault,' she said with a sniff. 'You didn't know.'

But I should have, she thought. I had the chance to know and I blew it.

Wait, though. There was one card she hadn't played. 'Queenie, what about Jake Andrews? Could he help us? I already told him about the tape and he said he'd look into the whole Landview thing. He has influence in high places still.'

Queenie's lovely china-doll face brightened. 'You're right. It's worth a chance.' She reached in her bag for her cell phone. 'By the way, did you mention my name when you saw him?'

'He said he didn't know you. I figured it was a lie, but I didn't push it.'

Queenie smiled, the look of a woman who kept the secrets of many men, well and in order. 'Good girl. You'd go far in my business, you know.'

Cassie couldn't help giving Travis a little smirk. 'What do you think, baby? Would I make a good dominatrix?'

He gave her just the reaction she wanted. 'I don't think so,' he said, arching a possessive brow. 'I'll be wearing the pants in this relationship, thank you very much.'

Queenie shooed them away as Jake answered her call. Travis had Cassie down on her knees in the bedroom working on yet another erection when Queenie knocked on the door several minutes later.

'I got Jake to talk to me,' she said.

The couple arranged themselves hastily and met her at the door. As a professional sex worker, Queenie took their dishevelled appearance in her stride.

'He was reluctant,' she explained, 'but I used some persuasion. He was a whole lot more forthcoming when I told him I was with you, Cassie, and that you were safe. It turns out Bryce has actually been in contact with him. They are making arrangements to see one of the mob bosses tonight.'

'But that's insane,' exclaimed Cassie.

'I know it is, that's why we have to stop them,' Queenie agreed.

It was Travis who offered a different point of view. 'Not necessarily. They must have some plan or they wouldn't take the risk, am I right?'

'Yes,' said Queenie, 'but there is no way it's going to work. They'll just wind up getting themselves killed.'

'I'll bet they are going to go in wired, aren't they?' said Travis. 'They want to get this whole thing on tape. Bring the whole crooked scheme to justice. It's brilliant.'

'It's also dangerous as hell,' Cassie pointed out. 'What if they get themselves caught?'

Queenie nodded fiercely. 'I agree. I won't let Bryce and Jake be exposed to that kind of danger alone.'

Cassie could almost hear the wheels turning in Travis' head. 'Who says they have to be alone?' the trooper asked.

'You'll never get Bryce to accept your help, though.' This objection came from Cassie, who at this point knew the man as well as anyone in the world. Maybe better.

Travis' eyes twinkled. The man was clearly loving the intrigue. Cassie had a feeling he was not destined to remain a mere highway trooper his entire career.

'In that case,' he said. 'We don't have to tell him we're helping him, do we?'

'No,' agreed Cassie, feeling rather proud of him at the moment. 'We don't.'

Queenie remained silent, still sceptical.

'I know, it's not the greatest solution,' Travis admitted. 'All things considered, we'd rather not be in this place at all. But as I see it, there's only one way out. And that's straight ahead.'

Queenie looked at Cassie, who nodded in affirmation.

'OK,' said the redhead with a sigh, steeling her resolve. 'Count me in.'

'Now you're talking,' said Travis. 'OK, here's the plan. First we get Jake back on the phone to give us details about tonight. Most especially, we need to figure out if there might be anyone on the inside who could help us.'

'I'll get right on it, Travis, and thank you.' She gave him a peck on the cheek. 'I can tell you're a good man.'

Cassie pulled possessively on the trooper's arm.

'What about me?' She pouted. 'What do I get to do in this little operation of yours?'

'You, my dear,' he drawled, once again showing his propensity for sounding like a man Cowell's age, 'are going to keep your pretty little behind safe and sound and out of the firing zone.'

'Don't you dare patronise me, Travis Jones,' she snorted, though secretly she was thrilled the man wanted to protect her.

Stick that in your pipe and smoke it, Queenie Amazon. As if the woman cared in the first place. Face it, Cassie sighed to herself, you're the one who's hung up on Trooper Jones and if you don't watch out it's going to get a whole lot messier.

And quite possibly a whole lot more permanent, too.

13

Bryce patted the reporter on the knee. 'Relax, it'll go just fine.'

Jake Andrews clutched the steering wheel, sweating like a schoolboy on the way to the prom. 'Who says I'm not relaxed?'

The Governor laughed, secretly hiding his own dread as they drew ever nearer to the estate of the infamous Big Vinny. 'It's written all over your face, Jake. If you were any more nervous we'd be up to our ankles in a yellow flood.'

'Yeah, well, it seems to me we ought to both be pissing our pants. Not to mention having our heads examined. You realise the odds we'll be facing in there?'

Bryce adjusted his shirt, checking the electronic wire and recorder. 'Same odds I faced to beat everyone else in the state to the Governor's office, if I had to guess.'

'One in four million, great,' said Jake, quoting the state population. 'Compare that to the odds of ending up in cement overshoes tonight. One pair for each of us. Four shoes. Four feet. Ding! We have a winner.'

'You're a stitch, Jake. You ought to write comedy.'

'I prefer to live it.' Jake turned the car into the drive, stopping just shy of the tall iron gates. A big man in a suit, somewhere between a Cro-Magnon and a gorilla, came out of a security booth, motioning for them to roll down the window.

'We've got an appointment,' said Jake.

'I know,' said the big man with a nod, laying the muzzle of a sub-machine gun on the window ledge. 'That's why you ain't dead yet.'

Two more of Big Vinny's men emerged from the shadows to look the car over, top to bottom, front to back. Finally they were allowed through.

'That was pleasant,' said the Governor.

'You ain't seen nothing yet,' quipped Andrews.

'Listen,' said Bryce, 'before we go much further, I just want to thank you for helping me to arrange this meeting. You're putting your own life on the line and I want you to know I won't forget that.'

'It's all right, Mr Governor. Just make me press secretary when you become President.'

Bryce laughed. 'I knew it. You are an optimist after all.'

'Nope. I've just decided to be as nuts as you are for the night.'

'Good choice. It's a lot more fun this way.'

Were they crazy? Bryce wondered. Probably. But what he had here was a clear chance of vindication, an open road to restoring the people's trust, not to mention the honesty of the government. And that was worth the price he might pay. Besides, he had a debt, for letting Landview get this far, for being so oblivious in the first place. He'd helped create the monster and now he would destroy it.

'Jake the Snake, how's it hanging?' The voice of Tony the Jackal boomed through the night air as they pulled up in front of the huge rococo mansion, a kind of grotesque version of the Governor's house. There were more men with machine guns here, though this group was hanging back, clearly under the Jackal's command.

Bryce got out of the passenger side, watching the

two men embrace. A hug would not be a good thing for him, nor would a weapons search. If they found a wire on him, he and Jake were as good as dead. Still, the risk was greater for the wearer, which is why he was the one with the tiny recorder they intended to use to bring down the entire organisational structure of Landview. Including his own father-in-law.

'Tony, I think you know this man.'

Fortunately, Tony stopped at a handshake. 'I seen you on TV,' the big man said as he squeezed Bryce's hand. 'You look bigger in person.'

'Most people think I look smaller,' said Bryce.

Tony shrugged his shoulders, amply covered in a sharkskin jacket. 'Hey, what do I know? I only got a twelve-inch TV screen.'

They all enjoyed a laugh, mostly because Tony was laughing and he didn't seem the sort one contradicted, what with his slicked-back hair, three hundred pounds of bulk and banana-sized fingers.

There were more guards at the door itself, also armed. Again the pair managed to get past without a personal inspection, though the subject did come up.

'What? What are you talking about over here?' Tony exclaimed to a thin, nervous guy who tried to pat Bryce down. 'He's the fucking Governor. Show a little respect.'

'A few extra votes wouldn't hurt either,' Bryce added.

Tony squeezed Bryce's cheek. 'I love this guy. Is he a great fucking guy or what?'

Everyone confirmed that indeed the Governor was a great fucking guy. It was a great fucking house, too, with lots of marble and gold, tacky statues, even a Roman-style bath in the living room.

Big Vinny was coming out of the bath when they

met him. The first thing that struck Bryce was that he was not particularly big. As it turned out, the moniker had been applied ironically.

'I got a cousin, Little Vinny, who goes about three-fifty,' the mobster explained. 'It's kind of a joke we got going.'

Bryce smiled politely, trying to appreciate the humour.

Thank God they were not being invited into the bath, he thought. Although there were a couple of girls in there who would have been worth cavorting with under different circumstances. One had short black hair and small, high breasts, while the other was a strawberry blonde with huge double Ds. Both were naked, completely comfortable displaying their bodies. They were probably OK with using them, too.

'Why don't you gentlemen make yourselves at home in the den?' suggested Big Vinny with surprising gentility. 'I'll be along presently. Tony, where's Tomiko?'

The Jackal shrugged. 'I ain't seen her, boss.'

'I am here,' came a voice from the doorway, sweet and melodic, the accent distinctly Japanese.

'Ah, my Eastern Star,' said Vinny proudly. 'Come here and introduce yourself, Tomiko.'

Tomiko was a gorgeous slender beauty decked out in a sequinned gown of gold, her dark hair piled high on her head. She stood with the aplomb of a model and the delicacy of a china doll. Her walk more than confirmed her grace and her slinky desirability.

'I am honoured to meet you,' she said, allowing Jake to take her hand and kiss it.

Bryce did the same. It was an innocent enough action, though as she raised her head again he could see in her eye that familiar look he had been getting from women his whole life. Clearly she wanted him. Ordinarily this would not be a problem, but tonight Bryce wanted conversation and nothing more. Taped conversation, to be precise.

'May I show you to the den?' asked Tomiko, looking only at Bryce.

'Thank you,' he said.

Jake brought up the rear as they walked out together. Bryce could feel Tomiko's heat next to him, like a small cylinder engine.

'You, sit here, please,' she said motioning to them as they entered the book-lined den. Jake took up his position in one of the two leather chairs facing the desk. As Bryce tried to move past Tomiko, however, she managed to interpose herself, brushing her breasts against his side. It was a near miss with the tape recorder. He'd barely caught his breath when she grabbed his hand and pulled him towards her in a full frontal embrace.

There wasn't much chance to refuse the kiss, unless he wanted to raise suspicions. It was a deep, passionate lip-lock and she had no qualms about using her tongue. Small and wily, it found the recesses of his mouth, drawing instant response from his cock. More than anything he wanted her small, fit body. He felt the adrenalin pumping, the danger only serving to increase his lust. It was his judgement paying the price.

'Governor, I see you're making yourself right at home.'

Bryce leapt back as if the woman was on fire.

'It's all right,' said Big Vinny with a laugh. His hair was freshly combed, his body covered in a red silk robe. 'I expect Tomiko to take care of my guests.'

She took that as an invitation to plaster herself

against him. Fuck it. Her small tight tits were right against the recorder. Tomiko froze a moment and then looked into his eyes in recognition. Was she going to rat him out? No. With only the faintest acknowledgement, she continued her kissing, across his face and down his cheeks.

'Would you like to fuck her?' asked the mob boss, who had settled into his leather chair behind the desk to have his feet rubbed by the black-haired girl, who was still naked.

Tomiko fell instantly to her knees, probably saving his life. All he had to do now was come quickly in her mouth and he'd never have to undress at all.

'Tomiko, slow down,' complained Vinny. 'What's gotten into you? Take the man's clothes off, at least, will you?'

'Perhaps if I sat down a bit, first,' Bryce suggested quickly, 'and got a little more comfortable.'

'Fair enough,' Vinny said with a nod. 'Besides, I know you gentlemen aren't just here on pleasure, are you? Tomiko, get us some brandy so we can talk business.'

'Thank you. I only wish we didn't have any business at all,' Bryce lamented. 'That way we could better enjoy your hospitality.' He was watching Tomiko out of the corner of his eye. Why was she helping him? Did she have something against Big Vinny?

'Such is life,' said Vinny. 'Into every existence, a little rain must fall.' He took his brandy from Tomiko and leaned back. 'On the other hand,' he sighed, accepting the dark haired girl's oral caresses, 'there are some perks to living, too.'

'To the simple pleasures.' Bryce raised his glass as soon as he got it. 'To sex . . . and all the rest.'

It was a perfect opening for the mobster to turn the conversation toward financial profit, and, sure enough, he took it. Hook, line and sinker.

'To money, may it always wash clean.'

Bryce let the brandy burn his throat. This was it. Time to go into action. 'Well said,' he agreed. 'Which brings me to why I've come here.'

The mobster nodded. 'Yeah, I figured it wasn't just for the pussy.'

Big Tony, who was sitting in a third wingback by now, laughed at this, a deep belly roll. 'Yeah, the Governor gets plenty of that on his own, am I right?'

Bryce inclined his head. 'Like our host said, life should have its perks.'

'Absolutely,' Vinny agreed. 'Tomiko, you can suck the Governor's dick now.'

The beautiful oriental girl knelt at his feet. Her eyes confirmed what he suspected. She was an unknown ally. An angel sent from heaven. Or maybe just an earthly woman who hated the mob as much as he did.

Bryce's cock wasn't entirely hard when she took it out. He blamed this on nerves. Little Tomiko wasn't fazed, though. She went right about her business, kissing and caressing and readying him to fit inside her willing mouth.

'First of all,' the Governor said, painfully aware that he must in no way appear to be entrapping the man or leading him into incriminating himself, 'I want you to know I'm only here as a last resort and I am extraordinarily grateful to you for making the accommodation to see me.'

It was a fine line he was walking here. He had to pretend as if he didn't know that Vinny was behind the effort to blackmail him. At the same time, he had to dangle some bait, something that would attract the man's interest. In this case, he'd hinted at wanting to make a deal: Bryce's continued cooperation with Landview in exchange for a piece of the pie. There was always the possibility that the gangster would kill him here and now, but that would be risky even for him. More likely they'd arrange some fake accident later on. Hopefully he'd have time before then to go to the authorities with whatever evidence he garnered on the tape.

Big Vinny was more blunt. 'Sure. Anyone sees you here we're both fucked. Chloe,' he said, snapping his fingers at the strawberry blonde lingering in the back of the room, 'suck Jake's dick, he looks lonely.'

'You're too kind, Vinny,' said Andrews.

'Hey,' said Vinny, lighting a cigar for himself. 'You can pay me back. Write up something in the paper real nice. Tony, give these men cigars.'

Tony heaved himself from the chair to tend to the boss's orders. Bryce accepted the cigar, allowing the Jackal to light it for him. He was throbbing now, his penis having swollen to full proportions.

'Well, there are risks for you and me already, aren't there?' said Bryce enigmatically. 'Whether or not we meet. I mean, times aren't what they used to be. Used to be a man's word was his bond. Nowadays ... who knows.'

'True enough,' the boss agreed. 'In my day, we knew how to handle a rat fuck, pardon the expression. Nowadays, there's witness protection, federal reward programs. It's a freaking nightmare.'

'On the other hand, the stakes are higher, too, aren't they? A man can amass a lifetime's resources in the wink of an eye.'

'Eh, what do I know?' Vinny said a shrug. 'I'm a simple businessman.'

Bryce nodded. He was swelling nicely under the girl's ministrations. 'Of course you are. You work hard for your money. All the more reason to protect it, don't you think? Especially on something as big as Landview.'

Vinny sighed thoughtfully. 'You know, you're absolutely right,' he replied, his continued pleasant tone giving no indication of his intentions. 'In fact, that's why I'm going to blow you two away. I hope you understand.'

Jake reacted first, sounding all the more passionate for having his dick completely inserted into the mouth of the lovely Chloe. 'Hey, Vin, no offence, but are you thinking this through? I mean, this guy is the Governor here.'

Vinny growled. 'You telling me I ain't thinking, college boy? Just for that I'm gonna kill you first.'

'Vincent, you really should learn the art of subtlety if you want to get anywhere in life,' said a new voice from the doorway.

Bryce's skin crawled instantly. The voice of Richard Davenport was like a hundred nails on a hundred chalkboards, like a slithering snake on a family Thanksgiving table.

'Bryce, what a surprise,' said his father-in-law. 'Please don't bother to get up. You, on the other hand,' he said, looking straight at Vinny, 'can feel free to vacate my chair.'

Vinny's gaze narrowed, but he did as he was told, allowing Davenport to replace him behind the big mahogany desk.

'Tomiko, Chloe,' Vinny said, 'that's enough.'

The two females abandoned their work, leaving Jake and Bryce completely exposed and glistening wet. The two men zipped themselves, as quickly and quietly as possible. Tomiko moved to stand quietly in the corner while Chloe slipped out the door.

'To what do we owe the honour?' Richard asked Bryce with a smile, his grey-haired, cool exterior belying his black heart.

'I was in the neighbourhood,' Bryce replied.

So Andrews' information was right. Davenport was behind the whole scheme. It was so tempting to come out and indict him right here, but he had to get the man to indict himself for the tape. Bryce would have to draw him out, most likely using the man's own egomania.

Richard laughed. 'Haven't they got enough work for you back at the executive mansion, my boy? Then again, I imagine it's a bit lonely there without your wife.'

Bryce felt the instant pressure in his chest. 'You've heard from Lydia? Is she all right?'

'She called me from Mexico, actually. Indicated she was planning to divorce you and remarry, someone named Wilder. I'm assuming there was a breakup somewhere I missed?'

'It happened very quickly.' The smug bastard, Bryce thought. Always turning everything into an occasion of sarcasm. 'We had ... differences.'

'I suppose you could call it that,' Ricahrd mused, 'though in my day it was known as adultery.'

'A lot of other things have been going on lately, Richard.'

'Yes, I understand there's a tape circulating out there.'

Bryce didn't take the bait. Instead he decided to light a little fire of his own to see if he couldn't smoke the man out. 'Yes, there is. I'm going to go to the police with it.'

'What will that accomplish?' Richard snorted. 'That's exactly what they are threatening to do already.'

'Yes, but I could pre-empt them . . . at the same time I encourage the cops to look into Landview.'

Davenport's eyes showed just how far he was prepared to go. 'You do that and you'll end up in jail. Your fingerprints are everywhere,' he threatened.

'But I didn't sign anything.'

'You think that means anything? You think your signature can't just show up on documents?'

'You mean forgery?'

'I mean only what I say,' the old man declared. 'And right now I'm saying you need to cut your losses.'

It was no good. Davenport wasn't going far enough. He'd have to provoke him further.

He shook his head. 'I am just confused. Lydia is gone, I'm being blackmailed, and people are asking me more and more about Landview. The way it seems to me, the whole thing is spinning out of control.'

'The hell it is,' Davenport thundered, his ego bruised. 'I have everything under complete control.'

'No. It's no good.' Bryce shook his head dramatically. 'I have to go to the police.'

Davenport slammed his fist on the desk. 'Damn it, you listen to me and you listen good. How many times have I told you not to try and think for yourself? See where it's gotten you? You can't even keep your pants zipped for five minutes. You're pathetic, letting yourself get taped like that. Do you know who did that? Me, Bryce, it was me. It's been me all along. Setting up your career, rubber-stamping you, giving you everything you needed. Where do you think the money for all that comes from? Selling Trail Scout cookies? It comes from real-life business deals. Deals that I make. So you listen up and you listen good. Landview is my daughter's future, and you will not mess that up, divorce or no divorce.'

'I–I just can't believe it all,' Bryce said, hoping the overacting wouldn't show. 'What you're telling me about you doing all these things.'

Davenport couldn't resist the opportunity to brag. 'Believe it, son. I control the Syndicate, and the Syndicate is Landview. Everyone reports to me. Isn't that right, Vinny?'

'Yes, sir,' said Vinny, looking like a whipped dog.

Davenport was glaring at Bryce now, waiting to see him crack. It looked as if the man held all the cards, but only the Governor knew the man's secret vulnerability. Richard Davenport was about to self-destruct.

'What's to stop me going to the authorities and telling them all this?' Bryce asked innocently.

Davenport's face contorted with fury. If there was one thing he could not abide it was insubordination. Poor Lydia had grown up with the man and would likely be dealing with the effects of his tyrannical behaviour for the rest of her life.

'Don't you threaten me, you insolent pup!' he bellowed. 'You are a pawn and nothing more. I put you up high and now I'm taking you down. You served your purpose. Your usefulness is through. To Lydia and to me. You will play out the part I've handed you and swallow your disgrace like a big boy.'

'But we had so many plans,' Bryce lamented. 'I was going to run for President.'

'Plans change, wonder boy. I'm backing Jankinson. He's easier to corral. And his family owns a construction company. Perfect for our needs. Especially the cement division.'

Tony the Jackal laughed. Big Vinny, still standing like an errant schoolboy, didn't crack a smile.

'What do you mean, cement?' Bryce asked, hoping to get these men to be as specific as possible about the crimes they intended to commit.

The industrialist laughed under his breath. 'Why don't you tell him, Vinny?'

'The other five heads of the Syndicate,' he explained, 'are about to meet with some unfortunate accidents.'

'Very much planned accidents, I'm afraid,' boasted Davenport. 'And I think a few of my banking friends may also have some accidents.'

'Do you know what you are saying?' Bryce exclaimed, attempting to egg him on as much as possible. 'Does Lydia have any idea?'

'Lydia is not your concern, my dear soon to be ex-son-in-law. What is your concern, for the last time, is doing what you are fucking told. You think I can't manage to live without your pretty face in the world? Think again.'

Bryce tried to look as downcast as possible, though in reality he was ecstatic. He had more than enough to put Davenport away for life. All he had to do was make his getaway.

'I know I can't fight you,' he sighed, making sure not to seem to give in too easily. 'I hate what you've done to me, and to Lydia, but I have no choice. I accept your terms.'

'That's the first intelligent thing you've said all night,' Davenport approved. 'Trust me, I'm making you a hell of a deal. Probably too sentimental on my part, letting you walk away, but I think I've made my point.'

'I'm just so tired. I need rest.' Bryce ran his hand through his hair. 'In the morning. I'll take care of things in the morning.'

'Yes,' said Davenport, 'that would be the wise thing

to do. Tony, why don't you bring these gentlemen's car around?'

'Sure thing, Mr D.'

Jake and Bryce were at the door when Davenport stopped them. 'Oh, Bryce, I wonder if you'd do me one more favour before you go?'

Bryce's pulse raced. 'What's that, sir?'

Davenport smiled broadly, the expression belying his intent. 'I'd like you to take your shirt off for us, if you wouldn't mind.'

Bryce saw his life flash before his eyes. He'd come so close, only to fall infinitely far short of his goal. The game was over. As was his life. 'Certainly,' he said, his brain desperately trying to find a way out in the seconds he had left. 'Any particular reason, if I may ask?'

Davenport smiled. 'Oh, it's just to humour the suspicions of a foolish old man. We both know you'd never do anything to betray my trust. Especially nothing as outrageous as trying to record our conversation for outside consumption.'

'I would never dream of that, sir.'

'I know this. I really do. Still, I have to take care of those gnawing, irrational little doubts, don't I?'

'Of course, sir. I understand completely.' He gave Jake one last look and moved to the centre of the room, directly in front of his wife's father. There was nowhere to run and he knew it, so why not face the man with dignity? Let him meet his end with his head held high.

Not a bad life, all in all. I've seen more than most, he thought. Had more than my share of the glory. Was there anything he regretted? He'd certainly tried to do more good than harm. To leave the world a slightly better place. It might be a rationalisation, but he honestly felt he had given something to each person he'd ever met, and to each woman he'd ever slept with. Not that he was all that phenomenal a lover or some kind of philosophical genius, it's just that he'd opened his heart with each one, letting them know, for the moment he was with them, that they were the centre of the world.

Lydia would never see it that way, obviously, and maybe there was where his regrets lay. She'd paid a high price for him being the free-loving spirit he was. But hadn't he paid a price, too, marrying a woman he could only ever love in a certain way and not with all his heart?

Had he ever really been madly in love with anyone? Cassie had touched something deep, yes, and she had been on his mind so often. But real love, from what little he knew, had to do with feelings so deep they could bring both indescribable pain and ineffable joy. To lose the object of one's true affection was to know an emptiness and loneliness without equal.

There was one woman whose memory he had blocked, whose presence in his life had become too unbearable to recall. Her betrayal had hurt worse than any wound he'd ever felt. So much so that he had not allowed himself to think of it, or her, for a moment since. That woman was Abigail. His one regret was that he would never be able to look her in the eye and ask why she'd done what she had.

Bryce loosened his tie, in readiness to unbutton his shirt. His life was life measured in seconds now. One button. Two. Three.

At four it happened.

All hell broke loose. Outside there was a large explosion, accompanied by gunfire. Two armed gangsters rushed in to warn Vinny the cops were here.

Richard spied the wire just under Bryce's shirt and ordered them to shoot him, but Tony jumped to his feet first, pulling out a pistol. 'Federal agent. Drop your weapons.'

'Kill him,' Richard cried out to Big Vinny. 'What are you waiting for?'

The robe-wearing Vinny threw up his hands. 'Where do you think I got a gun? Up my ass?'

'Get one of theirs.' He pointed to the machine guns dropped by the two henchmen.

By this time Tony was screaming for everyone to get down as more shooting came from down the hall. Big Vinny scrambled for one of the machine guns, only to be tripped by Tomiko. He landed with a thud, face-down.

'Get out of my way!' Richard was trying to make a run for it. He got as far as the door, only to be intercepted by two burly police officers in special weapons gear. A half-dozen more swarmed in behind them and soon everyone was on the floor, under guard, waiting for the authorities to sort things out.

'This man is a criminal,' Richard screamed, pointing to Bryce. 'He's taken bribes, he conspired with the mob. I'm only here to expose him.'

A pair of officers brought him and Bryce to their feet.

'Just listen to this.' Bryce pulled out the tape player. 'It explains everything.'

The cops looked at each other.

'He's right!' cried Queenie, rushing into the room. 'He was innocent all along. It's Davenport, he's the one. He's behind everything!'

Bryce's expression froze. A storm of emotions clouded over him. What was she doing here, of all people? Had she somehow heard him voicing that silent regret? Still, it was one thing to make a wish before death and quite another to be confronted with an unpleasant reality. This was not the time to see her, nor the place.

'It's all right,' Tony was saying to the cops as he held up his badge, indicating that he was an under-cover federal agent. 'The Governor's in the clear. I can vouch for him. So can Agent Tomiko. We were gonna bust this case ourselves, but he moved faster, and you guys, too.'

'Mr Governor,' said a new man, a state trooper. 'I'm sorry for the inconvenience. We gave instructions for the men to hold everyone till things were sorted out. But we knew you came here to clear your name. We knew all about the tape you were making, too.'

'But how did you know where to find me?' Bryce asked, astonished.

The trooper, whose nameplate read 'Jones', pro-ceeded to explain about Queenie's intervention and how she'd gotten help from Jake. The Governor eyed the reporter sharply, and chided him mildly for leaving him out of the loop.

'It was Queenie who talked me into it. She figured the only way to save your ass was in spite of yourself,' explained the erstwhile reporter. 'And hey, I was ner-vous enough, even with backup.'

Bryce flashed Queenie a confused look. 'But why would you help me now, after . . . what you did before?'

It was Jones who spoke for her. 'If I may say so, sir, she was trying to help you all along. Davenport's people convinced her that if she didn't get you to make that tape something much worse would happen to you. She thought she was saving you.'

'Is . . . is this true, Queenie?'

She blinked, moist-eyed. 'I never meant to hurt you, Bryce. I swear it. If I ever thought I'd hurt you . . . I couldn't live with myself.'

That was all the answer the Governor needed. Bypassing all the discussions and explanations, he simply took the curvy redhead into his arms. 'My God, Queenie, how I've missed you.'

'I've missed you, too, Bryce, more than you can know.'

Their words dissolved into a kiss. As far as Bryce was concerned, the world was gone at this point. It may have been for a minute or an hour, it didn't matter. He was making up for lost time, a life's worth.

And the best part was what lay ahead. An adventure for two. For the rest of their days, inseparable.

'I see you're none the worse for wear,' said Cassie, who'd come into the room to stand by the mysterious Trooper Jones.

'Nor are you,' riposted Bryce, astonished to find her here talking to him. 'My goodness, how many more old flames am I going to meet tonight?'

Queenie slapped his chest playfully. 'Excuse me, Mr Governor, I am your only flame now, past, present or future.'

He pecked her on the cheek. 'I stand corrected.'

'Ah, true love,' Cassie sighed, entwining her arm in the trooper's.

'You are supposed to be at home,' said Jones reprovingly, though he didn't seem too upset.

'I know. I got bored. You'll find that happens a lot with me.'

'And you'll find out things that happen with me,' he growled good-naturedly, his hand straying to pinch her ass.

Cassie giggled. 'Seriously, though, I'm so sorry I didn't give you a chance, Bryce. I should have known all this would be Davenport's doing.'

'You have nothing to apologise for. You acted in good faith. Obviously you knew how to handle things. All of you did. I'm grateful for that. It's not easy for an old dog to learn a new trick, but I can see I do better when I have help. So, thank you. By the way,' he said, stretching out his hand to the trooper, 'I don't believe we're been formally introduced.'

'I'm Travis Jones,' the trooper replied, beaming. 'Pleased to meet you, sir.'

'Travis is the one that helped put all this together,' said Cassie proudly.

'Is that right?' Bryce looked at Jones' uniform. He was a basic level trooper. It would be quite a promotion to give him Cray's old job, but he'd shown a lot of initiative and Bryce did have a job opening right now. 'In that case, Trooper, how would you like a reassignment in duties?'

Travis Jones looked at him warily. 'I'm not sure, sir. With all due respect, sir, I like highway duty.'

Bryce gave a wry smile. 'Enough to turn down a job as head of my security team?'

The trooper's mouth hung open. Cassie had to prompt him back to reality. 'This is the part where you say, "I'd be honoured to. When do I start, sir?"'

Jones repeated the words, his eyes big as silver dollars.

'Good,' said Bryce. 'Now that that's settled, there's only one thing left to do.'

Davenport was outside already, in the back of a

police car. There were a lot of things Bryce could say to him, but there didn't seem much point to any of that now. The man was going to suffer plenty in the coming weeks and months, he didn't need any extra barbs from him. Really, there was nothing left to be angry about, anyway. Their relationship was over. Richard Davenport was a non-person to him.

Still, for his own sake, Bryce wanted to clear his conscience. 'Richard,' he said, leaning down and talking to him through the open window of the police car, 'there's something I need you to know. I didn't treat your daughter as well as I could have. And for that I owe you my sincere apology, late as it is.'

Davenport's face was screwed up with pure hate. 'I have no daughter,' he said. 'As for you, if I never see your face again, it will be too soon.'

Bryce smiled grimly. If anything he felt pity for the man. 'Don't worry, Richard, I'm sure that will be arranged by the judge.'

Queenie in his arms, he watched the police car drive away into the night. For some reason all he could think of was Lydia. 'I have to see her,' Bryce said, the realisation clearer in his mind than anything he'd ever known. 'I have to make my peace.'

'I know,' she whispered. 'And I'll be with you every step of the way.'

'Thank you,' he whispered back.

So this is it, thought Bryce, his eyes finally opened. This is human love. Never would he go without it again. And fortunately, with Queenie, he'd never have to.

Lydia saw the two of them coming down the beach. At first she thought her eyes might be deceiving her. They were too distinctive a couple, though, to be anyone else.

The man with his imperious gait, dark hair and lean frame, the much smaller, curvier woman with her fiery red hair, both of them matching in white slacks and tops. It was them all right. Bryce and Queenie. She'd read the e-mail that told her he would be here some time this week, but she hadn't believed it. Not really.

'Cray,' she called into their three-room bungalow on the sun-swept Mexican coast, their own palace for two, south of the border. 'They're here.'

Brown as a bear, and just as nude, Cray Wilder emerged into the sunshine to stand beside his wife. Lydia was also naked, her smooth, trim body having darkened to a healthy golden shade.

'The son of a bitch has a lot of nerve,' said Cray.

Lydia grasped the hand of the man she had opted to spend the rest of her life with, in perfect love and obedience. Yielding in every way. Still, there were times a woman needed to speak her heart. 'We have to listen to him, Cray. He came all this way.'

'Fine,' he grumbled, tossing her a sundress from the hook on the door and grabbing a pair of shorts for himself. 'We can listen. But I guarantee we won't like what we hear. That man is as stubborn as the day is long. That will never change and you and I both know it.'

'In my mind, yes,' she agreed, pulling the well-worn cotton dress over her head. 'But my heart hopes otherwise.'

Lydia noted how comfortable Bryce and Queenie were together. He certainly wasn't exaggerating it to get at her: he was truly happy. She got a lump in her throat as she realised she had never seen him so happy with her. This really has been for the best, she thought.

The approaching couple stopped about twenty yards away and Bryce came forward alone. Lydia instinctively did the same. They walked towards each other slowly, cautiously, eyes moistening, though whether from wind or emotion it was hard to tell.

'You look good, Lydia,' said Bryce.

'So do you,' she replied with a smile.

'You're happy,' he said. It was a statement of fact.

'And you are, too, I hope?'

He shrugged, a twinkle in his eye. 'You know me – always a pot of gold at the end of the rainbow to chase.'

Lydia's heart swelled. She'd never intended to hate this man. In many ways they'd both been the victims of her father's machinations. They'd made the best of things and for that she would be forever grateful. 'Bryce, there's something I want to say—'

He held up his hand. 'Lyd, please, let me do the talking. It's the only thing I'm really any good at. I didn't come all this way to get any praise or closure or anything, I just came to wish you well. You and your new husband. It's not much, this late in the game, but it's the only thing I have to offer.'

Lydia felt the start of tears. 'Oh, Bryce, you don't know what that means to me ... you don't know what it's been like, having an empty place in my heart for so long. I'm so sorry how it all worked out and—'

They were in each other's arms, enjoying what would be their final embrace. And yet in a way it was their first, too: an affirmation of the friendship they had shared, and a sealing of their parting from each other. After a few moments they invited their new mates to join them and there was more hugging.

Most emotional of all was the embrace of the Governor and his former security chief.

'Cray,' Bryce whispered as they clasped one another.

'Mr Governor.' Cray gripped him back.

'No,' said Bryce, shaking his head. 'I want to hear you use my name. You don't work for me any more. We're equals now.'

Cray smiled. 'All right, Bryce. You win. Now, are you going to come into our home for a cup of tea or do I have to spar with you first?'

'Let's save that for another day, shall we?'

And so they went, all four of them, to enjoy a cup of tea. The best any of them had ever tasted.

Cassie had the accelerator pressed all the way to the floor as she passed the police cruiser. It had been parked in the bushes beside the road, out of sight. She saw the lights in her rear-view mirror, recognising instantly that she'd been busted. The cop drove right up to her bumper, leaving her no choice except where to pull over. She could just stop at the shoulder, but that wasn't safe. The road was too narrow, and it was too likely that one of them would be hit by a truck doing a hundred on this Godforsaken stretch of highway.

He stayed right with her as she drove on to the next rest area. It was totally empty, as it often was at this time of night. It could be scary for a woman out here alone. Sometimes you heard about men impersonating police and pulling women over for lewd sex acts. That's why she would be sure to get the man's badge number and demand to see his ID, just as Travis had taught her.

The tall trooper pointed his light through the window, blinding her. 'Licence, insurance and registration, please.'

Cassie reached for her purse. Fuck. She'd left it at the office. 'Um, there's a little problem with that, officer . . . I don't actually have them with me.'

She tried to sound cute and ditzy and she made a point of tugging up her short skirt a little bit, too, because that usually helped her get away with stuff. The officer did indeed shine his light on her bare legs, but he remained unimpressed.

'Out of the car please, miss.'

Oh, shit. She was in for it now.

'Is this really necessary, sir?' She couldn't make out his face. He seemed attractive, with a solid physique.

'Yes, it is. Against the car, please, and spread your legs.'

Cassie swooned. 'But surely you have women troopers to do this?'

'Budget cuts,' he growled. 'Now, are you going to cooperate or do I have to bring you in for resisting an officer?'

'Yes, sir.' She assumed the position meekly, her palms on the roof.

A pair of hands, strong as steel, gripped her waist. 'Legs wider,' he commanded.

Cassie felt her pussy flood in response. She was helpless; the man could do anything he wanted.

'Do you have any concealed weapons?'

'No, sir.'

He bent to feel her calf, moving his hands up one leg. She shuddered as he ignored the barrier of her skirt, moving his way clear up to her crotch. Could he smell her arousal? Was she making it that obvious how ready she was to be molested?

As he worked his way up the other leg, he went farther, pressing his thumb against the silk of her panties, making her little clit swell in response. 'You know the dangers of speeding?' he asked. 'To you and others?'

'Oh, yes, officer,' she moaned.

'That kind of behaviour can't be tolerated, can it?'

'N—no, officer.' He was working her now, making her squirm like a little slut.

'What should be done to naughty little girls who speed?' he wanted to know.

'They should be punished,' she told her husband.

'Punished how?' Former Trooper Jones, now Security Chief Jones, continued to masturbate his wife.

'They should be ... spanked,' she gasped.

It never failed to excite her, saying these words. No matter how many times they played this game, with him in his old uniform, it was always fresh.

'Anything else?'

'Yes,' she cried, feeling his clothed erection against her skirted ass. 'They should be fucked, too. Hard. Like the naughty little sluts they are.'

'Lie over the hood of the car,' he commanded. 'Pull up your skirt and take down your panties.'

Cassie could hardly walk. She had to lean against the car for support. It was so erotic, submitting like this, the hot metal against her chest, the open air against her exposed pussy. Sometimes it was all she could do to take her punishment without begging to be fucked right away.

Travis went quickly tonight, giving her ten ripe smacks to the bottom. She could tell he was excited as she was. All this so far, from the pretend pulling over of her vehicle to the creative sentencing on his part, was just the foreplay, their own special brand of appetiser leading up to the main course of his cock moving deep in and out of her wet and willing pussy.

'Oh, yes,' she cried. 'That's it, that's what I need.'

Travis knew this well and he never disappointed. Each new day, each new time of lovemaking brought new wonders and Cassie was sure now that she could happily grow old with just this one cock between her legs. Or in her mouth or ass, whatever the case might be. Yes, no matter how she thought about it, she had finally found a man who could keep up with her, and was happy doing it. As for politics, there would always be elections. Like the next presidential election, when she fully intended to put Bryce Clarkson in the White House. Then she and Travis could play their little games in Washington. On the steps of the Lincoln Memorial, maybe, or the Lincoln Room. Yes, indeed, she sighed, preparing to climax with her kinky beloved. Only in America.

The orchestra was just moving into the second movement of Beethoven's Fifth Symphony when the Governor slipped from his seat. He'd wanted to get away earlier in the evening, but up to now his very vigilant and controlling second wife had been by his side, watching him like a hawk.

Signalling to Security Chief Jones to call off the plainclothes watchdogs, he made his way alone to the rear of the great vaulted hall. It was a stroke of luck that the Museum of Modern Art was doing a second fundraising event so quickly. For the museum the in-house concert meant money to bid on a collection made available following the sudden death of the painter Bonifacio Morel. For Bryce, on the other hand, it meant an opportunity to fuck a certain familiar lady in red back in the film room, the one with all the futons. Bryce felt a little guilty since he'd already counted Morel as dead his last time here with Lindsay, but then all was fair in love and war.

The idea of having the city orchestra play to a small audience in the museum had been the First Lady's. The influence of Mrs Abigail Auvignon Clarkson in state affairs had already been remarkable in the three months since they'd been married. And it would only grow over time. Especially since she had taken such a, shall we say, dominant role in Bryce's life.

The museum hallways were just as he'd remembered them. He followed the path, through the exhibits, all the way to the secluded room Lindsay had introduced him to before. It was dark inside and at first he wondered if his tryst partner hadn't arrived yet.

'Hello?' he whispered into the void.

Bryce felt fingers grazing the back of his neck, small and feminine. 'Were you followed?' she wanted to know, moving around in front of him.

'I don't think so.' His cock swelled instantly at her touch.

'Better not have been,' said the woman as she unzipped the fly of his tuxedo trousers. 'You'd catch hell from your wife if she found out.'

'You don't know the half of it.'

The woman in the red dress took out his cock and began to play with it as if she owned it. 'Just out of curiosity,' she asked, 'what would Mrs Clarkson do if she caught you cheating?'

'I'd be punished,' he said without hesitation. 'She would whip me, probably take away most of my privileges, too.'

'Privileges?' She seemed intrigued by the idea of the woman having such power in a relationship. 'Like what?'

'I have to earn everything,' Bryce explained, his breathing growing more laboured. 'My orgasms, my recreational activities, even whether I'm allowed to sleep in the bed or not.'

'Wow. She sounds like hell on wheels.'

Bryce moaned lightly. 'No ... she's my mistress. I submit ... happily.'

'In that case,' said Abigail Auvignon Clarkson, his eternal woman in red, 'why are you still on your feet?'

The panting, exposed Governor fell immediately to his knees. 'Forgive me, my lady.'

She ran her hands through his thick dark hair, drawing him to her belly, lovingly, possessively. 'You may kiss my feet ... slave.'

Obediently, he put his lips to her painted toes, fully visible in the wispy red heels. A few hours ago he'd applied that very toenail polish after delivering an expert pedicure. It was one of many things she had taught him as his wife and mistress. Above all, she had helped him find peace in his life, not to mention order and discipline. He would no more think of cheating now than he would of switching political parties.

'On your back, my slave,' she ordered. 'It's time for me to take a ride on that big hard cock of mine.'

'Oh, yes, mistress, thank you, mistress.' Bryce appreciated sex these days as he never had before. He had to work for it now, and when and if he was allowed orgasms, he took them gratefully.

The former Queenie Amazon waited till he was flat on the carpet before turning on the light and preparing herself. He nearly cried out in pleasure as she walked over to him in all her glory, pulled up her sexy dress and worked her panties down over her hips.

'I better come hard,' she warned him, 'or you'll be going back out there with a mighty sore ass.'

'Yes, mistress,' he croaked, loving every minute of her sweet domination.

'You know the drill.' She tossed him the fragrant panties.

Indeed he did. They played games like this all the

time. Sexy, dangerous, public games. Games that made him burn with desire. No two sessions were ever alike. Being with Queenie was like having a thousand different women, each better than the last.

Bryce snatched the panties off his chest, breathed their scent greedily and then wadded them up in his mouth. He was too disciplined now to ever scream out during sex, but his wife enjoyed gagging him just the same. It was a psychological power game, really, being made to suck on his wife's moist underwear while she had her way with him.

Queenie was wet and hot for him, more than ready for penetration, as always. It was part of her love for him. Giving the most delicious sighs, she straddled his hips and settled down, taking him deep inside her, to the hilt.

'Oh, Bryce, I want your come inside me,' she declared. 'I want you to give it to me.'

He nodded, letting her know with his eyes that he was with her on this, beginning to end. The ride was ecstatic, Queenie squeezing and bouncing and Bryce pushing up from underneath, thrusting, the two of them meeting in a hot, liquid fusion born of a love so deep it had snuck up on them unawares and now enveloped them entirely. But then, the best loves always did that, didn't they?

They came together, their bodies electrified beneath their clothes, their movements in sync, their explosions timed to the second. Onward and onward they soared till at last they fell back to earth, as one. She showered him with a thousand kisses, nuzzling his neck, as he ran his hands over her back in utter devotion.

'That was good, lover,' she said with a smile, pulling the sopping panties from his mouth. 'But I'm afraid

I'm going to have to tell your wife what you've been doing behind her back.'

His leer was as wicked as it was spent. 'Oh, I hope you do, Mrs Clarkson, I sincerely do.'

LOOK OUT FOR THE ALL-NEW BLACK LACE BOOKS – AVAILABLE NOW!

All books priced £7.99 in the UK. Please note publication dates apply to the UK only. For other territories, please contact your retailer.

OFFICE PERKS
Monica Belle
ISBN 0 352 33939 X

This is the story of Lucy Doyle, a red-haired and hot-tempered London Irish girl with her eyes on the prize – and young men's trousers. Her family have got her a job in a Parochial House in North London for the summer, between leaving school and going to university, but she is sacked on her first day for doing something she shouldn't with the groundsman. Determined to stay in London she signs up as an office temp, faking her references and chancing her luck. Along with fellow recruits – the ladylike but filthy Bobbie and the completely dirty Sophie – this cheeky 'flower of Erin' carves a swathe of debauchery through London's office land, collecting lovers, outraging her bosses and drinking far too much as she causes havoc in the way only a bad girl can. **A wildly entertaining XXX-rated story of girls on the pull, causing mayhem and loving it!**

UNDRESSING THE DEVIL
Angel Strand
ISBN 0 352 33938 1

It's the 1930s. Hitler and Mussolini are building their war machine and
Europe is a hotbed of political tension. Cia, a young, Anglo-Italian
woman, escapes the mayhem, returning to England only to become
embroiled in a web of sexual adventures. Her Italian lover has
disappeared along with her clothes, lost somewhere between Florence
and the Isle of Wight. Her British friends are carrying on in the manner to
which they are accustomed: sailing their yachts and partying. However,
this serene façade hides rivalries and forbidden pleasures. It's only a
matter of time before Cia's two worlds collide. **Literary erotica at its best,
in this story of bright young things on the edge.**

THE BARBARIAN GEISHA
Charlotte Royal
ISBN 0 352 33267 0

When Annabel Smith jumps overboard from her father's sailing vessel
she expects to die – but is instead washed up on the shores of feudal
Japan and into the hands of the brutal warlord, Lord Nakano. Enchanted
by her naked blonde beauty, Nakano takes her to Shimoyama, his
fortress home. There Mamma San teaches Annabel the arts of sensual
pleasure. Shimoyama is a world of political intrigue and Nakano's
brother warns Annabel of the dangers that surround her. Will she ever
be accepted as a barbarian geisha? **Unusual story of arcane erotic ritual
in a hidden society.**

MS BEHAVIOUR
Mini Lee
ISBN O 352 33962 4

Santa is a university student with a wonderful new boyfriend and bright future. However, she's also a bad girl with a wild streak who cultivates an illicit and obsessive relationship with her law professor. The older Professor MacLean's attractions are too numerous and beguiling to avoid and Santa cannot stop herself from teasing him and rousing his ire with her saucy behaviour – in and out of class. Caught up in this dangerous game, she is neglecting her studies but honing her sexual skills, driving all the men around her to distraction. When MacLean sets Santa a defence assignment that mirrors their own highly charged situation, the sexual tension reaches boiling point and threatens to spill over into something far more dangerous. **A sizzling hot story of forbidden lust with a modern twist.**

FRENCH MANNERS
Olivia Christie
ISBN O 352 33214 X

Gilles de la Trave persuades Colette, a young and beautiful peasant girl from one of his estates, to become his mistress and live the life of a Parisian courtesan. However, it is his son Victor that she loves and expects to marry. In a moment of passion and curiosity she confesses her sins to the local priest, unaware that the curé has his own agenda: one which involves himself *and* Victor. Shocked, Colette takes the only sensible option for a young girl from the provinces: she flees to Paris to immerse herself in a life of wild indulgence and luxury! **An erotic and beautifully written story charting a rural young girl's journey into adulthood and sophistication.**

Also available

THE BLACK LACE SEXY QUIZ BOOK
Maddie Saxon
ISBN 0 352 33884 9

- What sexual personality type are you?
- Have you ever faked it because that was easier than explaining what you wanted?
- What kind of fantasy figures turn you on – and does your partner know?
- What sexual signals are you giving out right now?

Today's image-conscious dating scene is a tough call. Our sexual expectations are cranked up to the max, and the sexes seem to have become highly critical of each other in terms of appearance and performance in the bedroom. But even though guys have ditched their nasty Y-fronts and girls are more babe-licious than ever, a huge number of us are still being let down sexually. Sex therapist Maddie Saxon thinks this is because we are finding it harder to relax and let our true sexual selves shine through.

The Black Lace Sexy Quiz Book will help you negotiate the minefield of modern relationships. Through a series of fun, revealing quizzes, you will be able to rate your sexual needs honestly and get what you really want from your partner. The quizzes will get you thinking about and discussing your desires in ways you haven't previously considered. Unlock the mysteries of your sexual psyche in this fun, revealing quiz book designed with today's sex-savvy woman in mind.

Black Lace Booklist

Information is correct at time of printing. To avoid disappointment check availability before ordering. Go to www.blacklace-books.co.uk. All books are priced £6.99 unless another price is given.

BLACK LACE BOOKS WITH A CONTEMPORARY SETTING

☐ SHAMELESS Stella Black	ISBN 0 352 33485 1	£5.99
☐ INTENSE BLUE Lyn Wood	ISBN 0 352 33496 7	£5.99
☐ A SPORTING CHANCE Susie Raymond	ISBN 0 352 33501 7	£5.99
☐ TAKING LIBERTIES Susie Raymond	ISBN 0 352 33357 X	£5.99
☐ ON THE EDGE Laura Hamilton	ISBN 0 352 33534 3	£5.99
☐ LURED BY LUST Tania Picarda	ISBN 0 352 33533 5	£5.99
☐ THE NINETY DAYS OF GENEVIEVE	ISBN 0 352 33070 8	£5.99
Lucinda Carrington		
☐ DREAMING SPIRES Juliet Hastings	ISBN 0 352 33584 X	
☐ THE TRANSFORMATION Natasha Rostova	ISBN 0 352 33311 1	
☐ SIN.NET Helena Ravenscroft	ISBN 0 352 33598 X	
☐ TWO WEEKS IN TANGIER Annabel Lee	ISBN 0 352 33599 8	
☐ PLAYING HARD Tina Troy	ISBN 0 352 33617 X	
☐ SYMPHONY X Jasmine Stone	ISBN 0 352 33629 3	
☐ SUMMER FEVER Anna Ricci	ISBN 0 352 33625 0	
☐ CONTINUUM Portia Da Costa	ISBN 0 352 33120 8	
☐ FULL STEAM AHEAD Tabitha Flyte	ISBN 0 352 33637 4	
☐ A SECRET PLACE Ella Broussard	ISBN 0 352 33307 3	
☐ GAME FOR ANYTHING Lyn Wood	ISBN 0 352 33639 0	
☐ CHEAP TRICK Astrid Fox	ISBN 0 352 33640 4	
☐ THE GIFT OF SHAME Sara Hope-Walker	ISBN 0 352 32935 1	
☐ COMING UP ROSES Crystalle Valentino	ISBN 0 352 33658 7	
☐ GOING TOO FAR Laura Hamilton	ISBN 0 352 33657 9	
☐ THE STALLION Georgina Brown	ISBN 0 352 33005 8	
☐ DOWN UNDER Juliet Hastings	ISBN 0 352 33663 3	
☐ ODALISQUE Fleur Reynolds	ISBN 0 352 32887 8	
☐ SWEET THING Alison Tyler	ISBN 0 352 33682 X	
☐ TIGER LILY Kimberly Dean	ISBN 0 352 33685 4	

☐ RISKY BUSINESS Lisette Allen	ISBN 0 352 33280 8	£7.99
☐ OFFICE PERKS Monica Belle	ISBN 0 352 33939 X	£7.99
☐ UNDRESSING THE DEVIL Angel Strand	ISBN 0 352 33938 1	£7.99

BLACK LACE BOOKS WITH AN HISTORICAL SETTING

☐ PRIMAL SKIN Leona Benkt Rhys	ISBN 0 352 33500 9	£5.99
☐ DARKER THAN LOVE Kristina Lloyd	ISBN 0 352 33279 4	
☐ THE CAPTIVATION Natasha Rostova	ISBN 0 352 33234 4	
☐ MINX Megan Blythe	ISBN 0 352 33638 2	
☐ DIVINE TORMENT Janine Ashbless	ISBN 0 352 33719 2	
☐ SATAN'S ANGEL Melissa MacNeal	ISBN 0 352 33726 5	
☐ THE INTIMATE EYE Georgia Angelis	ISBN 0 352 33004 X	
☐ SILKEN CHAINS Jodi Nicol	ISBN 0 352 33143 7	
☐ THE LION LOVER Mercedes Kelly	ISBN 0 352 33162 3	
☐ THE AMULET Lisette Allen	ISBN 0 352 33019 8	
☐ WHITE ROSE ENSNARED Juliet Hastings	ISBN 0 352 33052 X	
☐ UNHALLOWED RITES Martine Marquand	ISBN 0 352 33222 0	
☐ LA BASQUAISE Angel Strand	ISBN 0 352 32988 2	
☐ THE HAND OF AMUN Juliet Hastings	ISBN 0 352 33144 5	
☐ THE SENSES BEJEWELLED Cleo Cordell	ISBN 0 352 32904 1	

BLACK LACE ANTHOLOGIES

☐ WICKED WORDS Various	ISBN 0 352 33363 4
☐ MORE WICKED WORDS Various	ISBN 0 352 33487 8
☐ WICKED WORDS 3 Various	ISBN 0 352 33522 X
☐ WICKED WORDS 4 Various	ISBN 0 352 33603 X
☐ WICKED WORDS 5 Various	ISBN 0 352 33642 0
☐ WICKED WORDS 6 Various	ISBN 0 352 33690 0
☐ WICKED WORDS 7 Various	ISBN 0 352 33743 5
☐ WICKED WORDS 8 Various	ISBN 0 352 33787 7
☐ WICKED WORDS 9 Various	ISBN 0 352 33860 1
☐ WICKED WORDS 10 Various	ISBN 0 352 33893 8
☐ THE BEST OF BLACK LACE 2 Various	ISBN 0 352 33718 4

BLACK LACE NON-FICTION

☐ THE BLACK LACE BOOK OF WOMEN'S SEXUAL   ISBN 0 352 33793 1
    FANTASIES Ed. Kerri Sharp

☐ THE BLACK LACE SEXY QUIZ BOOK Maddie Saxon   ISBN 0 352 33884 9

To find out the latest information about Black Lace titles, check out the website: www.blacklace-books.co.uk or send for a booklist with complete synopses by writing to:

> Black Lace Booklist, Virgin Books Ltd
> Thames Wharf Studios
> Rainville Road
> London W6 9HA

Please include an SAE of decent size. Please note only British stamps are valid.

Our privacy policy
We will not disclose information you supply us to any other parties. We will not disclose any information which identifies you personally to any person without your express consent.

From time to time we may send out information about Black Lace books and special offers. Please tick here if you do <u>not</u> wish to receive Black Lace information.   ☐

Please send me the books I have ticked above.

Name ....

Address ....

....

....

....

Post Code ....

Send to: Virgin Books Cash Sales, Thames Wharf Studios, Rainville Road, London W6 9HA.

US customers: for prices and details of how to order books for delivery by mail, call 1-800-343-4499.

Please enclose a cheque or postal order, made payable to Virgin Books Ltd, to the value of the books you have ordered plus postage and packing costs as follows:

UK and BFPO – £1.00 for the first book, 50p for each subsequent book.

Overseas (including Republic of Ireland) – £2.00 for the first book, £1.00 for each subsequent book.

If you would prefer to pay by VISA, ACCESS/MASTERCARD, DINERS CLUB, AMEX or SWITCH, please write your card number and expiry date here:

....

Signature ....

Please allow up to 28 days for delivery.